THE REVELATION OF EDEN PRUITT

THE REVELATION OF EDEN PRUITT

BOOK 3

K.E. GANSHERT

For Kara

*You are pure sunshine. Thanks for being such an encouraging reader.
Your cupcakes are divine!*

REVELATION

THE ACT OF REVEALING WHAT
WAS ONCE HIDDEN;
AN ANNOUNCEMENT

1

f he is the snake, Electus is his head. We are going to cut it off.

The words became a trapped echo reverberating in Eden's skull. The girl with the glass eye had said them inside the White House Bunker, without a clue Eden Pruitt was part of that head. For the first eighteen years of her life, Eden didn't have a clue either. She'd operated under the assumption that her parents were her biological parents and her biology was the same as every other person's biology. Until she took a knife, sliced open her hand, and watched it heal before her eyes.

If only Cleo could heal as quickly.

Eden's chest tightened as she sat beside her friend lying on the floor, hooked to a portable IV. Her complexion, usually aglow with health, had turned a muted and alarming gray. Scratches and scrapes mottled the left side of her face. An angry gash sliced through the skin above her right eyebrow. These injuries weren't concerning, but the one on her leg twisted Eden's guts. Blood had soaked through the bandage wrapped around Cleo's thigh where a piece of sharpened marble had struck her femoral artery.

She needed professional medical attention, not the crude care the condescending young man had provided. Cleo needed a doctor; she needed her mother. But Dr. Beverly Randall-Ransom was in Chicago and Cleo and Eden were trapped beneath Washington, DC, in an outdated bomb shelter designed to protect the president of the United States at a time when America still elected presidents. Eden's attention traveled up the wall to an archaic seal mounted above the wood paneling. An eagle clutched an olive branch in its right talon, thirteen arrows in its left, and a scroll in its beak that bore the words *E Pluribus Unum.*

Out of many, one.

The motto used to be on their money and their passports. It was a bygone ideology that considered diversity—of people, of opinion—to be one of the country's greatest strengths. That was before The Attack and the massive restructuring of government that followed. A restructuring that no longer prized diversity, because diversity was a prelude to division and division was clearly the enemy. The seal was replaced by Concordia, the Roman Goddess of Harmony and Peace. A cruel irony considering the smoking war zone above.

Cleo turned her head.

Pinpricks of sweat beaded along her brow.

Eden bit back a scream. How could she get Cleo help when they were stuck underground with two hostile members of a mortally wounded resistance? Francesca Burnoli, with her glass eye and her pixie haircut and her pale, androgynous face streaked with grime and smoke. And the giant named Asher, with his broad shoulders and his bronze skin and his NBA height made even taller by his hair—a stack of tightly wound curls fading neatly into buzzed sides.

They radiated accusation.

Eden didn't blame them. If the roles were reversed—if these two had shown up uninvited and shut down her emergency alert system—she would be just as outraged.

Bile burned in the back of her throat.

Fifty rebels. Reduced to ten.

Because of her and Cleo's blasted curiosity. They'd been

tracking Amir Kashif, the son of Lillian Kashif. She was Bella Bryson's sister, and one of ninety-three names on the back of a strange pamphlet Eden and Cassian had stolen from the Bryson's safe. Amir had passed something to Asher, and Asher had led them to a tunnel.

Cassian warned them against following that tunnel. They didn't know where it led or who it led to. He didn't want to make a rash decision. But Cleo had insisted and Eden had agreed, so Cass had been outnumbered. They'd gone. And because they'd gone, over thirty people were now dead and Cassian had been captured.

The room began to spin. Soldiers had shoved him into the back of a military truck with several others, one of whom was the infamous Prudence Dvorak. Not a member of a terrorist regime called Interitus, but the leader of a resistance working to defeat the Monarch. Who was, according to Francesca, *Oswin Freaking Brahm.*

Eden pictured him in her mind's eye. Charming and handsome. Generous and admired. A successful entrepreneur and philanthropist who had donated millions to fund programs that provided long-term care and assistance for those still suffering from The Attack. Apparently, *he* was the one who orchestrated The Attack.

The news hit her with the same shocking jolt she'd experienced in Dr. Norton's basement when he finally told her the truth about who she really was. *What* she really was. A weapon supposedly created by the most notorious terrorist of not only her lifetime, but *all* lifetimes. Karik Volkova. The name struck fear into the hearts of Americans everywhere. Turned out, that man was nothing more than a puppet. A disciple. Of the true villain.

Eden tried to wrap her mind around it, but her brain refused to grasp this new information as reality. She crouched down to wipe Cleo's brow, to check her pulse.

At the opposite end of the room, Francesca held a walkie-talkie to her lips as she guided a survivor from Bunker Three to Metro Center, her attention glued to the wall of surveillance monitors. Eight screens captured a variety of footage—from the smoking, apocalyptic scene above ground to the subway system underneath. One of those screens featured a prison-like room. A young man sat inside, slumped in a corner with his ankles and wrists bound by steel. He was the primary source of Francesca's escalating panic—a prisoner they were calling 'the asset'. A prisoner with the same biology as Eden.

Francesca's walkie-talkie squawked. "I'm here. Over."

"The dose will be in the inside pocket of his jacket," Francesca said. "Handle it carefully. Over."

On one monitor, the survivor Francesca was guiding bent over a dead body. He was retrieving a dose of something—tranquilizer, Eden assumed. Some specialized, super potent cocktail they must use to keep the asset in line. Otherwise, he would have no trouble breaking his steel restraints and busting down the door.

Asher sat with his chin propped on his fist, watching the scene with laser-like intensity. But he didn't notice it. Neither did Francesca.

A glint of metal.

A tiny mechanical sparrow on the periphery of the screen. Eden barely had time to cock her head before the sparrow swept the air with an infrared laser.

Francesca came out of her seat, shouting into the two-way radio.

The survivor stood abruptly. He spun in alarm, his eyes wide as the sparrow released a spray of bullets.

He fell.

The gunfire went silent.

With a roar, Francesca slammed her walkie-talkie onto the conference table.

Asher kicked a chair.

Horrified, Eden stared at the screen where two men now lay, side-by-side. Both of them dead.

"What *was* that?" Francesca asked.

Asher pointed a remote at the wall of monitors. He flipped channels from one area of the metro to another, until he found four more mechanical sparrows—so small, they were easily missed. He released a long sigh. "S and K drones," he muttered.

"S and K drones?" Eden repeated. "What are those?"

"Military drones programmed to search and kill."

An uneasy silence filled the room.

Cleo broke it with a moan as her head tossed restlessly.

The scream came back. It rolled up Eden's throat. She had to swallow it down. She wanted to sprint into the tunnels, grab every one of those drones, and crush them in her fist. It wasn't a foolish desire. She could do it with relative ease. But then what? She would give herself away. Francesca and Asher would know she was part of the snake's head and they would lock her up alongside the asset, where she would be of no help to Cassian or Cleo.

"This is why they evacuated." Asher continued flipping channels. "They dropped bombs above ground. They sent these below."

Francesca grabbed her assault rifle from the table and turned to the door.

Asher took her elbow. "What are you doing?"

"Someone has to administer that dose," she said.

"Don't be an idiot," Asher replied.

"Any minute, the asset will be strong enough to join the drones and we'll be toast." She shot Eden a murderous look, her good eye shining with animosity. This was, after all, Eden's fault. "What's left of the Resistance will be completely decimated."

"If you go out there, you'll be decimated." Asher took the gun from her hands. "How about we come up with a plan that doesn't require more body bags?"

"I don't think there is one, Ash."

"We can't afford to lose you." He rubbed his jaw, his attention swiveling slowly to Eden. "But we can afford to lose her."

Eden took a step back.

Asher narrowed one eye as though seeing her properly for the first time—a disposable heartbeat. "Let's make her get the dose."

2

Eden's ears caught fire.

Make her get the dose?

"You said no more body bags," Francesca said, regarding Eden with a look of utter disdain. "If we send her out there, she'll be dead and we'll be back at square one."

Eden gaped. They were discussing her like she was completely inconsequential. Her life of no value whatsoever. She pulled back her shoulders, tempted to leave right now and prove Francesca wrong. Eden wouldn't die. She could dodge bullets as easily as swatting a fly.

"Neither of us is going out there without a solid plan," Asher said.

The two argued.

Eden clenched her jaw. They were wasting valuable time. Cassian was slipping further away. Cleo, too. She turned to the screens. Her attention jumped from one to the next as she tracked each of the mechanical sparrows. Then she focused on a single screen, watching intently as the drones passed. "Thirty-eight seconds," she mumbled.

Asher and Francesca stopped bickering.

"They're flying in a pattern," Eden said. "Thirty-eight seconds apart."

Asher's brow furrowed. He turned to the wall, his furrow deepening as he traced his pointer finger through the air like one connecting an invisible dot-to-dot.

"What are you—?" Francesca began.

He held up his hand, his lips moving as his finger followed the same drone from monitor to monitor. Francesca tried speaking again. He gave his head a sharp shake and repeated the process. "She's right," he finally said.

"About *what*?" Francesca barked.

"The drones are flying thirty-eight seconds apart in a uniform pattern." He pulled a framed map off the wall and set it on the conference table. Eden pointed out Metro Center. Asher shooed her off and drew a line instead from the bunker they were in now to a room much closer. "Once a drone passes outside these doors, we have thirty-eight seconds to get from here to there."

"I thought you wanted to get the dose," Eden said.

"Right, but we can't unless we shut down the drones now, can we? And I can't shut down the drones unless I get here." He tapped the spot on the map. "Once I'm here, I can jam the drones and spoof their GPS systems. Then I can direct you to Metro Center."

"You mean *me*," Francesca objected. "We can't trust her to administer something this important."

"The asset's way overdue, Fran. If he's strong enough to snap, she's a goner. That happens, you're still alive and we can come up with a Plan B."

Eden gritted her teeth. They were talking about her in third person again.

"Besides," Asher continued, "I'm not trusting *her* to be my eyes and ears once I'm out there. I need *you* to direct us." He handed Eden the semi-automatic.

She recoiled.

Francesca scoffed. "You expect her to properly inject the asset when she can't even take a gun?"

He shoved the weapon hard against Eden's chest. "If she doesn't want us to throw her and her mangled little friend to the wolves, she'll just have to figure it out."

Eden glared. She had half a mind to take the gun from his condescending hands and show him exactly how well she could *figure it out.* But then a memory intruded, one that made her want to hurl the weapon as far away as possible.

Wind in her hair. Mordecai's arm around her waist. Sirens wailing and people screaming as she aimed the gun at Cassian. As she aimed the gun at her mother. As she curled her finger around the trigger and squeezed.

"Keep your eyes on the screen," Asher said to Francesca. "Let me know as soon as the next drone passes."

With a shaky breath, Eden wrapped her hands around the weapon. She wasn't afraid of her death or injury, but she was afraid of Cleo's. She didn't want to leave her friend, but staying would be of no help to Cleo or Cassian. Proving her worth—gaining their grudging respect—just might.

She followed Asher out of the room, past the dusty pallets of water and folded blankets, toward the sealed entrance. There he stopped. "Follow my lead. Do exactly what I say. Try anything funny and I won't hesitate to put a bullet through your head. Got it?"

She nodded, her mouth pinched.

Asher entered a code.

The airtight mechanism released with a loud hiss.

"Ready and waiting," he called to Francesca.

But Eden didn't need Francesca. She could hear the drone through the bomb-proof door. It was six seconds away. If she cast her hearing far enough, she could pinpoint the sound of the others.

"Next drone approaching," Francesca called back, "in four ... three ..."

The whirring of the mechanical sparrow grew closer. Louder.

"Two … one!" Francesca shouted.

Asher pressed a button.

The door slid open.

He held up his hand.

They waited on the threshold for one second. Two seconds. Three seconds. Then they stepped into the corridor as the drone ahead flew around a corner. Asher waved at her to follow. She did so quickly. They stopped at the turn. He peeked around the corner with his back against the wall, his lips moving silently as he counted the time. Then he gave his head a jerk. They stepped around the turn as the drone ahead flew out of sight.

They hurried after it, making their way in fits and starts. Eden's heart hammered. Asher's, too. Francesca issued directives whenever they had to divert from the path of one drone into the path of another.

Halfway, Francesca made a deadly miscalculation. She told them to go; the coast was clear. Eden's superhuman hearing said otherwise. She grabbed Asher by the shirtsleeve just as he was about to step into the open.

His giant hand tightened around his gun so fast, she had no doubt he would make good on his threat. Thankfully, a drone flew around the corner before he could, right into the path he would have been walking if Eden hadn't stopped him.

At its unexpected appearance, his face lost color. Francesca apologized profusely, her tone seeped in horror as Asher eyed Eden—not gratefully, but warily. Her hammering heart picked up speed as they made their precarious way to the entrance of the room Asher had pinpointed.

He used his thumb to press a code into the keypad. Eden waited for the lock to disengage. For the airtight seal to hiss.

No sound came.

Asher tried again.

This time, a small red light blinked above the keypad.

He swore.

Eden shifted.

The next drone was only twenty-one seconds away.

Asher tried again. Failed again.

Eighteen seconds.

"What are you doing, Ash?" Francesca's unease carried through his walkie-talkie. "Get inside *now*."

The keypad beeped.

The red light blinked.

"I need the override sequence."

His radio squawked. "I don't have the override sequence!"

Asher swore again, then plugged in a different number.

Beep.

Fail.

Twelve seconds.

He tried again.

Beep.

Fail.

Eden's grip on the semi-automatic tightened. She imagined the drone coming around the corner. She imagined throwing Asher to the ground. Dodging the spray of bullets. Hurtling herself forward. Diving at the mechanical sparrow and catching it in her hand. She imagined Francesca watching it unfold with her mouth ajar. How long before she realized what Eden was? And what would she do to Cleo once she did?

Six seconds.

"Get out of there, Ash!" Francesca yelled.

But Asher didn't listen. He hunched over the keypad, his bottom lip tucked beneath his front teeth, staring hard at the numbers in front of him.

Four seconds.

Eden braced for the infrared laser beam. The spray of bullets.

Three seconds.

Francesca shouted frantically as Asher punched in one last code.

There was a long beep.

A flash of green light.

The lock disengaged.

The seal hissed.

The door slid open.

They hurled themselves inside as the drone came flying around the corner. Asher slammed his palm against a button and the door closed behind them.

3

The room blinked with technology—computers and gadgets and another wall of monitors. Asher didn't wait for his heart to settle before taking control. He sat in front of the mainframe, typing in passwords like Jack Forrester 2.0. He was faster, smoother. Almost choreographed in his movements.

He communicated with Francesca as he swapped the walkie-talkie for a Bluetooth earpiece. He projected holographic command logs. He scrolled through streams of code in that determined way a person does when they are looking for something specific. His long fingers flew across the keys. His hands transitioned from one device to the next with a faint smile tucked into one corner of his mouth, like his near-death experience had been nothing more than a game.

"Time to play," he said, slipping on a VR set and picking up a remote that looked like it belonged to a gaming console.

Eden watched in begrudging admiration as the drone pattern changed. Shifted. Shrunk. Until all the mechanical sparrows were flying in a small circle under Judiciary Square.

"The pilot will notice," she said.

"I spoofed the GPS *and* I looped in old surveillance." Asher pulled up footage of the tunnels from the drones' perspective. "So no, the pilot won't notice. At least not until they catch sight of *that*."

The footage changed angles as the drone flew around a corner, and there, in the bottom right of the projection, was a flash of something dark. The heel of a boot. *Her* boot, right before she and Asher dove inside this very room. It was a blip. A fraction of a second. But visible to the naked eye. How long until the pilot spotted it? How long until the pilot realized it occurred every time that particular drone turned that particular corner?

Asher opened the top drawer of a nearby desk and removed another Bluetooth earpiece. He tossed it to Eden. It sailed across the room. She caught it cleanly.

"I'll be directing you to Metro Center where you will get the dose from Xavier. Then I'll direct you to the asset, where you will do exactly as I say. Don't ask questions. Don't mess up."

"Or you'll put a bullet through my head?"

He stared at her unapologetically.

She stared back. "Do you really have such little regard for human life?"

"You hurled us into survival mode, sweetheart."

The patronizing pet name set her teeth on edge.

"Survival 101. When you find yourself in situations like these, you can be one of two things—cutthroat or dead." He picked up the semi-automatic she'd been all too quick to abandon on the floor and handed it over.

Eden bristled. "Why do I need that?"

"In case they send actual human beings down here to finish the job."

She leaned away.

He rolled his eyes. "If you can't be cutthroat, that's your prerogative. But it would be really swell if you could do something helpful before you die."

"I saved your life back there."

"If we're still alive tomorrow, remind me to thank you." He

pushed the gun into her hands so hard she took a step back. "Don't go off script."

"I heard you the first time," she retorted, then stepped into the corridor.

The door slid shut behind her with a hiss of finality. She took a shaky breath, desperation stretching inside her like a yawn. She needed to get back to Cleo. She needed to find her way to Cassian. This was the best way to do it. Follow orders, even though she'd rather see the person giving them put in his place. She would prove to them she was on their side. She would prove to them she could be useful. But not so useful as to give herself away.

She suppressed her superior sense of direction. She ignored her photographic memory. She followed Asher's commands like she didn't know exactly how to get to where he was guiding her. She stepped around piles of debris, retracing the path she had traveled with Cleo when she wasn't injured and Cassian when he was by her side. Until finally, she strode through a rusted subway car and came out the back end, straight into Metro Center where the scent of decay and human excrement assaulted her nostrils.

A wave of revulsion rolled up her throat.

She swallowed hard, cursing her extraordinary sense of smell. She forced her feet to keep going as Asher commanded her to hurry. Around an abandoned ATV, to the bodies lying in pools of blood. One face down. One face up, his eyes open and unseeing, just like Mordecai on the rooftop of The Sapphire. Death surrounded her. It was in these tunnels below and on the ground above and at her feet now. It was in her past, and right here in her present. How much more would she have to witness before the end?

"Xavier is on the right," Asher said in her ear.

The one on the right was lying face down.

Her mouth flooded with saliva. She swallowed again—her revulsion thick and persistent as she reached out a trembling hand and pulled Xavier's shoulder. He flopped onto his back. Sucking in a sharp breath, Eden snatched her hand away. His body was stiff with rigor mortis. His skin, a pallid gray. Nausea churned in her stomach as she lifted the flap of his coat and reached inside his pocket. Her fingers curled around a small container. She removed it quickly and backed away.

From the smell.

From the cold impression of his skin.

From his blank, unseeing eyes.

"Confirm the syringe is still inside," Asher said.

The syringe.

Eden looked down at the small container and lifted the lid. A needle rested inside, the same shape and size as the one Jack Forrester had used on her in the Eagle Bend Police Department. Her body broke into a cold sweat. Asher was telling her where to go, how to get to the asset. But she couldn't hear. She was back in the interrogation room, huddled in the corner with her hands pressed over her ears as a man pretending to be her father stalked closer with a syringe just like this one.

My name is Eden Pruitt. I live at 3235 West Buckle Lane. My parents are Ruth and Alexander Pruitt. My name is Eden Pruitt. I live at 3235 West Buckle Lane. My parents are Ruth and Alexander Pruitt ...

"Drive the ATV and you'll get there faster," Asher said. "We have no time to waste."

Eden shut the lid. She tucked the container inside the pocket of her hooded sweatshirt and was about to climb onto the ATV when something in Xavier's hand caught her attention. A small, familiar magnet. The very one they had used to shut down the surveillance system. And by default, the emergency alert system, too.

The magnet was powerful. The magnet could very well come in handy. But Eden couldn't pick it up. Not without shutting herself down. She strapped the semiautomatic around her shoulder, mounted the ATV, and started the engine.

It rumbled to life.

She peeled away, leaving the dead men and the magnet behind. She hit the gas, turning when Asher told her to turn, trying her hardest to erase the memory of Xavier from her mind and the syringe tucked into her pocket. She drove at full speed until she reached her destination. Then she slammed the brake and came to a skidding stop in front of the door.

She cut the engine.

"We've been injecting him every four hours. At the moment, we're five doses behind schedule," Asher said. "For all we know, he's operating at full strength. If you can get to his neck, great, but anywhere will suffice."

Her body shook.

This was the moment. She would have to stab him with a syringe—against his will—like she had been stabbed. She wasn't worried about being overpowered. She was just as strong as the person trapped inside, with adrenaline coursing through her veins. But she did worry about giving herself away.

The back of her neck broke out into a cold sweat. Her fingers fumbled to press the code Asher recited.

The lock unlatched.

The door opened.

A young man sat inside the room. A boy her age with shaggy blonde hair and the same perfect symmetry as Eden and Barrett and Violet and Ellery. His face had no blemishes. No scars. No flaws. It was a face that would fit in perfectly at a college frat house. A classically handsome peer she might have crossed paths with next year on campus. But his wrists were shackled. His ankles, too. He was slumped in one corner with his head drooping like he didn't have the strength to lift it.

Asher was commanding her to go. To hurry. To remove the syringe from the container.

The case rattled in her hands.

She moved closer, imagining herself in an alternate universe. One where she was not Eden Pruitt. She never lived at 3235 West

Buckle Lane. Her parents were not Ruth and Alexander. Her father never worked for the CIA. The government never uncovered her existence. In that universe, she was part of the Electus. She was this boy. Inside this room. Locked up against her will.

The tremble in her hands grew.

She took another step when a splitting stab of pain pierced her temple. The same pain that made her fall on Lou's treadmill. The same pain that would have made her fall from a moving train had Cassian not been there to catch her. On instinct, she clutched the spot. And the young man who appeared too weak to lift his head capitalized on her distraction.

The steel chains snapped.

His body barreled into hers, slamming her against the opposite wall. Asher shouted in her ear. And in a moment of self-preservation, Eden tightened her hand around the needle and shoved it into the young man's neck.

She expected his eyes to roll. She expected him to go limp, to collapse in front of her.

Instead, his body seized. He screamed an ear-splitting scream as he rolled and writhed like every cell of his body was on fire.

Eden scrambled away. She clapped her hands over her ears. But she couldn't block out the sound. The scream continued—on and on and on—echoing inside the small room. Echoing inside her skull. Even when it was over, when he was silent and still on the floor, it continued. A bloodcurdling wail that would haunt her dreams forever.

4

sher's deep voice shouted in her ear, but she couldn't process his words. Not in light of the prone figure gasping on the ground in front of her. She stared in horror, her gaze fixed on the base of his throat, the notch between his collarbones drawing inward, skin pulling tight over bone as he sucked for air.

What had she just injected him with?

"Move," Asher commanded. "You need to get him here before we lose our window of paralysis."

Window of paralysis.

Did that include his lungs? Was he not able to breathe?

"Are you strong enough to get him on the back of the ATV? Is that something you can handle?"

His condescension made her want to snarl. Of course she could handle it. She could handle Asher if she wanted. She could lay him on his back in two seconds flat. But then she'd probably end up like this boy on the floor. This boy who couldn't breathe. With a shudder, she hooked her hands beneath the asset's arms and dragged him from the room. Aware that she was being watched via a surveillance camera, she pretended to struggle as she draped him over the seat of the ATV.

As soon as she arrived outside the control room, Asher came out to meet her, his expression renewed with wariness. Maybe even accusation. "I can't believe you were able to inject him."

She cut the engine and rubbed the back of her head, trying to sell it. It wasn't hard to act rattled. She *felt* rattled.

"We only have plastic zip-ties," someone called from inside.

Francesca.

Not in the White House Bunker, but here. Had she left Cleo behind? Eden's heart leapt into her throat as she barged into the room. She didn't exhale until her eyes landed on Cleo. She was here—semiconscious, sitting crooked in a chair, no longer connected to the portable IV. Eden rushed to her side and helped her into a more comfortable position on the floor.

Cleo smiled wanly. "Hey, Six."

The incriminating nickname came like a jolt. Eden shot a look over her shoulder. Thankfully—concernedly—Cleo's voice had been barely more than a whisper.

Asher clomped inside with the asset draped over his shoulders in a firefighter's carry. He dumped the young man in the far corner of the room, where he retched on the floor.

"What was in that syringe?" Eden asked.

"Something that keeps him under control," Francesca replied.

"Why aren't you using tranquilizer?"

"Because that would require injecting him every ten minutes." Francesca handed Asher a zip-tie.

He yanked the asset's hands behind his back and secured his wrists. "This won't hold."

"We'll have to increase the dosage," Francesca said.

"And the frequency," Asher added.

Eden's stomach rolled. She imagined injecting him with more poison. At more frequent intervals. It was inhumane. Awful. Appalling. And yet, they talked about it as matter-of-factly as a pair of coaches preparing for a last-minute exhibition match. All the while, the asset's scream was entombed in Eden's memory.

"This is torture," she said.

"If you have a better solution, we're all ears." He tightened another zip-tie around the asset's ankles. "Right now, sweetheart, we're working with what we've got."

There it was again.

Sweetheart.

Her hands clenched into fists. She stood there—furious, gobsmacked—as Asher and Francesca conferred and Cleo struggled to retain consciousness.

"I do, actually," Eden said.

Asher and Francesca paused from their conversation.

"You do, what?" Francesca asked.

"Have a better solution."

Asher raised his eyebrows.

"It's a small magnet made from a rare material."

"A magnet?" Francesca's acrimonious tone dripped with contempt.

"It shut down your entire surveillance system. It can shut down *any* system. Including his." Eden nodded at the asset without looking at him. She couldn't bear to look at him. He was so uncomfortably bound. Lying in a pool of his own vomit. And she had done it. *She* had injected that poison.

Asher folded his arms. "How do you know he has a system?"

"From my dad."

"Right," Francesca practically spat. "The CIA agent."

Asher shifted his weight, cocked his head. "Where is this magical magnet?"

"With Xavier."

"With Xavier?" he repeated.

"Yes."

"If it's really so powerful, why didn't you bring it with you?"

"I didn't know we would need it." She lifted her chin when she said it, refusing to squirm no matter how long Asher stared.

Finally, he pressed his finger against the Bluetooth in his ear and radioed Bunker Three. He told the survivors to make their way to the Control Room. But first, they needed to get a UTV from Union Station. One of them would drive to Metro Center and retrieve a special magnet.

After checking on the drones to ensure they were still circling beneath Judiciary Square, Asher turned his attention to the smoking sky above, where several more drones circled. Francesca joined him.

Eden knelt beside Cleo, who was unconscious once again. Her complexion, worse. Her breathing, painfully labored. Eden checked the bandage around Cleo's thigh. Infection seemed inevitable, especially without the IV. Eden pictured Cleo the first time they met. Garage band music on full blast. Bantu knots in her hair. Snake bite piercings in her lip. Brimming with life as she threw her arms around Cassian Gray's neck like he wasn't the most intimidating specimen Eden had laid eyes upon. Shoot-straight, irreverent, punk rocker Cleo. Eden refused to let her die. There had to be something she could do.

Closing her eyes, she focused on the whispered conversation unfolding behind her. Asher and Francesca were huddled together on the far side of the room, discussing what came next. Apparently, they needed more poison, which was stored in frozen vials somewhere above ground.

Asher broke from their huddle with a clap. Eden resisted the urge to shake her head. She knew what he was going to say, but she would not be their gopher. Not for this.

"Girl with the nine lives," he called.

"Eden," she replied, gritting the name between her teeth. She wasn't *girl*, and she wasn't *sweetheart* either.

"We require your services."

"They aren't available," she said.

"If you care about your friend, you'll have to make them available."

She spun around to meet his eye—this boy who had threatened to put a bullet through her head. He looked completely unfazed by her animosity.

"She obviously needs some TLC. We won't be able to get her

any until we have more of our ..." He moved his hands as though juggling invisible balls, in search of the right word.

"Devil venom?"

He smirked. "Call it what you like. That devil venom is keeping us alive right now. We can't leave until we have it."

"Leave?" Eden asked.

"We have a backup location. One with its very own medical center."

"They can't come with us, Ash," Francesca said. "They probably won't even let *us* in. Not with him." She tipped her chin at the boy on the floor.

"They have to," Asher replied. "It's part of the deal. And if she wants to be part of it, we'll need her cooperation." He turned to Eden. "The choice is yours. Moral superiority or your friend's wellbeing."

Eden ground her teeth. "This place has a medical center?"

"Qualified nurses and antibiotics, too."

With that, he had his answer.

Eden went.

She traversed the ravaged war zone above, carefully avoiding the drones in the sky. She retrieved an entire box of frozen vials. They clinked in her backpack as she made her quick return. When she arrived, Cleo was still unconscious and the rag-tag group from Bunker Three had joined them—four women and two men covered in grime. Their faces streaked with blood and tears. Each person eyed Eden with varying degrees of suspicion as Asher studied a small magnet in his hand.

When he was finished with the examination, he crouched beside the asset and pressed the magnet against his arm. It attached like the young man's skin was made of metal.

The mainframe beeped.

Asher strode toward the noise and punched in a command. His brow furrowed.

"What is it?" Francesca asked.

"His system is gone."

"What do you mean, it's gone?"

"His network disappeared." He typed several keys in quick succession and moved strings of code around a screen with his finger. When he finished, he slowly swiveled his chair—looking first at the asset, then at Eden. If he was wary before, he was brimming with suspicion now. He walked toward her and grabbed her by the hair. "Where did you get this magnet?"

"The Bryson's safe," Eden blurted.

"The Bryson's safe," Francesca repeated, her tone as belligerent as ever.

Before Eden could double down on the lie, something else beeped. This time, the sound came from a small device Asher had placed next to the mainframe. He let go of her and craned his neck to have a look. "We just got the go ahead," he said, turning to the rag-tag group of six. "I'll stay here and monitor the drones. Once you're secure, I'll catch up on the ATV. Fran will drive the UTV with the asset and *her*." He shot a scathing look at Cleo, like her injury was gum on the bottom of his shoe. "Everyone else will have to walk."

Eden shifted. "Walk where?"

Asher didn't answer.

Nobody did.

They might take Eden and Cleo with them, but apparently, they would not acknowledge her questions. Wherever they were going, Eden would find out along the way.

5

A girl called Jane walked along a lonely gravel road, past a creaky farmhouse with tinkling chimes and a giant, blow-up monster that flapped in the wind. She wasn't alone. The missing eighteen-year-old boy named Barrett Barr was with her. According to him, the monster belonged to a mad scientist named Frankenstein. It was a Halloween decoration, a holiday that was only a few days away.

Except for a mud-covered Jeep Wrangler that rumbled past an hour ago, the road was deserted. It was just her and Barrett and the moon and the crickets, which were chirping extra loud in a last-ditch effort to reproduce before winter.

"I can never decide which one is my favorite," Barrett said. "Pumpkins and haunted houses and a sack full of candy or Santa in his sleigh with a sack full of toys." He held out his hands like he was weighing the two options against one another. "I used to love trick-or-treating. Mom never let us dress up as anything too scary, but I think she would've allowed Franken-stein's monster. Psychotic serial killers from horror films, on the other hand? Not a chance. Jameson and—"

He looked at his hand where he'd scrawled three names in

25

blue ink. Every few days, a new name would drop out of his head. This last one had unsettled him greatly.

"*Graham,*" he said with an obvious note of frustration. "Graham, Graham, Graham." Graham and Jameson were Barrett's older brothers. Fraternal twins featured in so many of Barrett's stories, the girl called Jane felt like she knew them personally.

"Anyway," he continued. "Graham and Jameson always fought her on it. They wanted to be Freddy or Jason or Michael Meyer or It. The gorier, the better. Personally, I never understood the appeal. For me, it was superheroes all the way. I dressed up as a different one every single year until it got really uncool to dress up."

Barrett listed all the superheroes he had been through the years.

She tried to let his words wash over her, relax her. But every step they took brought her that much closer to the angry red X on the map. She gripped the rolled-up parchment in her hand while the knots in her stomach twisted tighter. They were going to the bad place. They were going there to get answers.

Something about her system was different. She was missing a piece. Jack Forrester called that piece the Queen Bee. The master node. The thing that commanded all the other nodes. Without it, she couldn't be controlled by the bad guys. But Barrett could. The red-headed girl named Ellery could, too.

"*She's free from that control, which means we can be, too!*" Ellery *had yelled.*

"*But I don't know how!*" Jack *had yelled back.* "*And the only person who could give us a clue refuses to talk!*"

The clue was Father.

Somehow, he made that piece go away.

Which meant she needed to go back. She needed to be brave. She needed to find out how Father had done it. Then they could replicate it so Barrett and the red-headed girl named Ellery would be safe. Eden, too, if she was alive.

"When I ran for student council in third grade, my dad said

to me, 'Barrett, dress for the position you want.' On Election Day, I wore a suit and a tie. I didn't win. It wasn't even close. But I took those words to heart whenever Halloween came around. I mean, what kid doesn't aspire to be a real live superhero?" He looked at her sideways, like maybe more of her words might come.

So far, she had said two of them.

Yes. And *Okay.*

If Barrett expected those words to be some prelude to a flood, he was in for disappointment. On the contrary, her voice felt like a rodent that had lifted its head from its burrow for a quick peek outside before ducking out of sight.

"My brothers were always the brave ones. Whenever Dad was gone and Mom needed a spider killed or a mouse chased out of the house, that's who she'd call on. Jameson and—" He glanced again at his hand. "*Graham.* Maybe that's why they didn't really care about dressing up as Captain America."

Barrett kept going.

He was trying to distract her. Maybe he was trying to distract himself, too. From the place they were going. From the place they had left. From the news they couldn't process. Cassian, arrested. Cleo, confirmed dead. Eden, presumed dead. The memory of those awful, terrible, pain-soaked sobs from Eden's mother.

The hoot of an owl made her jump.

She laughed nervously—a pathetic squeak of a sound.

Barrett smiled, his eyes twinkling in the moonlight. He had the warmest smile and the kindest eyes.

"You know what's interesting," he said. "Some of my favorite superheroes have the saddest backstories. Batman saw his parents getting murdered when he was a kid. Black Widow watched her mom die before she was recruited into the KGB. Bruce Banner had an abusive father. Clark Kent's entire planet blew up."

Murder.

Abandonment.

Abuse.

Destruction.

They were all terrible things that somehow made these superheroes special. The disquieting thought had all the knots in her stomach pulling tighter. She didn't want to be special, not if it required that much pain.

Behind them, headlights sliced through the night.

A red pickup truck approached.

Barrett stuck out his thumb.

He called this hitchhiking.

They'd been walking for hours and still had hours more to go. According to Barrett, they could get to Minneapolis much faster on a set of wheels, and he wasn't too worried about being recognized. His face hadn't been on the news much recently. Plus, his hair was considerably longer, and he was wearing a baseball hat. As for her, she was a nobody without an identity.

Brakes squealed as the truck slowed, then came to a stop a few paces ahead of them. Barrett had told her this was how it worked, and yet, the idling truck seemed to catch him completely by surprise. Clearly, Barrett didn't think anyone would stop. The mud-covered Jeep Wrangler certainly hadn't.

Barrett gave her a meaningful nod and pulled his hat lower. If the person behind the wheel recognized him as the missing 18-year-old, she was supposed to run. Straight into the woods as fast as possible. He would follow.

The truck's window rolled down. The scent of grease and cheeseburgers and a minty-sweetness wafted into the air. So did voices from the radio. The driver was an old man who leaned across the passenger seat. He had gray, scraggly hair pulled back into a low ponytail, a haggard face covered in a grizzled, patchy beard, and a fat bottom lip like something was packed inside. "Where you two headed?"

"Minneapolis," Barrett said.

The man looked from Barrett to her. She was hiding behind

her hair and holding onto a backpack bulging bigger than his lip. He spat a stream of black sludge into an empty bottle of Mountain Dew. "That city's crawling with drones and police officers. You sure you want to go that way?"

Barrett nodded.

"Hop in, then. I can get you as far as the border."

They climbed inside.

The floor was littered with crumpled McDonald's wrappers and empty red French fry cartons. A crucifix hung on his rearview mirror and a plastic creature had been stuck to his dashboard—a human with fangs and a white face and a black cape.

"I like your Halloween decoration," Barrett said.

"It's for my grandson. He's gonna be a vampire." The man sat with one hand on the steering wheel, the other wrapped around that bottle of black sludge cradled in his lap as he pulled onto the highway.

The glass beads of the crucifix tinkled.

The plastic creature's head bobbled.

The man spit into his bottle and turned up the radio.

"Mark my words," the host was saying, "this is the beginning of the end for this regime. Interitus will no longer have its tenterhooks in our great nation."

The man shook his head and spat once more. "Crazy times we're living in. Crazy times."

6

In all eighteen years of Eden's life, she'd never been to an airport. Her parents preferred driving. At least, this was what they'd always said. In truth, they were probably avoiding the security measures required for air travel. They weren't Ruth and Alexander Pruitt, after all, and Eden wasn't their biological daughter. The reality took her breath away. She couldn't dwell on it for long without feelings of sadness and betrayal creeping in, so she chose not to dwell on it at all.

Despite her lack of experience with airports, she'd always been able to picture the setting. According to everything she'd seen in movies and shows, they bustled with life and emotion—goodbyes and reunions, tight hugs and "Welcome Home" signs, characters racing through the crowd to catch a flight or frantically purchasing a ticket so they could declare their love before the final boarding call. Eden had spent plenty of time daydreaming about her first air travel adventure—an international flight to Paris, France.

Not once in all those imaginings had she pictured this—bearing the weight of her injured friend as they made their way through the giant crypt that was once Reagan National Airport. It wasn't ruined like Union Station. But it was empty, the air unnervingly still, their footsteps echoing through the concourse as they passed baggage carousels long out of use.

They were meeting a man named Jericho. Eden knew this, not because anyone had deigned to fill her in, but because she had used her superhuman hearing to eavesdrop. Jericho was part of the Resistance—a council member like Prudence and Asher and Francesca. But he didn't live underneath Washington, DC, with the rest of them. He lived in Alexandria—a revelation that had Eden biting her tongue. She knew of Alexandria. So did Cleo.

They first learned about it from a digital map in Mona's office —a virtual atlas of communities and safe houses for people living off the grid. Alexandria was one such community. She learned about it again from the gentleman who helped care for Elmer and Eloise Miller of Bethesda. A gentleman who was as infamous as Prudence Dvorak—the at-large media mogul named Dayne Johnson. Cleo's role model. And also, Editor-in-Chief of the largest illegal newspaper in the country, *America Underground.*

Alexandria was the hub of this illegal newspaper. And apparently, Jericho was the leader of that hub. Dayne didn't live in Alexandria, but as Editor-in-Chief, he was an integral part of their operation. As such, he had to work closely with Jericho. So, did Dayne know about the Resistance?

Eden rifled through her memories. When she'd asked him if he knew anything about the Monarch, he'd acted oblivious. When she'd shown him the pamphlet from the Bryson's safe, his face had registered nothing but genuine fascination. She didn't think he could be that good of an actor. As Eden shuffled forward, taking up the rear of the group, supporting as much of Cleo's weight as she could without rousing suspicion, she wondered if Dayne Johnson was alive and well. She wondered if he was still with the Millers.

She had her doubts, and those doubts made her stomach hurt. She strongly suspected this was all her doing. Not just shutting down the emergency alert system, but the reason the military showed up in the first place. The Resistance had known Eden was in Bethesda. Amir Kashif was part of the Resistance. He was also an employee of the NSA. They probably knew she was in Bethesda because of the intel Amir had intercepted through his job. And if that was the case, the government had probably known where Eden was staying.

She pictured Eloise Miller, tucked away in her sewing room, watching her scandalous show. She pictured Elmer doing his word search at the kitchen table, smiling kindly if not confusedly any time Eden walked into the room. The elderly couple had taken them in, given them refuge. Fed them hearty meals. Eden couldn't bear to think of Elmer and Eloise as anything other than perfectly okay.

Asher stopped in front of a set of half-opened sliding glass doors. A sign above read Delta. He unloaded the asset, who flopped onto the conveyor belt like a sack of potatoes. Eden assisted Cleo to the carousel, where she sat with a labored exhale, sweating profusely. Francesca rummaged through the backpack filled with poisonous vials, mumbling in dulcet tones with Asher. The others loitered nearby looking around like they'd never seen an airport either.

Cleo hugged herself and shivered.

Eden sat beside her, lending her body heat. She wrapped her arm around Cleo's shoulder, trying hard to ignore the unconscious young man behind them when footfalls sounded in the distance. Two sets. Nobody reacted. Nobody could hear. And Eden was struck—not with her own power, but the fragility of everyone else. How vulnerable they were to attack. To injury. To infection. To death.

Finally, two figures stepped through the doors. Eden came to her feet. "Dayne!"

He cut a sharp look in her direction.

"You two know each other?" Asher asked.

Eden ignored him. Dayne was alive. He was *here*. Hope

blossomed in her heart. "Elmer and Eloise. Are they—?" She didn't finish the question. The look on Dayne's face stopped her cold.

"They're dead," he said, squeezing her blossom of hope into dust. "They shot Eloise as soon as she answered the door. They shot Elmer in his bed."

She sat down, feeling dazed. Sucker punched. Hopeless. Her worst fears confirmed. This *was* her fault. The military had come because they'd been tracking *her*. Now two more deaths had been heaped upon her shoulders. Only this time, those deaths were more than numbers. More than a concept. They involved a kind, elderly couple she'd known. Two individuals she'd grown to care about.

"There wasn't anything I could do but hide until they left." Dayne looked old and angry as his attention moved from Asher and Francesca, to the six battle-worn stragglers, to Cleo and Eden sitting on the conveyer belt, to the unconscious asset, to the unarmed gentleman standing beside him—a baldheaded Black man with a salt and pepper goatee. "Now here I am, completely in the dark about some *deal*."

"That deal has kept us well fed," Jericho replied, stepping forward to shake hands, first with Asher, then Francesca. "You're sure you weren't followed?"

"Positive," Asher answered.

"This is everyone?"

"Seven were taken in the raid. The rest are dead."

Jericho scratched his goatee. "We could hear the airstrike from Alexandria. As far as my people are concerned, you're members of Interitus. They won't risk their lives for terrorists."

"Then we'll have to tell them the truth," Asher said.

Francesca shook her head. "We can't."

"Why not?" Dayne shot. "I don't understand why you've kept yourselves a secret. Especially from me."

"You didn't know?" Eden asked.

"I've been completely clueless," Dayne said. "So has

everyone else working for *America Underground*. Jer here has kept us completely in the dark."

Eden stared—perplexed. Frustrated. In full agreement with Dayne. Maybe if the Resistance had been more forthright, none of this would have happened. As soon as Eden showed Dayne the pamphlet, he would have told her who the Monarch was and who Amir Kashif was. She and Cleo and Cassian could have joined the Resistance instead of inadvertently destroying it.

"The more people who know about us," Francesca said, "the more vulnerable we become."

"The fewer people who know about you," Eden retorted, "the more likely you are to be mistaken for something you're not."

Francesca shot Eden a scathing look with her good eye. "You don't think Pru tried in the beginning? The rumors that resulted nearly got her killed. She learned the hard way that if she wanted to build an army, she would have to do it slowly, with extreme caution."

"The time for slow is over," Dayne said, tipping his chin toward Jericho. "If even half of what he's told me in the last hour is true, you're going to need the entire off-the-grid community on your side."

"Do you think they will join us?" Asher asked.

"None of us are receiving an invitation to Brahm's future Utopia," Dayne said. "Which makes the choice simple: we join or we die."

7

A chilly breeze ruffled Eden's hair. The smoky scent of it triggered a memory so vivid that for one disconcerting moment she could hear Mordecai's snake-like voice whispering in her ear, *"I would like you to shoot them."*

She shoved her hands deep into the pocket of her hoodie and pushed the intrusive memory away as a lone leaf scuttled past her feet. She was standing on the edge of an empty parking lot outside a deserted strip mall beneath a full-bodied sky. A tapestry of gray and purple clouds roiling overhead. It smelled like rain.

She didn't know what time it was. She didn't even know what day it was. She felt as though she'd been underneath Washington, DC, for a lifetime. And now suddenly she was here in Alexandria without Cassian, watching Cleo ride away in a UTV. The driver was taking her to the community's medical center, a building they called Kaiser.

Eden was relieved Cleo would get the care she needed, but not as relieved as she'd be if she was going with her to get that care. When she tried, Asher had grabbed her by the elbow and told her she wasn't going anywhere. Not with Cleo. Not with the survivors from Bunker Three, either. All six had been shuttled off to The Landing, a former retirement facility turned residence hall.

Thanks to the airstrike, the people of Alexandria were on high alert. There was an edge of panic in the air. While Cleo could slip into Kaiser with little fanfare, and the six from Bunker Three could walk through The Landing without drawing too much attention, Eden was a different story. Over the past few weeks, her face had been plastered all over Concordia News. Until Jericho could call for a proper assembly and explain her presence, she would need to stay close.

So here she was, marveling at how very different this place was from the Damen Silos in Chicago. The people in that community existed in a dank underground labyrinth with mold in the air and dirty sheets hanging in the doorways. The people here had an entire campus with a medical facility and a residence hall and a PA system from which Jericho could call for an assembly. Granted, that campus appeared to be abandoned and neglected, preyed upon by time, overrun with weeds. But it was above ground, and it had basic amenities and access to fresh air. If the off-the-grid community was a ship, the Damen Silos were steerage; the Potomac Yard in Alexandria was first class. Made possible by the very man they were forming an alliance to fight.

Oswin Brahm.

Thanks to him, Alexandria was part of the no-go zone. Off limits because of its supposed toxicity. But it hadn't been directly hit in The Attack. Everything was in working order, powered by a privately owned solar farm courtesy of their backer, a man named Harlan. Apparently, this was part of the deal. A power grid in exchange for an emergency evacuation plan.

"What did you do to him?" Jericho asked, finally addressing the young man Asher had dumped into the back of Jericho's UTV.

Asher showed Jericho the magnet on the asset's arm.

"What is it?" he asked.

"She had it with her." Asher's attention lifted to Eden. "She claims it was a trinket she found in the Bryson's safe."

"The Bryson's?" asked Jericho.

Asher nodded meaningfully. Eden Pruitt was wanted for their murder. It was the reason her face had been all over the news. Jericho's dark brown eyes took on the same suspicious glow as Asher's hazel ones.

"We need a secure place to store him," Asher said, nodding at the asset.

"And her," Francesca added.

"What?" Eden choked, taking a lurching step backward.

"We have important matters to discuss. *Confidential* matters. And according to Jericho, we can't have you wandering about."

"I won't go wandering about."

"That's nice, but we don't know you and we don't trust you."

"I know her," Dayne said. "And I can vouch for her."

Francesca's attention jerked to the Editor-in-Chief. She looked like she might say the same thing to him, but Jericho intervened. "I can vouch for Dayne."

Dayne's jaw ticked with annoyance, like he didn't want to be vouched for by a person who had left him so blatantly in the dark. "She came to the Millers wanting to take down the Monarch, not the Resistance. Like me, she didn't even know about a Resistance."

Eden jumped in. "And I've done nothing but cooperate with you guys. I did everything you asked of me. I even saved your life." She glared at Asher.

A taut face-off ensued.

She would not look away. She would not be intimidated. After an extended moment of simmering silence, he blinked first. With a huff, Asher took Francesca's backpack. The glass vials clinked inside. "These need to be stored in a deep freeze and kept somewhere easily accessible."

"Easily accessible?" Eden blurted.

Everyone looked at her.

She blinked at the bag. She wanted to snatch it from Asher's hands, race across the train tracks and the neglected parkway beyond, and dump every vial into the Potomac River. "You wanted a better option. I gave you one. The magnet works just fine."

"His system is offline," Asher replied.

"So?"

"*So*," he said, "he has a network; I'm trying to breach it. I can't do that unless his network is online."

"You haven't breached it yet?"

Asher gave her a look of utmost annoyance. "His network is one of the most complicated and secure networks I've ever come across, and we've only had him since the Prosperity Ball."

Eden made a quick computation. The Prosperity Ball had been on October fourth, the anniversary of The Attack. The last time Eden had a confident grasp of the date had been the morning of the twenty-sixth, when she and Cassian and Cleo followed a tunnel into Washington, DC. Which meant they'd had the asset for over twenty-two days, a timeline that made no sense. Eden had watched Asher hack into government drones. She'd watched him spoof their GPS systems like it was nothing more than child's play. Jack Forrester knew his way around a computer system, sure. But comparatively, Asher was—as her old friend Erik would say—a Jedi Knight, and Jack Forrester was a Padawan. So how was it possible that Jack had breached her network in a handful of days while Asher was still working after twenty-two of them?

"I don't understand what you're doing with him," Dayne said.

"Trying to gain access into his inner workings," Asher replied. "Once I do that, I should be able to figure out how he's controlled. And once I know how he's controlled, there are a myriad of ways we can use him."

Use him.

"Imagine the Monarch's surprise when we turn his most precious weapon against him," Francesca said, practically crooning the words.

Eden blanched. They planned to control him. Force him to do things against his will. Just like Eden had been controlled and forced. "If that's your strategy, how are you any different from Brahm?"

Francesca's good eye flashed. "We won't be decimating entire cities."

Another awkward silence ensued.

This time, Jericho was the one to break it. "I can bring him to the commissary," he said, glancing at his watch. "Nobody should be there this early in the morning. We can keep the vials in one of the chest freezers. We can keep him in the walk-in refrigerator."

A shudder rippled up Eden's spine.

They were going to store the asset *in a refrigerator*?

Jericho climbed behind the wheel. "Once I get him situated, I'll meet you in the east tower."

Asher handed him the bag. "We'll send an alert to Amir. The others, too."

"The others?" Dayne asked.

"Fellow council members," Asher replied. "We need to apprise them of the situation."

"And call for a vote," Francesca said, the corners of her mouth tight. "If we're going to make a move as big as inviting everyone here into the Resistance, then it needs to be a majority decision."

"Fair enough," Asher said, shrugging in acquiescence. "Hey, Jericho. Does this place have any handcuffs?"

Jericho glanced at the plastic zip-ties wrapped around the asset's wrists and ankles. It was obvious he wouldn't get them off anytime soon.

"They're not for him," Asher said.

The ominous statement came with no elaboration. Jericho seemed to understand just fine without any. With a nod, he started the engine and accelerated to The Landing. The asset's head flopped over the seat, dangling lifelessly above the weed-riddled road as the UTV sped away.

8

The steel door opened with an echoing groan. Light stabbed his eyes, but Cassian Gray could not shield them. His hands were bound behind his back. His left shoulder throbbed. He imagined a fire poker in a blacksmith's forge, glowing red with heat. Thrust through muscle and sinew until its pointed tip rested between the ball and socket of his joint. A fierce, demanding pain. And yet, it was nothing compared to the inferno of helpless rage blazing in his chest.

Eden.

She had to be alive. She was designed to be alive. He couldn't consider any other possibility.

Boots clomped across the cement floor. Rough hands yanked him to his feet. The pain in his shoulder howled. But not him. Cass gritted his teeth. He ground his molars as the guard shoved him out of the prison cell, into a dank corridor. His head swam. His throat ached. He was dizzy and weak and consumed.

Eden.

Where was she? What had they done with her?

He had to escape. He had to find out. Which meant he had to be stronger than the pain and smarter than his captors. He forced his eyes to adjust. He inspected his surroundings, determined to collect information like a miser collecting gold. He would hoard every detail until he found a way to escape.

The guard escorting him through the hallway had a slight limp. Something was wrong with his left leg. Could Cass use that to his advantage? They passed several doors. He needed to see what was behind them. *Who* was behind them. Was she behind them? But the guard shoved him onward until they reached one last door at the end of the corridor.

He pressed his thumb against a keypad.

The door slid open.

Cass was pushed inside a room as dank and dim as the hallway. A bare, dangling lightbulb cast a halo of yellow light upon a small table in the room's center. It was empty except for a bottled water. Beyond, set in the concrete wall, was the kind of mirror found in interrogation rooms. His reflection glared back at him— a mangle of bruises and dried blood. He wanted to charge forward and ram his fist through the glass. He wanted to reach through to the other side and wrap his fingers around the neck of whoever was watching. Whoever was in charge. He wouldn't let go until that person told him where she was.

It was a lovely fantasy. One he wouldn't hesitate to carry out if his hands weren't bound.

The guard shoved him into the chair.

Another pair of cuffs snapped into place behind him, securing him to his seat. The guard strolled around Cass with the same slight limp, his lips thin and bloodless as he swiped the bottle of water off the table. The plastic crinkled in his grip. "You must be thirsty."

Cass glared. He was, in fact. Terribly so. But he would not give this man the satisfaction of saying it.

The guard untwisted the cap and held the bottle to Cassian's lips. "Time to hydrate."

Cass ground his teeth.

The guard chuckled, then—without warning—shoved the bottle into Cassian's mouth with such force, his lips smashed into his teeth. The guard poured the water down his throat. Cass reared back, but the man kept pouring. Cass choked and coughed until the guard yanked the bottle away as aggressively as he'd forced it in.

Cass spit what he hadn't swallowed into the man's face.

For a shocked moment, the guard did nothing. A mixture of water and spit dripped from his long nose. Then, with a curse, he backhanded Cass. Hard.

The metallic taste of blood filled his mouth.

Cass spit that, too.

Before the guard could deliver another blow, a middle-aged woman with copper-colored hair strode into the room, fire blazing in her eyes. She raised her hand sharply. "This isn't how we treat prisoners."

The man yanked a handkerchief from his back pocket. He whipped it open with a sharp shake and wiped the bloody spittle from his nose. "He's a terrorist."

"I am not a terrorist," Cass said, gritting the words between his teeth.

The woman pulled at the hem of her blazer and arched her eyebrow. "Enlighten us, then, Mr. *Ransom*—who are you?" She emphasized the surname as she dropped a thick file on the table. It landed open with a picture on top that came like a brutal, unexpected punch to the gut.

"Allow me to introduce Atticus Belby, an investment banker who lives in Gary, Indiana, with his wife and two children. But this isn't his first marriage." The woman plucked a second photograph from the file and set it beside the first.

It came as another sucker punch.

"His previous marriage was to Rebecca Wilder," the woman continued. "The daughter of a wildlife biologist who lived in Wyoming. Grayson Wilder. Or *Gray*, as many called him."

She perched on the edge of the table. "Atticus and Rebecca met and fell in love. They settled in Denver where Rebecca gave birth to a son. Tragically, Rebecca and her son died in a boating accident on Sloan Lake. Their bodies were never recovered."

Cass glared.

The woman crossed her arms. "Imagine Mr. Belby's surprise when a few weeks ago, he sees his dead son on Concordia National News, responsible for the bombing in Chicago."

Bile burned in his throat. If his father was shocked, it wasn't because he thought he'd lost his son in a boating accident on Sloan Lake. It was because he thought he killed that son with the same baseball bat he'd used to kill Rebecca Wilder.

The woman stood. She strolled around the table until she reached Cassian. She lifted the torn sleeve of his shirt, revealing the tattoo beneath—a wolf framed in Celtic knots. "It would seem little Cassian Belby didn't drown in Sloan Lake, but grew up to become a ruthless fighter known as Cassian 'The Wolf' Gray."

The woman released his shirt sleeve. "What's less clear is what happened to Cassian Belby's mother. Is she alive, too?"

"Why don't you ask Atticus?" Cass replied, his voice low and mutinous.

The woman peered at him, her carefully lined eyes narrowed into slits. Her face was freckled, but those freckles had been muted by makeup. "How did you come to know Prudence Dvorak?"

He didn't answer.

She rubbed her earlobe, then strolled back to her spot on the other side of the table. A golden brooch pinned to the lapel of her blazer caught the light as she removed a third photograph from the file and set it on top of the other two. This one, a mug shot Cass knew well. It had led him to Eden.

"What about *her*?" the woman asked.

Fire burned in his chest.

"How did you two meet?"

He jerked against his restraints with nostrils flared.

The woman picked up the file. She began an unhurried,

short-routed pace as she studied the contents within. "As I understand it, Mr. and Mrs. Pruitt were very troubled by their daughter's arrest. So troubled, in fact, they moved from San Diego, California, to a small, obscure town in Iowa."

She removed a fourth photograph and dropped it onto the table—a candid of Eden's parents carting boxes into their new home in Eagle Bend. Then she pulled out a fifth photograph. She set the file back on the table with this photograph on top—a picture of Eden's parents on their wedding day, when they weren't Alexander and Ruth Pruitt, but Alaric and Molly Taylor. "All kinds of familiar faces have been cropping up in the news these days."

The inferno beneath his sternum turned into something cold and desperate. They knew. Of course they knew. As soon as Eden's parents made national headlines, the government had undoubtedly connected the dots. Cass had known it. So had Eden. But now, that knowing stared him in the face.

The woman set her hands on the table and leaned forward. She tapped the photograph taken in Eagle Bend. "Alexander and Ruth Pruitt." She moved her tapping finger to the wedding photo. "Alaric and Molly Taylor. An uncanny resemblance, wouldn't you say?"

Cass swallowed.

"Alaric Taylor worked for the government once upon a time. That is, before he and his wife disappeared. As thoroughly as Rebecca and Cassian Belby. Alexander and Ruth have a daughter who is eighteen, but they didn't have a daughter when they disappeared sixteen and a half years ago." The woman shut the file. "Perhaps if you could tell us something of value. Something that might lead us to the girl, a deal could be arranged."

His mouth went dry.

He stared at the woman, processing her words.

Lead them to the girl?

Then that meant …

A flood of relief extinguished the fire.

She wasn't here.

They didn't have her.

"Freedom could be yours," the woman said, mistaking his expression. Like he was enticed by this offer of immeasurable irony. Hand over the girl and freedom would be his. It was the same offer Yukio had issued. The same offer that had entangled him in this mess to begin with. Only then, the girl had meant nothing to him. Now she meant everything.

"What do you think, Mr. Gray?"

He smiled a slight smile, the taste of blood still on his lips.

The woman arched her eyebrows, higher this time—waiting. Expectant. Like the game might really be this easy.

"I think …" Cass leaned forward, watching as the woman's pupils dilated. "That you and your guard can *go to hell*."

The man lurched forward with his fist cocked.

The woman held up her hand with an irritated jerk, stopping him before he could pounce. She peered at Cass for a long moment, then she gathered up the photographs and tucked them into the file. "It would seem our interview is done for now. Perhaps time will make you more cooperative."

The guard unlocked Cass from the chair.

"We know she was there, Mr. Gray," the woman said. "We know she was with you in Washington, DC. Which means she is hiding beneath the city with what remains of Interitus, *if* anything remains at all."

Interitus doesn't exist.

The words belonged to Prudence Dvorak.

Her scathing proclamation played through his mind as the woman straightened her blazer. "Or she escaped above ground during the chaos. We have drones searching the tunnels, and we have drones searching the streets. Drones with facial recognition, able to identify specific targets. They have been programmed to kill on sight."

His brow furrowed. A drone wouldn't kill Eden. Surely they knew this.

The woman examined one of her nails, then scooped up the file and met Cassian's gaze. Hers was unwavering. "Unless, of course, they come upon Eden. For her, we have tranquilizer."

————

*T*ranquilizer.

They had loaded their drones with tranquilizer. Which made it official. They knew exactly what Eden was and how to capture her. Once they did, how long until the government finished the job her father couldn't all those years ago?

The guard wrenched Cass to his feet. His shoulder flared with pain. White-hot adrenaline coursed through his veins as the guard shoved Cass into the corridor and pushed him forward, the metal restraints biting into his wrists.

Ahead, two figures stepped into view.

Prudence Dvorak—her face bruised, her dark hair askew—flanked by her own burly guard. She stared at Cass as hard as he stared at her—as if each were a book, and if the other found the right page, they might glean vital information before they passed one another. Their arms brushed. He looked over his shoulder. She looked over hers. But they were shoved forward, and all too quickly, Dvorak was gone and Cass was being pitched off course —a sharp pivot down a dark hallway. The guard rammed him against the wall. He jammed his forearm into Cassian's neck with such force he choked.

"Where is he?" the guard hissed.

Cass couldn't speak. He could barely breathe. But even if he could hiss out an answer, he had no answer to give. He didn't even understand the question. *Where is he?*

"Where are they keeping him?"

He coughed.

The guard thrust his face so close, Cass could count the black pores on his nose. The guard pushed harder, applying so much pressure, the blood trapped in Cassian's head became a pulsing pressure that pressed against his eyes. He clenched his fists, wishing his hands were free as the guard pulled him forward and slammed him against the wall. "If you want your girlfriend to live, you better start talking."

Rage swelled. A blinding, explosive rage.

Cass sunk his knee into the guard's groin. The man doubled over with a wheeze, then tried to force himself upright as Cass reared back and used his head like a hammer. With a sickening crunch, he connected with bone and cartilage.

The guard fell back, a spray of crimson splashing against the floor.

Cass charged. He used his uninjured shoulder to shove the guard into the opposite wall as the man screamed for help.

Boots came running.

Someone tackled Cass from behind.

A kick landed hard in his ribs.

The guard he attacked scuttled away, clutching his bleeding nose as a third man jumped into the fray. Cass fought without his hands. He bucked and kicked, heedless of the pain. Heedless of the odds.

Eden.

Her face filled his mind like a bright and shining beacon.

He had to get to her.

But then something hard cracked against his skull.

A loud ringing sounded in his ears.

Stars danced behind his eyes.

The world went black.

9

The downshift woke her.

She'd been sleeping with her head on Barrett's shoulder. She blinked at him groggily. His head was leaning against the headrest, his hat askew, his mouth open. Sunlight caught the crucifix as the truck came to a stop. Its reflective glare winked in her eye.

She sat up straight.

The old man turned down the radio. His bottom lip no longer bulged. The bottle of sludge was capped and on the floor, resting against Barrett's boot. Up ahead, the St. Croix River stretched in front of them, along with an on-ramp that led to a bridge in the distance and a sign that said *Welcome to Minnesota*.

"There ain't ever been a checkpoint here before," he said, nodding at a slapdash booth with a camera mounted on its roof. "I suppose with the state of affairs, more and more of 'em will be cropping up." With the shake of his head, he started muttering about surveillance. About Big Brother. About how much harder it was to live an unbothered life in this day and age.

Meanwhile, her heart was in full gallop.

There was a line of three cars ahead of them. Orange cones on the road. A patrol vehicle parked on the shoulder next to the booth. And a uniformed officer standing at the driver's side door of the car in front.

The old man peered into the rear-view mirror. "Not a soul behind us. Why's that always happen—getting places at the exact wrong time?"

She shook Barrett. Hard.

He awoke with a start as the car in front of the line drove off and the other two crept forward.

Barrett wiped drool from the corner of his mouth, blinking like one trying to gain his bearings. A second later, he went ramrod straight, his attention jumping to the door handle by her elbow like he might make a dive for it so they could run away. Instead, he pulled his hat lower.

She could hear his heart beating the same as hers—wildly.

Fear swelled in her belly. Sweat prickled under her arms.

They watched as the patrol officer took the driver's license and registration, then scanned the driver's retinas. Was there a passenger? There seemed to be someone in the back seat, but the officer didn't identify this person. With a nod, he allowed the driver to go through. The vehicle maneuvered around the cones and sped off toward the bridge.

The old man shut off the radio. He shifted into first gear and inched forward.

The crucifix glinted.

The vampire's head bobbled.

The car ahead of them passed through.

They were up.

The old man pulled to a stop and rolled down his window.

The officer bent over with one eye squinted against the sun, the other fixed on the old man's hands at a perfect ten and two, his gnarled knuckles white with tension, like he had a reason to be tense.

"Mornin' officer," he said.

The officer looked past him, toward Barrett with his hat. And her, hugging the bulging backpack in her lap.

"License and registration," he said in a flat tone.

The old man reached past Barrett and removed the paper-work from his glove box.

"Where you headed?" the officer asked, examining the license.

"Rochester. Visiting my grandson for Halloween."

"And these are …?"

"My other grandchildren. Excited to see their cousin."

The officer held up the retinal scanner.

The old man acquiesced, looking straight into its infrared light.

The officer studied the screen with a frown. "Several unpaid tickets here."

"Yessir. I plan to take care of those as soon as my next paycheck arrives."

The officer studied the old man for a long, nerve-wracking moment, then said, "Could I ask you to step out of the vehicle?"

"That really necessary?"

"All three of you, please."

She squeaked, then quickly clamped her mouth shut.

Barrett slid out after the old man. She could have opened her own door and exited the vehicle the normal way, but it felt safer to follow Barrett. She scooted across the bucket seat, leaving her backpack behind, and stepped out into the morning sun, the two-lane highway behind them empty, the cars that had been in front, disappearing over the bridge.

A second officer stepped out from the booth. "What's the …" His voice fell away mid-question, and despite Barrett's hat being low, despite his hair being longer, the officer's eyes went bright with recognition the moment they landed on him. "Hey, you're that kid! The one who's been missing."

As if on cue, the officers pulled guns from their holsters at the same time and turned on the old man. "Hands on the truck."

His face paled. "What?"

"Hands on the truck now!"

The old man did as he was told.

It was all the distraction she needed. Without hesitating, she dropped in a twirling foot sweep and knocked the closer patrol officer onto his backside. In a matter of seconds, she'd disarmed the other one, too. Both officers were without their guns, belly-down on the ground with their hands over their heads, pleading for their lives as the old man and Barrett ogled like a couple fish. She handed a gun to Barrett, which seemed to free him from his frozen state. He asked the group for duct tape.

When nobody answered, he asked louder.

"In my glove box!" the old man shouted, his arms going over his head like he was preparing to protect himself from the inevitable gun shot.

Barrett quickly retrieved the roll. He tied up all three, apologizing the entire time.

"I don't understand why you're doing this," the old man blubbered. "I done nothing but help you two get to where you wanted to go."

"This way, they'll know you didn't kidnap us," Barrett said, fumbling around inside their pockets. He removed keys and walkie-talkies and phones. He put each gadget on the ground and shot them one by one. He turned and shot the camera mounted on the booth, too. Then they climbed into the truck and Barrett drove away.

"We just committed a major felony," he said, his voice shaking as he shifted into third and hit the gas harder, leaving the three men behind—tied up, with no way to report them. Until, of course, another car arrived.

———

Barrett cut the engine. "Is this—why are we—?"

She held her finger to her lips like the drones circling the city might hear. With her eyes on the dumpster ahead, she climbed out of the red pickup truck they had stolen and stepped into the shadowed alley. Barrett hadn't known where he was going. With their adrenaline pumping, she had guided him with points and nods while his attention darted between the rearview mirror and the road in front until they reached a rundown business district on the outskirts of the city.

He climbed out after her.

They left the doors open. It was best not to make any sound.

With her heart still galloping, she pulled at the hem of her jacket and crept toward the dumpster on silent feet. It was impossible. She knew this. Too much time had passed. They were gone or dead. But she had to look. She had to check. When she came around the dumpster and saw the tarp—tattered and stained and crumpled—her galloping heart leapt. If the tarp was still here, maybe they were, too.

Her insides warmed at the memory—tiny little puppies with eyes that could barely open, mewling as their proud mama stood by. Then the men had come. The mama had growled low in her belly with ears flattened and hackles raised. After that, Jane couldn't remember anything else. One second, those bad men were creeping closer, and she was curling her hand around a broken piece of glass, prepared to protect the mother and her babies. The next, she was waking up in Dr. Norton's basement.

She couldn't hear any heartbeats now. But maybe, just maybe …

Holding her breath, she ripped the tarp off the ground with a whip and a rustle. There was nothing underneath. No puppies. No mother. They were gone, and even though she knew they would be, their absence stole every ounce of warmth within her. In its place, an overwhelming sadness unfolded.

Had those men taken the babies? Had they taken the mama? Did they kill her like Father had killed Kitty? The babies wouldn't have survived on their own. They would have died. Because babies needed a mother. The sadness kept unfolding. It smelled like sesame oil and talcum powder. It felt like the soothing stroke of her hair. It sounded like a low, secret whisper as Mother read her stories at night from the forbidden books they kept hidden beneath a loose floorboard under the bed. Then Mother left and all Jane had were those stories and a photograph in her pocket that was no longer in her pocket, but lost somewhere between those men in this alley and Dr. Norton's basement. The sadness grew bigger and bigger until she thought it might swallow her whole.

Why did Mother leave?

The tests and the training got so much worse after she left. The pain and the torture and her failure and his anger. Then Kitty. Oh, how she missed Kitty.

Barrett touched her shoulder.

She jumped.

His brow furrowed. "Are you okay?"

She dropped the crumpled tarp and took a step away from the empty slab of cement. Fear swirled with the sadness—a deep and fathomless pit. She was close. Too close to that red X. The nearness had her knees knocking, her words burrowing deeper. She let her hair fall in her face. She wanted to hide. She wanted to run.

"You know he can't hurt you, right?" Barrett dipped his chin to meet her eye.

Oh, but he could.

Somehow, someway, Father always could.

"You're stronger than him, Jane. I'm stronger than him, too." He looked over his shoulder at the open-doored truck behind them. "But we don't have to go. You don't have to do this. We can go back to Milwaukee. Or anywhere, really. We probably just can't drive the truck."

She didn't have to do this.

It was a choice.

She could turn back, and Barrett would go with her.

He'd go with her anywhere.

As far away from the Red X as possible.

But then, what would happen if the bad guys found them?

Maybe Father really couldn't hurt her. Maybe Father really couldn't hurt Barrett. But the bad guys could. If she ran, the possibility would forever hover over her shoulder. A ticking time bomb waiting to explode.

Barrett was right.

She wasn't trapped.

She had a choice.

She closed her eyes and forced her lungs to expand, to breathe. Then she imagined a seed of courage sprouting. She imagined its roots reaching deep, taking hold. With shoulders squared, she marched to the truck and grabbed her bulging backpack. She grabbed Barrett's, too, and the guns they had taken from the patrol officers.

She tucked one into her belt and handed him the other.

Then she motioned for him to follow.

Through the abandoned business district, where she had once slept and scrounged for food. Into the woods beyond. Deep, deep in the woods, where Father's house hid. Fear sucked at her boots like thick, viscous mud. Her steps were slow and plodding.

Barrett didn't rush her.

He walked at her pace. He followed her lead. His words and his voice a calming stream of water that made her courage grow.

10

Eden sat inside the executive boardroom of a building that once belonged to the Institute for Defense Analysis. Floor-to-ceiling windows looked out into a central courtyard that wasn't overrun by weeds like the grounds outside, but neatly kept with autumn crocuses still in bloom.

Early morning dawn had melted into a moody day.

Her hair smelled like smoke. Her clothes like war. She needed to shower. She needed to sleep. But more than either of those, she needed to know what happened to Cassian. Across from her, Dayne looked equally exhausted and equally determined. He insisted that he be included in this meeting, even though he wasn't a council member. A fact Francesca kept muttering under her breath.

Asher worked at the conference table, its normal height unable to accommodate him. His shoulders hunched considerably as he pulled up a holographic interface. Apparently, their meeting wouldn't commence here, but in a virtual war room. One that existed on the Amber Highway—an illegal metaverse created five years ago by someone named Gollum. Cleo was obsessed with this highway. Dayne, too. Since its inception, his newspaper had been one of its biggest beneficiaries. According to him, the highway not only enabled superior, secure communication with correspondents across the country, it allowed them to streamline in ways that freed up valuable time and resources.

Dayne watched Asher keenly as he synchronized and navigated layers and systems, demonstrating not mere proficiency with this virtual world, but mastery. How was it possible that he had not yet breached the asset's network? Eden was stuck inside the question, unable to make heads or tails of it.

Dayne leaned forward and set his elbows on the table. "Are you Gollum?"

Asher paused from his work just long enough to give his eyebrows a saucy lift.

Eden gaped.

Dayne, too.

The door swung open, and Jericho entered. He set an opened container, a white carafe, and a stack of styrofoam cups on the table. Francesca poured herself some coffee and took a long drink. Asher removed a chess piece from his pocket—a queen—and set it on the table with a sharp tap. Then he helped himself to some coffee, too. He crossed one long leg over the other and peered at the queen over his cup. Two sips later, her head flashed.

Eden pointed. "What was that?"

"Our cue," Jericho said, pulling a domino from his pocket. It was flashing the same as Asher's. So was the locket around Francesca's neck. She wrapped her hand around it, then reached inside the container Jericho brought with him and removed a pair of handcuffs, her good eye pinned on Eden. "Give me your hands."

"No way," Eden said.

"You're not coming to our meeting, and we can't have you leaving either."

Eden pressed back in her chair.

"Cooperate," Asher said, setting his cup on the table, "and

maybe we'll start to trust you as much as he trusts you." He tipped his head toward Dayne.

She *had* been cooperating. So far, all it had gotten her was Asher's animosity, Francesca's accusatory stare, and now, handcuffs. But this wasn't a hill to die on. If an emergency arose, the cuffs couldn't hold her anymore than a plastic zip-tie. With her lips pursed, she held out her hands.

Francesca cuffed her wrists to the chair, then returned to the container. She pulled out three headsets, tossed one to Asher, one to Jericho, and took the last for herself. Dayne came forward in his seat like he might take one, too. She yanked the container away.

He glared.

"Let us talk to the rest of the council," Jericho said in his deep baritone. "As long as they're okay with it, you can join us."

Dayne muttered angry words under his breath. So did Francesca as she sat next to Eden. With a nod, the three of them slipped their headsets over their eyes and ears.

They went completely still.

It was more than creepy. She sat in a boardroom with four people, but three of them weren't really there. For all intents and purposes, it was just her and Dayne Johnson, his fists clenched on the table. In all their time at the Millers, she'd never seen him so visibly angry.

He belonged to the same demographic as Dr. Norton—white, older male. And yet, the two gave off very different vibes. Dr. Norton radiated pleasant grandfather with his silver mustache and his woolen flat cap and his kind eyes. Dayne Johnson made a person forget he was old enough to be a grandfather. Twenty-one years in hiding and he still radiated charisma. TV ready, superhero chin, dazzling smile with a physique made for expensive suits. Instead, he wore a white cotton shirt beneath a nubby, double-breasted cardigan. The same clothes he was probably wearing when he had to flee the Millers.

"I'm really sorry," Eden said.

He looked at her across the table, his fists unclenching. His jaw, too. He didn't have to ask what she was sorry for. "This isn't your fault."

Au contraire. She had a strong feeling it most definitely was.

Dayne ran his palm down the length of his face. "Elmer and Eloise knew the risks they were taking when they decided to house fugitives."

Eden wasn't Catholic. She'd never been inside a confessional. But she imagined this was what it felt like. Guilty. Self-conscious. Alone, but not really. She looked at Jericho sitting beside Dayne, as still and unresponsive as a statue. "I don't know how aware Elmer was of anything." Let alone the risk she'd put him in when she knocked on his door.

"He was aware in the beginning," Dayne said. "It was his idea to take me in. Eloise agreed and they've been treating me like their son ever since." His eyes went dewy. Probably at his use of present tense, which no longer applied.

"I thought about moving here several times over the years. It would have been easier. But Elmer and Eloise enjoyed having me with them. Eloise specially, when Elmer's memory started to go. I suppose Jericho liked the arrangement, too. It was easier to keep his secret, anyway."

His jaw clenched again. His fists, too. "I think some of this might have been avoided if he hadn't kept me in the dark." Dayne shook his head. "It doesn't even make sense. Why wouldn't the Resistance use *America Underground* to advance their cause?"

"They must have been happy with the numbers they had." Maybe they didn't need any more people to carry out their aim. Maybe they saw themselves less like an army in need of numbers and more like special ops. "And it sounds like they've been burned before."

According to Francesca, Prudence Dvorak tried to grow the Resistance once upon a time. The rumors that circulated nearly squashed them before they could get started. Eden suspected those same rumors led to the scrambling device implanted in her ear.

"A few years later, your father started hearing rumors," Dr. Norton had told her.

He'd been making tea at the time. She'd been sitting at the small table in his basement kitchenette, in shock after learning the truth. Because of those rumors, her parents had taken her to Dr. Norton when she was four. They told her she was getting tubes in her ears. In actuality, the doctor had implanted a scrambling device. He'd done the same to Ellery Forrester. And because of those scrambling devices, Eden and Ellery weren't taken like Violet and Barrett. On the contrary, Eden had helped rescue Violet and Barrett.

In all likelihood, those rumors had prevented four more weapons from passing into enemy hands. But she could hardly share this without letting a giant cat out of the bag. She was one of the superhuman soldiers the Resistance wanted to destroy.

Dayne cracked a knuckle. "So, Cassian was apprehended?"

She nodded, a strong ache burning in the back of her throat. She felt like she was sinking into quicksand with nothing to grab onto. Where was Cassian now? What had they done with him? And how could she get the Resistance to care about his well-being as much as they cared about Dvorak's?

Dayne cracked another knuckle. "Cleo will be back to herself in no time. They have a good medical team here."

Eden tried to respond, but her throat was too tight. She cleared it and tried again. "Once she realizes where she is, I'm sure she'll be thrilled."

The girl who'd run an illegal newspaper from her dorm room was quite obviously a big fan of *America Underground*. Now here she was, in its epicenter.

Dayne smiled.

Asher moved. With no warning at all, he removed his headset. "The council just voted," he said. "Amir hasn't arrived yet, but at this point, his vote doesn't matter. Majority will still be majority, and majority's in favor of debriefing Alexandria. It's also in favor of letting you join us." With his attention on Dayne, he nodded at the container of headsets and scooted closer to his makeshift work station. He made several adjustments on the three-dimensional interface, then stood from his seat and unlocked Eden's cuffs.

She rubbed her wrists.

"Lark has questions," Asher said, gesturing for her to take a headset, too.

Eden looked up at him, shocked.

"She wants *you* to answer them."

11

The moment Eden put on the headset, she was no longer in the boardroom. The floor-to-ceiling windows disappeared, replaced by a dimly lit octagonal room. Curtains covered six of the walls. Two were alight with intel.

One featured the enemy—a dossier on the Monarch. The other was a bit more jarring. It featured her and Cassian. Eden's mug shot—taken after her arrest in California—stared back at her. Next to it, a promotional picture from Cassian's fighting career. Beneath each, information the Resistance must have acquired about them. Thankfully, her information was sparse. His was much longer. It included his former occupation as a fighter. His more recent occupation as a tracker. His connection to Mordecai, a high-stakes gambler in the world of Underground Fighting and a known member of Swarm. Along with information Eden felt certain Cassian wouldn't want so visibly displayed. Like the photograph of his mother. And another of a man who had to be his father.

He had Cassian's strong jawline, Cassian's straight nose, Cassian's caramel eyes and full lips. Their likeness was uncanny, and yet, she knew they were nothing alike. This man was a monster. An abuser who hunted down a mother and her child, beat that mother to death, and nearly did the same to his son, forever altering that smiling, gap-toothed six-year-old boy so safely tucked between his mother and Mona.

Longing burned in her chest. It throbbed in her arms. She wanted to hug him. Hold him. Be with him. She felt it so intensely, Cassian might as well be a limb that had been torn from her body. The phantom pain was almost unbearable. She bit down on her lip—wanting to break skin, wanting to taste blood, wanting to feel anything other than this terrible ache in her heart—and turned away from the photographs.

The oblong conference table had been replaced by one much more intimate—a circle with eight chairs.

One was occupied by Jericho, another by Asher, another by Francesca, who looked like she'd been forced to chew on a mouthful of rocks. Three more were occupied by strangers. Two of them, old men. One had an elfin face with caterpillar eyebrows and large ears sprouting with hair. He looked rough around the edges, like life hadn't been particularly kind or easy. The other wore a tweed suit. He had a bulbous nose, a thick head of silver hair, and a matching beard. Beside him sat a woman who was younger, but not young. Of east Asian descent, slim with choppy, shoulder-length hair and a familiar face.

"*Lark*," Eden exclaimed. *Shangguan*. An actress and martial artist known for doing her own stunts. "You were at the Prosperity Ball."

"So were you," Lark replied, her voice as deadpan as her expression.

There were two empty chairs at the table, and a ninth not at the table at all, but placed several feet in front. Stark and alone, swathed in light from the bulb overhead. Asher snapped. He pointed at this seat and told Eden to sit.

She did so stiffly. She didn't like being snapped at any more than she liked being called sweetheart.

Jericho invited Dayne to the table. Eden watched him sit hesitantly, looking so much like himself, she wondered how Asher had done it so quickly. How had he created an avatar from scratch with all the nuances of an actual person? Everything was so realistic that had she not been sitting inside a boardroom in Alexandria mere seconds ago, she would absolutely believe she was sitting here, in a physical space.

The two old men stood from their chairs and offered Dayne their hands. The hairy-eared fellow was named Emmett. He spoke with an Irish brogue. Dayne shook his hand first and when they let go, he looked down at his palm in wonder, as though he'd felt the interaction. Eden had been in the metaverse before. Plenty of times, in fact. Usually, if a participant wanted the fully immersive experience—one which involved all the senses—they needed more than a headset.

The man in the tweed suit introduced himself as Harlan Wallace.

Eden's attention caught on the surname. *Wallace.* That was familiar, too. "Any relation to Renata?" she asked.

Harlan's face paled, which was answer enough.

"How do you know that name?" Lark asked.

"I read it on the back of a pamphlet I took from the Bryson's safe."

Harlan cleared his throat. "Renata was my granddaughter."

Which meant Harlan's granddaughter was dead. Along with every other woman on the back of that pamphlet. Not from grueling labor, but from poison forced upon them after giving birth to Oswin Brahm's special soldiers, of which Harlan's great grandchild was one. Was he aware that his counterparts were torturing one of those soldiers right now? Did he know they'd tossed him into a refrigerator like a piece of meat? Did he care? Or was he as cutthroat as Asher and Francesca?

Eden glanced at the other wall of intel which contained a plethora of pictures, all of them of Renata Wallace's murderer. One in particular caught her attention. It had been taken when he was young. A fresh-faced student in his teens. She'd never seen it before, not even in his biography, which had been one of her dad's favorites. Eden had never read it, but she had flipped through the pictures a time or two.

Her eyes traced the shape of his young face—this man who had kidnapped her from an IVF clinic when she was nothing more than a frozen embryo. This man who had altered that embryo using nano-science. Then grew her and five others in a laboratory. It was his first successful test group. Until CIA agent, Alaric Taylor, found and dismantled the operation when those test subjects were eighteen months of age. He was ordered to extract the nanobots. Upon carrying out that order, Alaric discovered the babies could not survive the extraction process. Two of them died before he came upon Subject 006. A little girl who somehow had his eyes.

"Where did you get that photograph?" Eden asked.

"From my yearbook," Lark answered.

"You were classmates?"

"We went to the same boarding school."

Eden's mouth fell open. The urge to know everything there was to know inflated inside her. Who was Oswin Brahm, really? On the outside, he was a rich and upstanding philanthropist. But in secret, he played God. At least, his own twisted version—a deity who pulled puppet strings and manipulated truth and altered human life and blew up entire cities. He called himself the Monarch, a butterfly. But to her, he was a venomous spider spinning a web he wouldn't stop spinning until the entire world was trapped and at his mercy. "Did you know him well?"

"Unfortunately," Lark said, in the same deadpan way she'd said everything up until this point.

"What was he like?" Eden asked.

"Brilliant and dangerously charismatic. He had the entire staff and half the student body hopelessly charmed two weeks into our first semester."

"Were you part of that half?"

Lark's dark eyes went flat, but not before she shot a fleeting glance toward Harlan. Despite its brevity, Eden was able to catch the blip of emotion inside that glance. Shame. Terrible, all-consuming shame.

"I was one of his first followers," Lark said. "I helped recruit people to his cause. It took many years before I saw his true colors. And it will take many more to undo the damage I inflicted."

Eden shot a curious look at Harlan. Something told her Renata Wallace was one of the people Lark had recruited.

Lark blinked, as if coming out of whatever stupor she'd gotten stuck inside. She folded her hands on top of the table. "Cassian Gray is affiliated with Nicholas Marks, a known member of Swarm. Which led us to assume, as one could understand, that you were both members of Swarm. But you're telling a different story."

Eden nodded.

"I'd like to hear it," Lark said.

Eden obliged. She gave Lark the version Cassian had given Dvorak before the raid. They were hunting the Monarch because the Monarch was after Eden's father, a former CIA agent who helped bring down Karik Volkova. She kept her voice even, her breathing steady. Her heart rate, however, was harder to control. Thankfully, nobody here had the superhuman hearing required to register it.

When she was finished, Lark narrowed her eyes. "If this is true, how did Cassian Gray come to be involved?"

"When he found out Mordecai was trying to kill my father, he sent us a warning."

Lark tilted her head. "This father of yours. Where is he now?"

Eden didn't want to give them his location, so she held her tongue.

"Why are you doing his dirty work?"

"He was badly injured. I decided to eliminate the threat. And Cassian decided to come with me. It's how we ended up in the Bryson's basement, where we got the pamphlet."

"And the magnet," Asher said, his stare so intense she felt like it was boring holes into the side of her face.

She nodded. "We never killed anyone. We were falsely accused, just like Dvorak was falsely accused."

"Just like *I* was falsely accused," Dayne said. "There seems to be a pattern. Innocent people. False accusations."

Before Lark could respond any further, a current of electricity ran through the room. Someone else had joined them. Eden knew his face. She'd been staring at it through the front window of a diner for the past week. Amir Kashif, with his dark hair and his long nose and his Harry Potter glasses, looking wild in the eyes—like he'd swum through alligator-infested waters to get here.

When his attention fell on her, sitting alone in a chair in front of two computerized walls, his wild eyes went wilder. "You!"

She pressed back in her seat.

"What are you doing here?" Amir whirled to face the others. "She's the reason Pru was taken. She's the reason the air raid happened in the first place. They were following *her* and her two friends."

Eden closed her eyes. This wasn't news, really. She'd suspected it all along. But to hear it confirmed so angrily made her heart sink into the soles of her feet.

"What did you call Pru's hamster when you were a teenager?" Francesca demanded.

Eden's eyes flew open.

It was the strangest question. And yet, Amir answered it like it wasn't strange at all.

"Cujo," he said.

Francesca seemed to relax.

"Avatar theft is a real problem," Jericho said, addressing Eden's confusion. "The simplest way to check someone's identity is by asking a question nobody but the real person would know the answer to."

Eden imagined eighteen-year-old Prudence Dvorak, forced

into pregnancy by her extremist father, owning something as normal as a pet hamster. She imagined seventeen-year-old Amir, dealing with the fact that his widowed mother was also pregnant, lounging with Prudence in her bedroom. Maybe Amir tried to hold the hamster. Maybe the hamster bit him. And thus, the nickname was born. Cujo, a rabid dog from a Stephen King novel. She pictured Prudence tossing a pillow at Amir in defense of her pet, then casually setting her hand over her baby bump. All of it was so normal. Which made it even more bizarre.

"We brought her here to ask questions," Lark said. "There's no harm in it. All classified information has been covered."

Eden looked at the six covered walls, wondering what intel was hiding behind the curtains.

"Her story checks out," Asher said. He filled Amir in. By the time he finished, Amir's hair was a mess; both of his legs bounced.

"We have to get Pru out," he said.

"We have to get all of them out," Harlan added.

"Please let me help." Eden came forward in her chair and nodded at Dayne. "He's vouched for me. And you already decided to invite Alexandria in. For the foreseeable future, I will be part of Alexandria."

They looked at her like she was speaking French.

"My father was in the CIA. I grew up with him imparting certain … skills." She was grasping at straws now, her desperation growing. But maybe this would work. Maybe this would also throw them off her scent. She wasn't superhuman; she was simply well-trained. "I can be just as valuable now as I was in Washington, DC."

Her attention darted to Asher, hoping he might confirm. He knew she was valuable. But he only stared back at her with half-lidded eyes, like her plea was boring him.

"Our goals are aligned. You want to get Dvorak back. I want to get Cassian back just as bad." Her heart was hammering now. Hammering into the silence.

It seemed to stretch on for an eternity.

Finally, Asher turned to Dayne. "If you vouch for her, we're holding you accountable if anything goes wrong."

He shrugged like the threat didn't bother him in the slightest.

Eden's heart continued to pound. Was that it? Were they going to let her in? Would Cassian be part of the prison break? One question toppled into the next like a string of dominoes as Amir set a small gadget in the center of the table and pushed a button. A three-dimensional projection appeared. A layout of what looked to be a military base. "This is where they've been taken," he said. "It's a decommissioned military prison outside Annapolis."

Eden stared at the place Cassian was being held. All too quickly, one thing became clear. There would be no easy way to get him out.

Jericho leaned back in his chair. "It's impossible."

Nobody argued.

It certainly seemed impossible.

He thrust his hand toward the projection. "We don't have the resources to break into that. Not even Harlan does."

The old man didn't object.

The room's gravitational force seemed to multiply, like the air itself had grown heavy and oppressive.

Eden refused to sink beneath the weight of it. "Then we don't break in."

They regarded her like she was daft.

Everyone except Asher. He didn't regard her at all, but peered at the projection as he fiddled with his queen. "We flush them out."

"Force a transfer," Eden said.

"By leaking their location," Dayne added.

By then, the others had caught on, too.

The only person resisting this newfound enthusiasm was Jericho, who was—for whatever reason—hellbent on holding on to his pessimism. "And then what?"

Silence followed his challenge. Glances were exchanged. Brows were furrowed as everyone considered.

Eden set her hands flat on the table. "We figure out their route and stage an ambush."

Jericho laughed. "That easy, huh?"

"Of course not. But it isn't impossible either."

The skeptic rubbed his salt and pepper goatee. "Do you have any idea how many moving pieces we'd have to control for this to be successful?"

"Not a problem, Jer." Asher propped his elbow on the armrest of his chair, spinning the queen between his fingers. "I'm an expert at controlling pieces."

Hope sprang to life in Eden's chest as the wheels of a plan began to move. A sense of motion. A small but strong seed of possibility—that Cassian wasn't lost. That she could get him back. With this group of unlikely people, she could break him free.

12

The door of Cassian's prison cell opened.

He squinted as the blurry outline of two people came into slow focus. The woman in the blazer held a tray of food, a bottle of water, and a neatly folded jumpsuit. A man in a white coat carried a black medical bag.

A deep-seated instinct lurched inside him, demanding his body to move. Go. Barrel through this woman and the doctor and escape. But his hands were trapped behind his back and the place he would barrel into came with surveillance cameras and more guards. Cass squashed the instinct and focused instead on the water. His tongue was dry and swollen.

The woman seemed to notice. She glanced from Cassian on the floor to the bottle on the tray. "I don't imagine you want me to feed this to you."

His lip curled. If she tried, he would spit it in her face like he'd done to the guard. Consequences be damned.

She set the tray and the jumpsuit on the bench and removed a bionic-looking cuff from her pocket. "Do you know what this is?"

He glared up at her.

"A motion taser cuff. Or, as we call them, an MTC. If you run

—if your foot so much as makes an attempt—you will be incapacitated. Painfully." She snapped the cuff around his ankle. "I recommend against it."

She nodded for Cass to lean forward so she could unlock the restraints around his wrists. As she did, he noticed the golden brooch again, pinned to the lapel of her blazer. It was a small rendering of a woman in a blindfold. She held a sword in one hand, scales in the other.

Lady Justice.

The doctor in the white coat set his bag on the floor and began removing salves and tinctures. Cass used his good arm to grab the bottle of water. He removed the cap with his teeth and chugged. The woman stood there all the while, watching. When he finished, the doctor applied antiseptic to the open cut above his left eye.

Cass hissed.

The doctor didn't even pause from his treatment.

"Is this how it works?" Cass asked. "Beat the prisoners, then patch them up?"

"Prisoners who beat the guards will inevitably get beaten," the woman answered. She crossed her arms and leaned against the doorjamb. "You broke his nose."

"He's lucky I didn't break more." Cass jerked as the doctor moved to another gash. The smaller injuries had always been the most bothersome. The sting of a cut more aggravating to him than a bruised spleen. The big ones were angry bulls. The smaller injuries, pesky flies. He'd take the bull any day.

The woman sat on the bench. She handed him the tray of food as the doctor continued, no more gently than Vick between rounds. Cass recalled the piercing tenderness of Eden's touch in the basement of Cleo's dormitory after she hit him in the head with a door.

Voila. Tout au mieux.

Was that when he'd started to fall, when she'd spoken those words? Would he ever hear her say them again? The possibility that he might not filled him with such misery, he was almost glad when a stabbing pain yanked his mind into the present. The doctor was prodding his shoulder.

The woman crossed one leg over the other. "How does a fighter like yourself get wrapped up with Interitus?"

Interitus doesn't exist.

Prudence Dvorak's statement echoed inside his head, and it was confounding. In its wake, more of her words emerged like fireflies floating to the surface of his memory.

Are you spies for Swarm?

Did you come for the asset?

Was this who the guard had been referring to when he asked his strange questions? *Where is he? Where are they keeping him?*

The woman arched her eyebrow, waiting for Cass to answer.

"I'm not wrapped up with Interitus. I already told you, I'm not—"

"A terrorist." Her eyes narrowed slightly. Her lips twisted to the side. "It's the same thing your friend, Ms. Dvorak, said."

"She's not my friend."

"Then why were you together?"

"Why don't you ask her?"

"I did."

"What did she say?"

"No more than you have."

The knots in his chest loosened ever so slightly. He knew they'd interrogated Dvorak. What he didn't know was what Dvorak had told them. Before the ambush, Eden and Cass had given her half-truths. Eden's father had destroyed the test group and because of that, the Monarch was after him. Cass didn't see how those half-truths could lead to Eden's whereabouts. Still, he was relieved to know Dvorak had remained as tight-lipped as he had, even if that relief was short-lived. Did they try to strike the same deal with Dvorak as they had with him? If so, how long until she put the pieces together and realized what the government already knew? Eden Pruitt was Subject 006.

His ribs tightened.

Who was she with now? What if they connected the dots, too? Eden wasn't invincible. She had a self-destruct function. The thought left his throat dry, his pulse elevated. He needed to get out of here.

The doctor shone a flashlight into each of Cassian's eyes. He removed scissors from his bag and began cutting off his shirt.

The shock of cold air against his skin made his muscles clench.

The woman's attention rolled up his torso. Not in a desirous, predatory way Cass had seen plenty of times before. This was a clinical and curious gaze, one that paused when it reached the scar on his side. "Was that from a fight?"

"Yes," he said. The fight hadn't been in a ring, but a parking garage. Dr. Norton had treated this injury in his basement while Eden stood by, on the cusp of unraveling. Maybe that was the moment he'd fallen—when she handed him his phone and told him she was dangerous. Brutal honesty mixed with a desire to protect, even as she was coming undone. Strength and vulnerability wrapped up in a selflessness that was convicting. He pushed the memory away and picked up the plastic fork on the tray. He wasn't hungry. Especially not in light of the astringent-smelling ointment the doctor was rubbing onto his shoulder. But he shoveled a bite of unidentified casserole into his mouth anyway. If he had any hope of escape, he needed his strength.

Cass ate while the doctor wrapped his shoulder. When the gentleman finished, he collected his equipment and picked up his bag. The woman dismissed him, but she didn't dismiss herself. She remained on the bench, her high-heeled foot bouncing casually. "You were one of the most ruthless fighters I've ever seen."

"Do you make a habit of watching many fights?"

"A couple years ago, yes. It was part of my job."

"You worked undercover."

The woman nodded, her foot continuing its nonchalant

movement. She sat with one arm wrapped across her midsection, her opposite elbow propped against her forearm. She tapped her pointer finger against her chin, studying him with a keen interest that made him want to growl. He was done with his food. The doctor was done treating him. He was half-dressed, and this wasn't an interrogation room.

"You gave your money to the widow," she finally said.

He shot her a look of surprise.

"A few days after you killed her husband in the ring, she received over a hundred thousand dollars from an anonymous source. It was you, wasn't it?"

Cass pled the fifth.

The woman tilted her head. "You never returned to the ring after that."

"Why the play-by-play?"

"I'm just trying to figure you out." She leaned against the cement wall behind her. "You gave your money to the widow, which means you must have a conscience. But then, what about these new widows? Will you send all of them money, too?"

"What new widows?"

"The ones you made when you bombed The Sapphire."

"I didn't bomb The Sapphire."

"Because you're not a terrorist."

"No, I'm not."

"What are you then?" she asked.

"What do you mean?"

"If you're not a terrorist. If you're not Dvorak's friend. What are you? *Who* are you?"

He narrowed his eyes, unsure where she was going with this line of questioning. Unsure what she was trying to accomplish. *Who was he?* This wasn't a therapy session.

She waved her hand, gesturing to the prison cell. "Why are you here?"

"Why are *you*?" he shot back.

He didn't expect her to answer. Not honestly, anyway. But

she did. "I'm here to fulfill the vow I took when I went into public service. I'm here to protect the innocent."

"Eden Pruitt is innocent."

"Let me guess. She didn't blow up The Sapphire either."

"No, she didn't."

"Or kill an innocent family of three?"

"The Brysons."

The woman nodded.

She was referring to Gage and Isabella Bryson, along with their son, Clay. Cass and Eden had broken into their home after receiving a tip from Willow Bryson, their estranged daughter. *The answers they were looking for were in the Bryson's safe.* Cassian and Eden had broken in, confiscated several items, then escaped by the skin of their teeth. The next day, the Brysons turned up dead, and Cass and Eden were on national news wanted for their murder.

"Check out the room in their basement," he said, "then tell me if you think they're really innocent."

"What does that mean?"

"They abused their children."

"So you took justice into your own hands?"

"We didn't kill them."

"Of course not."

"They were shot in their home after we broke in and escaped. You really think we'd be dumb enough to return to the scene of the crime and kill them?"

"They were killed in the same way the security guards were killed at the SafePad compound outside Chicago. A crime scene to which you were also linked. It seems to be your modus operandi."

"When I left that compound, those security guards were alive."

She pinched the bridge of her nose and released a heavy sigh. "How very convenient, Mr. Gray."

"It isn't convenient. It's the truth."

"Who are you suggesting killed them, then?"

"A police officer. Several were there when I left."

She released a puff of unamused laughter.

"Wearing a badge doesn't make you good."

"Making an accusation doesn't make it true."

"So go find proof. Talk to the officers who were at SafePad. Talk to the officers who arrived on scene when the Brysons were found dead. Check out the room in their basement, while you're at it. See what you find. See if the facts line up. But tread carefully, lest you end up with a bullet through your head, too."

"Is that a threat?"

"It's a warning." His attention flicked to her brooch. Lady Justice. "You vowed to protect the innocent. But the bad guys are still out there, and Eden Pruitt isn't one of them."

13

Jericho called for a mandatory assembly in the auditorium. He needed to brief his constituents, who had been thrust into a state of unease ever since the airstrike. He planned to introduce Alexandria's new residents and explain why they were here. He broadcast the invitation from an intercom, like school announcements at the beginning of the school day.

Eden wasn't invited.

Jericho believed her appearance would only cause an uproar. He needed to get everyone up to speed first. She was to stay in the boardroom until everyone was in the auditorium. Dayne offered to stay behind with her. By the time the coast was clear, the sun was beginning to set and Eden was long past the point of tiredness. She was amped up on caffeine, adrenaline, and hope. The ball was rolling now, but she wanted it to roll faster. She wanted it to fly at warp speed.

She followed Dayne through the courtyard. "I'd love to get my hands on a copy of Oswin Brahm's biography, if possible."

"That shouldn't be difficult," he said. "There's an entire library of books in the basement of Kaiser. I'm sure his biography is among them. We can make a pit stop before we go to The Landing and see."

"Can we check on Cleo, too?"

"Of course," he said. "Let me stop by the newsroom first and we'll be on our way." He opened the door to the west tower of the IDA.

Eden stepped inside.

They hurried through the deserted lobby, his indignation as palpable as her eagerness. No matter how often Jericho apologized, Dayne couldn't get over it. All this time, his right-hand man had been part of something critical. Paradigm-shifting. *Newsworthy*. The falsification of an entire terrorist regime. The true culprit behind The Attack. A Resistance formed to fight him. People deserved to know. *America Underground* existed for this very purpose. Instead, Jericho had kept it secret. According to him, he had no choice *but* to keep it secret.

He'd been the leader of Alexandria first. Council member of the Resistance second. That council had recruited him in order to establish a deal. Jericho's community would be stocked with electricity and clean water and food in exchange for confidentiality and an emergency evacuation plan they hoped they would never have to use.

Eden and Dayne stepped inside an elevator. He pressed a button for the fourth floor and stood with his weight on his toes, watching the ascending numbers above the elevator door light up one by one. His hands fidgeted inside his pockets.

"Dayne."

He looked at her.

"If you didn't know about the deal, then how did you think Jericho was able to manage all this?" She motioned to the elevator, then lifted her hand higher to indicate everything beyond.

"I knew about Harlan," he said. "I just didn't know he was bankrolling a Resistance. Jericho made it sound like he was a family friend."

The elevator stopped.

The noise grew louder. She'd heard it from the ground level —the drone of multiple conversations unfolding at the same time. As the doors slid open, she immediately saw the voices weren't coming from people, but several flat screens mounted along the walls of a large, open newsroom. All of them were on, as if whoever had been here before left too quickly to turn them off.

"I need to check the newswire," he said, hurrying past cubicles and desks organized into groups of six, all with their own computers, toward two round tables in the back.

On one of the flatscreens, Concordia Entertainment was televising an interview with Brenda Lemming and a tearful Felicity McCoy, an actress who'd suffered multiple injuries at the Prosperity Ball Bombing. Felicity was immensely relieved to know Prudence Dvorak, the new leader of Interitus, was no longer at large. With her and Cassian Ransom behind bars, maybe the nightmares that had plagued her since that life-changing night in Chicago would finally relent.

Concordia Global was covering the worldwide response to the decimation of Interitus Headquarters in Washington, DC. Eden listened as the Prime Minister of France expressed her condolences to the families of military members who perished in the raid, sacrificing their lives not only for America, but for the world at large.

A late-night talk show on Concordia Sports had paused from their coverage of the World Series to pay tribute to the former Washington Nationals, who'd gone on a three-year World Series run and were on their way to a fourth when The Attack in Washington, DC, buried the franchise.

A myriad of Concordia Local stations discussed more nuanced, provincial reactions to this great victory while Concordia National aired a news conference with the press secretary.

Eden could process all of it. Every news feed simultaneously. With unsettling ease, she could tease apart each voice until there was no longer a buzzing chatter, but separate threads she could commit to memory and replay if needed.

This was a skill. A *superhuman* skill. People weren't made to hear and process multiple conversations at the same time. Brains didn't work that way. But thanks to Oswin Brahm, hers did.

Suddenly, she was no longer in a newsroom, but a glade. Sun dappled through the leaves in a world gone topsy-turvy as she stood face-to-face with Cassian. A lethal fighter ready to teach her how to fight.

"Then be a weapon. And use it against him."

His boot had flown toward her face in an expertly executed roundhouse kick. She'd caught it on sheer instinct, with no training at all. Another superhuman skill. But how could she be the weapon—how could she offer her talents—without ending up inside a commercial refrigerator alongside the asset? She could still hear his agonizing screams after she injected the poison. She could still see the unnatural way he had writhed on the ground. Would she scream just as loud, writhe just as unnaturally, if ever she found herself on the receiving end of that syringe?

The sound of Cassian's name punctured the disturbing thought.

Eden pinned her attention on Concordia National.

The press conference had ended, replaced by a brief address from Kendra Cruz, Chairwoman of America's Board. She was talking about the fate of the prisoners and the importance of sending a strong message to any and all enemies of America.

Eden's stomach churned.

They had sent a strong message before with Karik Volkova; he had been publicly executed. Would the same happen to Cassian? The possibility sat on her chest like an elephant.

It was a babel of lies. A snarl of deceit.

The air strike upon Washington, DC, wasn't a victory against Interitus. Interitus didn't exist. Oswin Brahm had concocted the regime to give the people a common enemy. Off-the-grid communities weren't a threat. At least, not a threat to the truth. Concordia was lying, like her parents had lied.

The room spun.

Her heart beat faster. And faster. Gathering speed and energy until it struck her temple like a bolt of lightning—this mystery pain that came and went with no rhyme or reason. With a sharp intake of breath, she clutched the side of her head, and when the room stopped spinning, when she finally caught her breath, she heard another familiar name.

Barrett Barr.

A young female news anchor was talking about an incident in Minnesota. She stared directly at the camera, her expression sober as she issued a warning. What they were about to see was disturbing and graphic. Viewer discretion was advised.

Eden took a step closer.

There was Barrett. And there was Violet. They were climbing out of a red pickup truck at a highway checkpoint outside the city of Minneapolis.

What were they doing in Minneapolis?

Why were they at a highway checkpoint?

With eyes widening, she watched Barrett disarm the man in uniform. She watched Barrett turn the gun on the patrol officer and shoot him, point blank, in the face.

14

A dusky sky outlined the house as it squatted in a clearing amidst a tangle of weeds and knee-high grass. A doorless, detached garage leaned beside the stumpy abode, the gravel drive unfurling from its dark, open mouth like a long, dusty tongue. The property looked as if it hadn't been tended to in over a year. It probably hadn't. That was her job, after all—the upkeep of the property. When Father wasn't working on her, she was working for him.

She listened for a heartbeat. But other than her own and Barrett's and the non-human heartbeats of squirrels and birds, there wasn't one to hear. Relieved, she exhaled forcefully and stepped out of hiding.

Together, they made their way toward the rickety porch. When she climbed the steps, the rotted slabs of wood bowed underfoot. Barrett drew his gun as she reached for the door handle and twisted. The rusty hinges groaned. The door creaked open, and the stench that escaped had her burying her nose in the crook of her elbow.

Barrett coughed.

Evening light poured through broken blinds, catching dust motes that floated in the air. Garbage overflowed from the bin.

Rotten food had spilled onto the floor. Stacks of dirty dishes and empty liquor bottles battled for space on the countertop. Gray, stagnant water filled the sink like bilge from a ship, leaving behind a ring of scum where the water had once reached. Black mold climbed up one wall. A drop of water dripped from a brown patch on the ceiling.

Barrett stepped inside. He nudged a chewed-open garbage bag with his boot. A pair of mice squeaked and scuffled out of sight. He lifted his eyebrows. "Does someone live here?"

She flipped a switch near the front closet.

The light didn't come on, but she could hear wires humming in the walls. The bulb was out, but the electricity was still working. At the sink, she turned on the faucet. With a deep groan, water ran from the spout. And at the table, a bowl of half-eaten congealed cereal sat atop a stack of newspapers that were only a few days old. Along with obscure scientific journals and even more obscure religious ones. Father enjoyed anything to do with the book of Revelation; articles about the apocalypse and the end of the world had always been his favorite.

Barrett set the cereal aside with a wrinkled nose and lifted a page of folded newspaper, his eyes going round as he looked from it to her. "This is *you*."

He was right.

The picture on the page was a picture of herself.

She watched Barrett grapple, taking it in—his mouth opening and closing. Back at Dr. Norton's, when he'd been trying to guess at her identity, he'd looked through every missing person's report he could find. She hadn't been in any of them. But those reports had been from Concordia. This newspaper was called *America Underground*. "Your name is Violet?"

She swallowed.

Barrett tilted his head, his expression as soft as Kitty's fur. "I can keep calling you Jane."

Jane.

It was a name with no past. It belonged to a girl who'd

woken up in a scary room filled with strangers and met a nice boy named Barrett and a nice mother named Ruth. Jane was a common name given to people without an identity. Violet, on the other hand? That name had a bad past. It belonged to a girl who was meant to stop the apocalypse from happening and had to endure agony to do so. But Violet was also the name Mother had given her. A name Father regretted.

Something about that final thought popped the bubble of words stuck in her throat. "Violet," she said, softer than the scuttling mice.

"Violet," Barrett repeated. He looked down at the picture and bobbed his head. "Violet," he said again. "It's a pretty name."

"Th-thank you."

"You're welcome," he said, nodding some more, smiling a boyish smile when something beyond her caught his attention—an old-fashioned radio. His boots clomped across the floor where the radio was perched atop a cheaply made end table beside a drooping couch. He turned it on and began twisting the dial, fiddling with the rabbit ear antenna.

Violet eyed the staircase for a moment or two, then slipped away.

By the time she reached the upstairs landing, a local news station had broken through the static. She crept away from the sound, toward the room at the end of the hallway that had once been hers. She set her backpack on the twin bed, got down onto her belly, and checked the loose board beneath. It lifted just like it always had, and unlike the puppies in the alley, these treasures were still here. She pulled them out—one-by-one—and sat cross-legged on the floor with her spine pressed against the metal bed frame, beholding her riches. She picked up the camera —a refurbished Canon—and tried to turn it on. When nothing happened, she snatched the black cord that might bring it back to life. She set them side by side on the floor. Then she gathered the rest of the treasure into her arms and carried them downstairs.

She thrust the loot onto Barrett's lap like these were her friends and she couldn't wait to introduce them.

He looked down at the tottering tower of dusty books while the radio blathered and lifted the first with a smile. "My mom used to read this to me."

With a nod, Violet sat beside him. She took *The Very Hungry Caterpillar* from his hand and gave him the second. *The Poky Little Puppy*. She kept going until Barrett had met every single one. *The Velveteen Rabbit. Stuart Little. Anne of Green Gables. The Secret Garden. Treasure Island. Where the Sidewalk Ends.* And her very favorite, *The Phantom Tollbooth*. This one had been read so often, half the pages had come loose from their binding.

"Where did you get these?" he asked.

Violet gathered the books and grabbed his hand and pulled him up. She showed him the loose floorboard beneath her bed and the camera with the black cord.

"This is yours?" he asked, nodding at the camera.

She sat beside her backpack. "M-mother's."

"Mother's?" he repeated. He looked at the books in her arms, his face stretching long. "Your mom gave you these?"

Violet nodded.

"Your mom," he said, his voice tinged with awe. He'd told her so much about his own mother, his whole family. She'd never spoken a word about hers. He sat beside her. The mattress springs squeaked. He took the book on top of her stack, *The Velveteen Rabbit*, and peeled it open. The binding creaked. "What happened to her?"

Violet frowned. "Sh-she left."

His brow dimpled. It was like he'd been expecting a different combination of words. Like a Mother who loved books couldn't also be a Mother who left. But then his ears perked.

Hers did, too.

The radio had just spoken his name.

They raced downstairs.

The broadcaster was alerting the public. He said Barrett was armed and highly dangerous. He said Barrett was on the run with an unidentified female the same age as himself. He said Barrett shot and killed two patrol officers, along with an elderly civilian named Thomas Mueller.

With a sharp intake of breath, Violet tugged the power cord from its socket.

The lying radio went silent.

15

Eden clapped her hand over her mouth.

Shock and horror tore a deep, dark pit in her mind as Barrett turned the gun on the second patrol officer. Then the driver of the pickup. All three men were dead. Barrett had killed them. Talkative, affable, Golden Retriever Barrett. He would never hurt a fly, let alone shoot three people in the face. No matter what the circumstances. No matter the stakes, he just wouldn't. Which could only mean …

The pit of horror stretched wider.

Eden shook her head, her hand still cupped over her mouth.

She could feel the gun in her hands. Her finger twitching over the trigger. Mordecai's snakelike voice in her ear.

Barrett was being controlled. It was the only explanation.

The pit of horror morphed into a black hole that consumed all hope.

Even if they won this war, even if Eden and Cassian survived and they freed Barrett from Oswin Brahm, how would he ever be the same?

The footage switched to a swirl of reporters, hounding a pair of young men as they fought to get to a house much like the one Eden had left in Eagle Bend. Only this house was in Idaho, and these young men were Jameson and Graham Barr, Barrett's older twin brothers.

"Did you know your brother was a member of Interitus?" a reporter asked.

"Do you have any idea when the recruitment began?" another shouted.

One twin shoved the cameraman away. Amidst a din of terrible questions, they disappeared inside their home.

Fear upon fear upon fear.

Eden imagined it expanding through the country like ripples in a pond.

How often had Barrett Barr's smiling face been shown on Concordia? Portrayed by his parents as a nice kid with a good head on his shoulders. Viewers of Concordia had just watched that nice kid brutally murder three people with a look of mild disinterest. If that could happen to this smiling boy with loving parents and two supportive big brothers, then surely it could happen to anyone.

The news anchor was back, discussing the identity of the girl. "Not even our most advanced facial recognition has identified her, which leads us to conclude she has been living off the grid."

More fear.

More ripples.

Further evidence that the rhetoric was true.

Off-the-grid communities were a breeding ground for terrorists. As such, they should be shown no mercy. People who lived amongst them were lawbreakers. Societal leeches. A cancer in need of eradication. It was nothing she hadn't heard before. This was simply a more extreme version for more extreme times. She imagined herself sitting on her couch in San Diego, watching with her best friend, Erik. Would she have swallowed the rhetoric whole, quietly agreeing with the newscaster?

"How to take over the world, 101," Dayne muttered. He'd come to stand beside her and was watching the same screen.

"Step one, convince the public that your enemies are their enemies."

First, the media. They were made into a scapegoat after The Attack. Dayne Johnson, chief among them. The media was to blame for the country's divisiveness. The rotten, greedy, agenda-driven media. Because of them and their constant stream of fake news, America was tearing itself apart, which had left America vulnerable to attack.

Freedom of the Press was part of the problem, so that right was taken away. Now, that press was owned by the government, and the government was in Oswin Brahm's pocket. Goosebumps marched across Eden's skin.

When she first visited the Damen Silos in Chicago and saw the conditions in which so many young children were living, she'd been struck by how wrong Concordia was getting it. They were mistaken. Off-the-grid communities weren't breeding grounds for terrorists. But now, she couldn't help but think that they were getting it precisely right. Concordia wasn't broken. Concordia had been built to do exactly this. Make Brahm's enemies the public's enemies. Free press had been his enemy. For as long as the press remained free, he could not control public thought. Now, off-the-grid individuals were his enemy. For as long as people lived off the grid, he could not control them either.

The news anchor returned to the terrible, awful footage of Barrett.

Acid burned up her throat.

She didn't want to see it, but she couldn't look away.

Beside her, Dayne pulled his hands from his pockets and picked up a remote from a nearby desk. He rewound the footage and played it over. Again, and again, and again. Confused, Eden closed her eyes. Why did he want to keep watching it?

"It's fake," he finally said.

Her eyes flew open. "What?"

"This footage is fake." He rewound to the spot where Barrett disarmed the patrol officer. He pushed pause and pointed. "Look there, at Barrett's hand."

Eden peered at the screen.

And she saw it. Easily, in fact.

A squiggle where Barrett's fingers were wrapped around the handle of the gun. It looked like visible heat waves.

"It's a deep fake." Dayne huffed and ran his palm down his whiskered face. He needed a good shave. "They made our jobs nearly impossible before The Attack. They were rampant and insidious and had conspiracy theories spreading like wildfire. We couldn't trust our own eyes."

He unpaused the footage. He set the remote back on the desk as Barrett shot the patrol officer. "They are highly illegal, for obvious reasons. But here Concordia is, airing one now."

"So … it's not real? Barrett didn't—?"

Dayne shook his head.

Relief came like a flood.

"Was he even there?" she asked. "Outside Minneapolis?"

"That part's real. Nothing's altered until the first officer is disarmed."

Eden tried to make sense of it. Barrett was in Minnesota with Violet and this stranger in a red pickup truck. They'd been stopped by highway patrol officers conducting retinal scans. What did this mean? Why were they there? And why the deep fake? Was it simply to feed the public an extra helping of fear? Or was this Oswin Brahm pulling more puppet strings? Did he know who Violet and Barrett were? Was this his way of apprehending two of his lost soldiers—get the entire country looking for them like the entire country had been looking for Eden?

She was so focused on the disturbing footage, on the tumult of questions spinning through her mind, she didn't notice Dayne staring at her until he asked a question. "Do you know him?"

She blinked.

Dayne nodded at the screen. "Are you acquainted with Barrett Barr?"

Eden swallowed nervously. She'd spoken his name with too much familiarity. Dayne had noticed. What would he make of her connection to Violet and Barrett? What would Asher and Francesca and the other council members? Three eighteen-year-olds, three months older than the Electus. And Eden's father, a CIA agent who supposedly destroyed a test group that would have been *three months older than the Electus.*

Asher and Francesca weren't dumb. They would put the pieces together. And then what?

The news anchor was talking about Violet again. But Dayne wasn't paying attention. He was too busy studying Eden.

"She was in your paper," she finally said.

Dayne looked at the television.

"Her name is Violet Winter. She was reported as a missing person." By her father. Who lived in *Minneapolis.* Barrett and Violet were supposed to be in Milwaukee with her parents and Dr. Norton and Jack Forrester. They were supposed to figure out how to disable the Queen Bee so Eden wouldn't be forced to shoot someone ever again. So they couldn't be controlled. Not by the Monarch. Not by a member of Swarm. Not by the Resistance, either. So what were they doing in Minneapolis, so close to Violet's father? Were Eden's parents okay?

"Dayne," Eden said. "If Violet's father reported her missing, would you have a way to contact him?"

"If Violet is listed as a missing person in *America Underground,* then yes, we should have a way to contact him."

Which meant Eden might be able to get in touch with them. She at least needed to try. As soon as possible. But how could she without asking Dayne for help? Her breath went shallow.

He slid his hands into his pockets and cocked his head. "So you *do* know them?"

Eden bit her lip.

Dayne was watching her, waiting for an answer. Waiting for the truth. This man who had vouched for her without really knowing who he was vouching for. She was keeping a massive secret from him, no different than Jericho. If she didn't share the truth with him now, she risked alienating the one person here besides Cleo who trusted her.

"Yes," she finally said. "I know them."

She could see the cogs turn in his mind. A missing 18-year-old boy and an off-the-grid girl. "How do you know them?"

Eden grappled for a lie. An innocent explanation. But then, what would stop Dayne from mentioning that connection in casual conversation? Whatever she told him now would have to be done so in confidence.

The tilt of his head deepened. She expected to see annoyance in his eyes. She was obviously holding something, and he was obviously sick of secrets. But he only looked curious, and sympathetic.

He wasn't loyal to the Resistance. Other than Jericho, he'd known Eden longer than any of the other council members. Could she trust him to keep her secret? She didn't see any other option. If she wanted his help, she would have to tell him. And hope with everything inside her he would keep that truth to himself.

16

"Asher is *Gollum*?"

"Apparently," Eden said.

Cleo gaped, her spoon paused halfway between her mouth and the tray in front of her. She was resting on an inclined bed in her own room in the Kaiser Medical Center. She wore a hospital gown. The gash above her right eyebrow had been glued. Her scratches and scrapes covered in antiseptic. She wasn't exactly the picture of health, but she did look significantly improved. Her complexion, at least, no longer had that alarming grayish tint that it did yesterday.

Last night, when Eden and Dayne finally arrived to check on her, the patient had been sound asleep. The nurse on duty wasn't happy about their visit. He'd taken one look at Eden, still dressed in the clothes she'd been wearing when the government dropped bombs from the sky, and began shaking his head and wagging his finger as he ushered both her and Dayne to the nearest exit. If he recognized her as the fugitive responsible for those bombs, he didn't let on. He was too busy shooing her away. She could come back in the morning when she didn't look like a walking health hazard.

Now it *was* morning. Eden had showered. Slept. She wore a

cheap but clean pair of light gray sweatpants and a matching crewneck sweatshirt, provided by the abandoned concierge desk of The Landing. Dayne had retrieved the clothes, a roll of toilet paper, a small stack of folded towels, and a key. He'd escorted Eden to her new living quarters on the fifth floor—a two bedroom, two bathroom suite with a kitchenette and a living room and a balcony that faced the Potomac River and the decimated capitol beyond. Dayne had let her in, then bid her goodnight, leaving her alone for the first time in a long time.

Eden didn't like it.

There'd been entirely too much space. To feel Cassian's absence. To worry about her parents. To theorize as to why Barrett and Violet had left Dr. Norton's cabin in Milwaukee, each possibility more dire than the last. There was too much space to think about the bombs, and death, and Xavier's stiff body, and the asset's agonizing screams, and Eloise and Elmer Miller killed in their own home.

The soft, king-sized bed in her new room had felt obscene. Even more so knowing Cassian was locked in a cold cell, probably with no bed at all. She'd distracted herself with Oswin Brahm's biography, which had been riveting. But that only lasted an hour. *Sixty minutes.* It had taken a mere sixty minutes for Eden to not only finish the thick tome, but commit everything inside to memory, making her wish she could switch off her superhuman powers. She would have liked more than an hour's reprieve.

By the time she fell into a fitful sleep, her bedside clock read three am. She awoke a few hours later with sunlight streaming through her windows. Her kitchenette had no food, so she made her way to Alexandria's commissary, feeling very much like a bug under a magnifying glass. The residence hall was no longer empty, and while the occupants had been briefed last night at the assembly, none of them seemed particularly welcoming. She'd grabbed a banana and a protein bar and headed to Kaiser, eager to tell Cleo all the things she hadn't been able to tell her last night.

"The jerk who did the hack job on *this*." Cleo motioned to her leg, which had been cleaned and bandaged, and was now hanging from a sling. "It was so bad, the nurse had to remove my stitches and put in new ones. That guy is *Gollum*?"

Of all the things Eden had told her—about Lark and Harlan and his granddaughter Renata, about the asset in the refrigerator, about their plan to leak the prisoner's location in order to force a transfer, about the deep fake that had made Barrett Barr look like a cold-blooded killer—this was what elicited the strongest reaction.

Asher as Gollum.

"He didn't come right out and say it, but yes. I'm ninety-nine percent sure he is Gollum."

Cleo gave her head a rattle, as though trying to shake this bit of news into place.

"Dayne should be here soon," Eden said, shifting in her chair.

He was coming with a device that would enable them to contact Violet's father. Or someone who would know how to contact Violet's father. According to Dayne, every missing person's report was assigned a reference number, and every reference number was connected to a digital code. That digital code was used within the confines of the Amber Highway to communicate information regarding the missing person, should any information arise. Dayne was meeting them here with that code and the device.

Cleo glanced at the door. "You really told him everything?"

"I didn't know how else to get the contact information." Eden ran her hands down her pant legs and resisted the urge to pick at her fingernails. Last night, when she told Dayne the truth, he'd reacted in the best possible way. He could have panicked. Sounded an alarm. Gone directly to Jericho. Instead, his trust in her only seemed to solidify. Even so, she'd spent a significant chunk of her fitful sleeping hours second-guessing. What if sleep changed his mind? What if he woke up with a new take on the whole ordeal? She was dangerous, and everyone ought to know.

Cleo scooped out the last of her yogurt with her lips pursed. She took the bite, then set the container on the tray. "I think it's fine," she said confidently. "Dayne Johnson isn't going to rat you out. Especially if you told him off the record."

"It was definitely off the record."

"Then you can trust him." Cleo licked her spoon.

Eden's leg bounced. Her instincts said the same, but her instincts had been incorrect before. In pretty egregious ways. Like following a tunnel to see what was on the other side. For all she knew, Dayne was in the boardroom with Francesca and Asher right now, telling them everything while they readied one of their poisonous vials.

Cleo set her spoon beside the empty yogurt container. "Tell me more about this biography."

"It was fascinating," Eden conceded. She understood why it was one of her father's favorites.

Up until last night, her familiarity with Oswin Brahm extended no further than her familiarity with her principal back in San Diego. She knew Brahm's face, his voice, his demeanor, his most notable accomplishments. She also knew he was an underdog who'd risen above his tragic circumstances to become a national hero. She just hadn't known any of the specifics. Now she knew plenty.

Eden shared the highlights.

He was an only child. His father had been a police officer. His mother stayed at home. The biography contained a picture of both. His father was handsome. His mother, hauntingly beautiful and unnaturally thin. When Oswin was eight years old, his father was killed in the line of duty during a riot. After which, his mother succumbed to addiction. Oswin was placed into the foster system where he was subjected to all manner of abuse. When he was twelve, his fifth-grade teacher noticed his exceptional intellect. He was awarded a scholarship to one of the country's most prestigious boarding schools. This was where Oswin's path had crossed with Lark's.

"Their boarding school was shut down halfway through his junior year, because of widespread protests," Eden said. "He had to go back into foster care."

Cleo took a deep breath, then let it out in a low whistle. "Suddenly, this utopian society he wants to create is making more sense."

Caelum In Terra.

Heaven on Earth.

A world where fathers didn't die in riots and schools weren't shut down by protests and children weren't abused in broken systems. Like Cleo, Eden could understand his motive. In a disturbing way, she could even appreciate his vision. Who didn't want to live in a world unmarred by death and war and suffering? What she couldn't understand, what she would never appreciate, was the means by which he was choosing to get there.

"He sees division as the enemy," Eden said.

"Of course he does," Cleo replied. "It's what led to the riot that killed his father and ruined his mother. It's what led to the protests that shut down his boarding school, the only place he wasn't abused."

"I guess in his own warped way he's trying to eliminate that division."

"By eliminating freedom."

Cleo's words reminded Eden of the first time they'd met, in Cleo's dorm room back when Eden hadn't known anything. Not the truth about herself. Not the truth about her parents. Or why this mysterious stranger named Cassian Gray had driven up on his motorcycle offering to help. Back then, Eden believed the forfeiture of their freedoms was a good thing.

"They brainwashed you good, little sis," Cleo had said.

Until that conversation, Eden hadn't thought to question or examine any of it. It just was what it was—the world in which she lived. But now, she could never view anything in such an uncritical light again. Nor could she ignore the fact that more freedoms were being stripped away at this very moment. The borders were closing. Authorities were radically enforcing fingerprinting and retinal scans—all under the guise of safety, with the public's full approval.

Eden shook her head. "Do you think this is how he's going to use his army—to eliminate freedom?"

"I don't think he needs soldiers for that," Cleo said. "Not when he's doing it just fine without them."

Eden made a humming sound in the back of her throat. "Did you know he had a wife who died in The Attack?"

"I did, actually. Mainly because I saw a picture of her once and she looked almost identical to my aunt." Cleo shuddered, like the thought of Uncle Oswin couldn't be creepier. "They had a son."

"I know," Eden said, just as surprised about it now as she was when she read it last night.

"Who, tragedy of all tragedies, went the same way as Oswin's dear mother." The declaration didn't belong to Cleo. The declaration belonged to Asher. He swept inside the room. Apparently, he'd been standing outside, eavesdropping on their conversation. "Addiction is said to be hereditary. Lucky for Oswin, it must have skipped a generation."

"His mother and his son died of addiction," Eden retorted. "I would hardly call that lucky."

Asher stopped at the foot of Cleo's bed, his six foot six, broad-shouldered frame making the room feel claustrophobic. Like Eden, he had cleaned himself up and was wearing basic clothing—a much larger pair of sweatpants in a darker shade of gray and a sage green henley with sleeves pushed up his forearms. He gave his eyebrows a challenging lift. "Are you defending him?"

"Never. But I won't make light of his pain, either."

"How very noble of you," he drawled.

The muscles across Eden's chest pulled tight. She kept her mouth shut as he adjusted the backpack slung over his shoulder and tapped the rolled-up newspaper he was holding against his palm.

Cleo pushed herself up. "Is that *America Underground*?"

"*Concordia Times*."

She made a face.

He tossed the paper onto her tray, knocking her empty yogurt container to the bed. "Your mom's on the cover."

She snatched the paper up and quickly unrolled it. Eden came out of her chair to see the cover for herself.

A black-and-white photograph of Dr. Beverly Randall-Ransom took up a significant portion of the front page. A candid of her looking distraught, attempting to shield her face from reporters as she made her way through a hospital parking garage. Above it, a headline read *Famous Neurosurgeon's Daughter Confirmed Dead*.

Eden scanned the article, noting the details Concordia had uncovered about Cleo, a resident advisor at Marquette who had been running an illegal newspaper called *The People's Press* out of her dorm room. She disappeared after her *cousin*, Cassian *Ransom*, and his partner in crime, Eden Pruitt, shot and killed the Brysons, a family of three in a suburb outside Chicago. Now she was dead, killed in a government raid upon Interitus Headquarters in Washington, DC.

Asher clucked his tongue. "It's a tough spot to be in, when a parent thinks you're dead." The words might have been sympathetic, but he packaged them in a dispassionate tone that rang of mockery.

Cleo looked up from the article and glared. "I need to speak with her."

Asher chuckled.

"Did I say something funny?"

"Oh," he said. "You're serious."

"As a heart attack."

He crossed his arms. "Are you an idiot?"

"Excuse me?"

"Or do you just like to say idiotic things?"

Cleo pulled back her chin.

"Your mother is being watched. Her phone. Her email. Her work. Her house. I guarantee you every aspect of her life is under surveillance. If you contact her, they'll know you're alive. And if they know you're alive, they'll deploy every resource to find you. They find you, they find us. That happened once. Let's not go there again."

Cleo scowled.

So did Eden.

Dr. Beverly Randall-Ransom had already lost her husband. Now she was being led to believe she'd lost her daughter, too. Eden understood Asher's point—trying to contact Beverly would probably be too risky—but did he really have to be so condescending when he made that point?

"Why are you here?" Cleo lifted the newspaper. It crinkled in her grip. "What's the point in showing me this if you won't let me do anything about it?"

"I thought you'd find it interesting."

Cleo huffed.

"And Fran is hyperventilating."

"About my mom?"

"About the volatility of our size these past forty-eight hours. We went from fifty to almost nothing, and now we're in the hundreds. Assuming everyone here is on board. That's the rub though. We don't know. She especially has a high level of distrust in the pair of you."

Eden thought about the asset locked in a refrigerator. The vials of poison stored in a freezer. If she were being honest, the feeling was mutual.

"I told her I'd come check in, make sure you weren't doing anything stupid. I also wanted to give you these." He slid off his backpack and removed a pair of tablets from inside. He handed one to Cleo, the other to Eden. "You insisted on being part of the prison break. Here's your part."

"What are we supposed to do with them?" she asked.

"Amir sent us a database of names. It includes every person even marginally connected to the prison outside Annapolis. The list is long, so I divided it into several subsets. Your tablet has one. Your tablet has another." He nodded at Eden, then at Cleo. "I installed a plug-in that will allow you to insert names from your lists. The plug-in will cull together all the information about the person available online, dark web included. Then it runs that information through an algorithm that will flag potential weak spots."

"Like?"

"Skeletons in the closet. Unsavory habits. Debts in need of paying. Anything we could use that might motivate a person to lend a helping hand."

"Blackmail," Cleo said, her voice wooden.

Asher made a clicking sound with his tongue and pointed his finger at her like he was shooting a gun.

Eden looked down at her tablet. She tried to imagine creating this plug-in, whipping up an algorithm capable of accomplishing what Asher had just explained. She wouldn't have the first clue where to begin, and yet, between last night's assembly and now, he had done both. The guy was obnoxiously impressive.

"Why did you name yourself Gollum?" Cleo blurted.

"What's that?"

"*Gollum.*" She folded her arms, looking disgusted. Like someone who had just yanked the mask off her favorite superhero, only to discover an arrogant jerk underneath. "Of all the names you could have given yourself, why that one?"

"The Amber Highway is my precious," he said with a smirk.

"Gollum dies at the end."

"Thanks for the spoiler."

"You haven't read the books?"

"I watched the first movie."

"You watched the first movie," Cleo repeated, speaking the words slowly, enunciating each syllable.

"It was really long."

The disgusted look on her face grew more pronounced by the second.

Asher rolled his eyes. "Can you handle this assignment or not?"

"Plugging in names and looking for flags?" Cleo asked.

"Yeah," he replied, his eyebrows raised like he really needed an answer. Like he really wasn't sure if they *could* handle it.

"We can handle it just fine," Cleo said.

"Good." He zipped up the backpack and slid it over his shoulder and headed for the exit when the half-opened door swung open all the way, nearly hitting him as it did. He side-stepped into its shadow.

Dayne stepped inside, freshly shaved and bright-eyed. Last night's worry was for naught. The camaraderie they'd built seemed just as strong this morning as he held a device aloft. He had yet to notice Asher, who was standing to his left, behind the opened door, outside the periphery of his vision.

"Look who's here," Eden exclaimed.

Dayne pivoted, spotted the young behemoth of a man, and quickly hid the device behind his back.

Asher stared suspiciously.

Eden squirmed.

Dayne forced a smile and bounced on his toes. "I was just stopping by to check on the patient," he said. "Who is—I must say—looking much better this morning."

"Thank you," Cleo said, but her usual excitement when in Dayne's presence was nowhere to be found. She kept glancing forlornly at the picture of her mother on the front page.

"What do we have here?" Dayne asked, gesturing to the tablets.

"Our assignment," Cleo said.

"I have one for you, too." Asher unzipped his bag once again and removed a third tablet. He handed it to Dayne with the same explanation he'd offered Eden and Cleo. Dayne updated him on the prison leak. His team was working on it now. Asher nodded, then invited Dayne to a meeting in the boardroom after lunch.

"Can I come?" Eden asked.

Asher gave her a dismissive once-over. "Why?"

Her cheeks flamed. "I—I thought I was going to be part of the plans."

"You are. By working on that." With a nod at her tablet, he exited the room.

Eden fumed.

Dayne ran his pointer finger beneath his collar and apologized for being late. "The newsroom is buzzing." He peeked into the hallway to make sure Asher was out of earshot, then closed and locked the door.

"Is that it?" Eden stared at the gadget he'd come into the room touting.

Dayne set it on her palm. "Everything's connected."

It was the same shape and weight as a phone—one of the newer foldable models. But when she flipped it open, there was no screen. Just a small numerical keypad on one side of the fold and a circular lens on the other. "How does it work?"

"You push this button here," he said, showing her. "The person on the receiving end will get a notification."

"Then what?"

"If the person's available when they receive the notification, they could answer immediately. If not, they call us back."

Eden took a deep breath and pushed the button. The device released a ping, and the circular lens projected a small holographic, scrolling ellipse.

Eden's heart fluttered. If someone answered, who would it be? Violet's father? An off-the-grid PI *hired* by Violet's father?

What would this person do when they saw *her*—a wanted fugitive presumed dead?

The device pinged again.

The ellipse continued to scroll.

Her palms grew sweaty.

She licked her bottom lip.

She needed someone to answer. She needed to know why Barrett and Violet had left her parents. And they needed to know they were in grave danger.

But the scrolling ellipse stopped.

Instead of a ping, the device *blooped*.

The holographic projection disappeared.

Her heart sank. "Now what?"

"Now we wait," Dayne said with a shrug. "Hopefully, someone calls back."

<h1 style="text-align:center">17</h1>

Barrett flipped to the next page in the scientific journal looking visibly troubled as he waited for the pot on the stove to boil. Violet could see the tension in the corners of his eyes, in the slant of his mouth. He'd gone to bed that way. He'd woken up that way, too. The radio had called him a terrorist. His picture would be splashed across Concordia again, only this time, he wouldn't be a missing boy, he would be a murderous boy.

Around him, the kitchen was no longer deplorable. Last night, they'd cleaned it together as well as they could with the supplies on hand until the floor was swept and the counters were clear and the sink didn't stink like sewage. When they were finished, hunger had gotten the better of them. Violet's jar of half-eaten peanut butter would no longer suffice. They needed sustenance.

Barrett had rummaged inside the pantry with alarming boldness. Violet had never been in the pantry. Father used to keep it padlocked. Now the padlock was gone. Barrett had found one can of beans and two cans of corn. He'd heated them on the stovetop in the same pot he was now using to boil water. As they ate, they'd kept their ears perked, listening for Father's truck. But Father never came. Barrett fell asleep on the couch. Violet tried sleeping in her old bed. But nightmares plagued her. So she'd taken her dusty blanket and her dusty pillow and she curled up on the floor by the couch until morning came.

Now they were going to have spaghetti for breakfast, and Barrett was looking through Father's scientific journals like they might provide the answers they'd come for. Violet kept glancing at the closet door with the moth-eaten coats, where the answers actually were. She tried to work up the courage to tell him, but every time the words got close, her ears would start ringing and her throat would squeeze shut.

Barrett flipped another page. "At least my parents know I'm not dead," he said, then immediately frowned. "I hate to think of what the media is putting them through, though."

They had yet to turn the radio back on, despite Barrett's longing glances at the unplugged cord. He wanted to hear more; she obviously didn't. So the radio remained off.

"Hey!" Barrett said, standing straighter. He pointed at the camera. Last night, they'd plugged the black cord into an outlet, then they attached the camera to the black cord. Nothing had happened. Now, a small, green light was on.

The camera had come back to life!

Her stomach did a strange pirouette as she snatched it off the counter. With a trembling breath, she held the power button until the screen illuminated. Then she covered her mouth with her hand, her fingers atremble as Barrett came beside her to see what she was seeing. A woman with raven hair and wide-set eyes the color of coffee. Shaped like a bird's tail, each with a single brush of straight lashes. Violet's eyes were a mixture of hers and Father's. A little like both, but not quite like either.

"Is that your mom?" Barrett asked in a tone as reverent as her breath.

Violet grazed her thumb across Mother's chin and nodded.

"She's beautiful," he said.

She was.

So very beautiful.

She toggled to the next photograph.

A little girl twirling in a meadow of violets.

That meadow was her namesake.

According to Mother, it was the most beautiful thing she'd ever seen. Until she held her own Violet in her arms. A child Father thought would never come, despite his prophetic vision. As he told it, an angel had visited him in the night. It flew through his window and told him he would bring forth a child who would save the world. A cruel joke at the time. His wife couldn't bear children. Fertility drugs hadn't worked. Not even IVF.

But then they received the strange phone call, and his prophetic vision had been magnified. Suddenly, his wife's infertility wasn't cruel at all, but the necessary path that led to the prophecy's fulfillment. For this reason, he allowed his wife to name their child. A decision he would later regret. Mother was weak, he liked to say. It's why she left. She didn't have the strength required to see the job through. Father hated that his daughter—a girl destined to save the world—had been named by someone so cowardly. With his own consent.

The water in the pot began to boil.

Something beeped. Or more like pinged.

They looked about, perplexed by the sound, then pinpointed where it was coming from.

The closet.

Barrett hurried toward it.

Violet's throat closed. She brought her hands to her neck and backed away—fear choking her. Strangling her. She couldn't breathe as he opened the closet door, unaware of the other door. The one behind those moth-eaten coats. He began digging inside pockets until he pulled out a device.

By then, the pinging had stopped.

"What is this?" he asked, turning the device over in his hand.

Violet didn't know.

Nor did she very much care.

All that mattered was shutting that door.

18

Dayne didn't stay. He would carry out his assignment between his ongoing work in the newsroom.

Eden sat in the chair by Cleo's bed while they entered the names into the plug-in and waded through the onslaught of information. They were looking for flags while *Concordia Baltimore* played quietly on the television mounted in the corner of Cleo's room. *National* had begun regurgitating news. About the raid in DC. About the prisoners. About confirmed deaths (Cleo Ransom) and suspected deaths (Eden Pruitt). About Barrett Barr and his unidentified friend and Interitus recruitment strategies.

A nurse came to check Cleo's vitals and change her bandage. Eden stepped out for a snack. There was a complimentary vending machine down the hall. She snagged a box of Whoppers for Cleo and a bag of Salt and Vinegar chips for herself. When she returned, the nurse was gone and the gadget Dayne left behind still hadn't pinged.

She tossed the Whoppers to Cleo.

She opened the box and rattled a few chocolates into her palm when a burst of dramatic instruments sounded from the television—a staccato arrangement that would have everyone within earshot looking up, paying attention as a male voiceover and a red screen with the Concordia logo interrupted the local broadcast.

"This is a Concordia News Special Report."

Eden's stomach dropped. She braced herself for any number of possibilities. The prisoners' executions. The apprehension of Barrett and Violet. The apprehension of her own parents, who would undoubtedly be framed as members of Interitus, too. The possibilities were so paralyzing, she couldn't pin any specific one down. All she could do was hold her breath as Cleo pointed the remote at the television to turn up the volume.

Chief anchor, Chuck Perez, replaced Concordia's logo. He sat behind his news desk in a suit, staring somberly at the camera while late-breaking music played in the background.

"It's 11:06 here in Chicago and I'm Chuck Perez. We understand that there has been a mandatory lockdown in Minneapolis after multiple incidents of unexplained civilian death and sickness. Hospitals are overflowing with patients who are experiencing the sudden onset of serious and disturbing symptoms. The National Guard has been deployed and is on the scene."

"What the heck?" Cleo exclaimed as the screen cut to footage of soldiers in hazmat suits, walking amongst bodies strewn along the city's central business district. All the while, Chuck Perez continued, informing the public of what they knew and what they didn't—the latter vastly outweighing the former. Was this bio-warfare? Retaliation by what remained of Interitus after the military bombed its headquarters? Or could this be an international adversary catching America unaware?

Eden clutched the gadget in her hand. Barrett and Violet were in Minneapolis. Was it a coincidence? Or was this late-breaking news and the presence of Barrett and Violet somehow intertwined? She gave the gadget a shake, as if doing so might force it to ping. But the thing remained frustratingly silent. Eden abandoned her bag of chips in the chair by Cleo's bedside and tucked her tablet beneath her arm.

"Are you leaving?" Cleo asked, pushing herself upright.

"I have to find out what's going on."

"So do I!" Cleo flopped against her pillow and growled at the ceiling. "Why is my dumb leg in this stupid sling?"

Eden shot her irritated friend an apologetic grimace. With a promise to return as soon as possible, she hurried from the room.

Outside, the sky was blue and cloudless. The leaves on the trees were vibrant shades of yellows and reds. An autumn chill permeated the air as she jogged across the street, past the east tower, into the west. She rode the elevator to the fourth floor and stepped into a newsroom so abuzz with activity, nobody noticed her at all. Keyboards clacked and phones rang as Dayne exited the glass doors separating the newsroom from an office beyond. He carried a stack of printouts to a group of people bent over a nearby table.

Eden waded through the chaos to meet him, her cheeks flushed from the brisk jog outside. "What's happening?"

"We're not sure yet," Dayne replied. "Our wire started buzzing forty-five minutes ago."

She looked at the flat screens circling the top of the large room—each one featuring Chuck Perez as the story unfolded.

A woman began spreading the printouts on the table when a frazzled-looking gentleman hurried from the same office Dayne had exited. "We've got more," he said, holding the papers aloft.

The woman grabbed them and quickly scanned the contents. "They're saying it could be a toxin."

Dayne read over her shoulder, his eyes slightly manic as they twitched back and forth like the pendulum of a grandfather clock.

Eden noted the time on the monitors. It was definitely past lunch, and Dayne didn't appear to be leaving soon. "Would you like me to go to the meeting on your behalf?"

"The meeting," he said, as if just remembering. He looked at his watch. "If you don't mind, that would be great."

She didn't mind in the slightest.

Seizing the opportunity, Eden exited the newsroom as quickly as she'd come and took the elevator to the ground floor. She cut through the courtyard between the west and east towers and was just lifting her hand to let herself into the boardroom when the gadget in her pocket pinged. She pressed her palm over the sound and hurried away, ducking around a corner, pushing into a ladies' room. She closed the door, turned the bolt, removed the gadget, and pressed the correct button before the pinging could stop.

The circular lens transmitted a three-dimensional hologram.

"Barrett!" she cried.

There he was, a smaller version projected inches in front of her, his mouth agape—a stunned holographic FaceTime. She let herself into a stall and locked that door, too.

"You're alive!" Barrett said, looking every bit as relieved as she felt. "We knew you had to be. But Concordia kept saying you weren't and—" He glanced down at his hand. "Cleo," he said. "What about Cleo?"

"She's fine."

Relatively speaking.

Barrett heaved a loud, relieved sigh. "Where are you? What's going on? How is this even possible?" He moved his finger from her to him. "This thing began pinging. We found it inside a coat, but we didn't know who was calling and it took me a while to figure out how to call back." Barrett pulled at his jaw. "I don't understand. Why were you using this thing to call Violet's father? That's her name—Violet."

"Barrett," Eden said, interrupting his freak out. She needed him to focus. "Why are you in Minneapolis? Where are my parents?"

"They're in Milwaukee with Dr. Norton. Jack found out why Violet's signal is weaker. She doesn't have a Queen Bee."

"*What?*" Eden exclaimed.

"The master node. It's not there. Her system doesn't have one."

"What does that mean?"

"She can't be controlled."

Eden's heart jumped.

"Jack doesn't know how to replicate it. But we think Violet's dad knows. So we came here, looking for him." Barrett shoved his fingers into shaggy hair, looking very much like his mind was spinning as fast as her own. "Ellery showed up! She hid in the back of Jack's car and came to Dr. Norton's. He totally freaked out. Then Annette came, too, and the news hit about the airstrike on Interitus Headquarters in DC. Cass, arrested with Prudence Dvorak. You, dead. Cleo, dead. Everyone lost their minds. Your mom started crying. Your dad looked like he was about to faint. That's when I caught Violet sneaking off. She told me I could come with. She said yes. Like, an actual word. She's talking, sort of. We hitched a ride with this old man in a red pickup. We ended up at border patrol. Now the news is saying I—"

"Barrett," she interrupted, putting some force behind his name. She'd forgotten how fast he could talk. How many words he could string together without pausing for a breath. "What's going on in Minneapolis?"

"I told you. It's where her dad lives and—"

"I mean the lockdown. The deaths."

"What are you talking about?"

"The National Guard is marching through the central business district in hazmat suits. A lot of people are dead. Even more are sick. They're saying it's some sort of … toxin." The more Eden talked, the wider Barrett's eyes became.

"I have no idea. This place doesn't have a TV. Only a radio. We turned it off because what they were saying was really upsetting. I could tell Violet didn't want to hear it."

"Where are you right now?"

He shot a quick glance over his shoulder. "Her dad's house."

"Near downtown?"

"Not even close. More like the outskirts of the city. He's MIA.

The place was a mess. A total dump. We're waiting for him to come back, but I'm not sure if he will. I think he's the reason Violet doesn't have a Queen Bee. I'm pretty sure he did a lot of really awful things to her. I also think—" He glanced over his shoulder, then leaned closer and lowered his voice. "I also think he might have killed Violet's mom. She thinks her mom left, but I don't buy it. Oh, and get this!" He held up his hand, where he'd scrawled three names in blue ink.

Hers.

Cleo's.

And his brother, Graham's.

"I keep forgetting names. It started happening after you left. Yours was first. It was like it just fell out of my brain. And Violet's hearing keeps going haywire. It's happening more and more frequently. We think there's some sort of glitch in our system, like maybe we need updates."

Eden touched her temple.

Updates.

Did that explain the unsettling bursts of pain that struck without warning?

"And the device! The one with the blinking dots. You know how there were five? When Violet and I left, there were twenty-eight. Twenty-eight! We have no idea what it means."

Barrett kept going as a shudder raced up Eden's body. She knew exactly what it meant. The Electus was coming online. They were ready for activation. Once activated, they would be poised to do whatever it was Oswin Brahm wanted them to do.

"You're in danger," she blurted.

Barrett closed his mouth.

She dove in, talking faster than she'd ever talked before, knowing he could keep up. She told him the truth about Karik Volkova and the real mastermind behind The Attack, Oswin Brahm. AKA, The Monarch. She told him about his army of ninety-four soldiers. About the Resistance and Prudence Dvorak and Dayne Johnson and *America Underground.* She told him about their plans to carry out a prison break. Then she told him one simple truth—Oswin Brahm had to know about them. And if he knew about them, he had to be looking for them. He probably orchestrated the deep fake to get the rest of the country looking for them, too. Now the National Guard was in Minneapolis. A man with Brahm's wealth and resources wouldn't have to work hard to dig up her father's address. Which meant Barrett and Violet needed to get out of that house as quickly as possible.

"Where are we supposed to go?" he asked.

Eden grappled for a suggestion. If the National Guard was in the city, they were probably surrounding the city, too. Leaving Minneapolis felt entirely too risky. "There's an off-the-grid community living in an old hospital building in Stevens Square. I can have a message sent ahead of you. I'll assure them you aren't terrorists. Maybe they'll let you take refuge there until the National Guard clears out and we're able to get you somewhere more secure."

She gave Barrett the address. She told him to avoid the central business district at all costs.

"What about the answers?" he asked.

Her stomach tied into knots. She wanted those answers as much as he did, but right now, their safety was more important. "I really don't think it's safe for you to stay there any longer. We'll find the answers some other way. Right now, you need to get out of there. Contact me as soon as you arrive."

Something crashed.

Barrett looked left.

"What was that?" Eden asked.

Before he could answer, the feed cut out and the hologram that was Barrett disappeared.

19

Gravel popped beneath tires.

Violet peeked down from the rafters of the detached garage and saw Father's truck ambling up the long drive. The vase in her hand dropped. It crashed on the concrete below—an explosion of glass that went everywhere as the truck pulled to a stop with brakes that squealed.

Like a nimble acrobat, she scampered across the rafters until she was pressed against the far wall beside a gabled window covered in cobwebs where she could spy. She sucked in her stomach and held her breath, going statue-still as the truck door opened. She could smell the booze immediately. He'd gained weight. The tail of his shirt was untucked. His thinning hair unkempt. He didn't notice the broken vase. He didn't see her in the rafters as he stumbled toward the house where Barrett was.

Violet's underarms broke into a clammy sweat. She needed to move, go. Right now. She needed to protect her friend like she should have protected Kitty. But her body was paralyzed, her grip on the wood beneath her so strong it splintered.

"You!" Father's booming accusation rattled the cobwebbed window pane. "What're you doin'n my house?"

His words slurred angrily.

She squeezed her eyes shut as Barrett replied with a measured voice that only seemed to make Father more belligerent.

"Don't tell me t'calm down! Where's m'daughter? What've you done with'er?"

Get down, Violet.

Go inside right now!

But her hands wouldn't let go. Her body refused to listen as her heart thundered and her ears rang. Father yelled. He shouted obscenities. Louder and louder until it sounded like he was in the rafters right beside her and every scrap of noise within a ten-mile radius screamed bloody murder in her ear.

She dropped like the vase. She fell between the rafters and landed hard on the concrete below. The camera around her neck landed hard, too—with a horrible crack. And somehow, Barrett was there, kneeling above her, his eyes panicked. "Violet, can you hear me?"

She sucked in a long, loud breath and thrashed—like a feral animal trapped in a cage. Barrett grabbed her wrists. He pulled her up into a tight bear hug. "It's okay," he said. "He can't hurt you."

He repeated the words until the wild creature inside stopped flailing.

She went still. Very, very still as Barrett told her what had happened. He knocked Father out. He hit him over the head with a frying pan. The man collapsed onto the kitchen floor when Barrett heard Violet fall. "He's unconscious," Barrett said. "But you don't have to come in. I can tie him up, and when he comes to, I can get the answers we need."

She breathed out, then in.

Out, then in.

Father couldn't hurt her.

Father was unconscious.

She needed to see it for herself.

One brave moment later, she was standing inside the front

door. Father was sprawled on the floor, face up with his shirt askew, exposing a belly that was hairy and pale and bulging over his belt. His face was puffy. In need of a shave. His neck, too. The frying pan Barrett used to do the deed lay beside him.

A twig snapped outside.

She pulled Barrett down behind the counter, out of sight from the windows. He opened his mouth like he might talk, but she quickly shushed him. Another twig broke. Without breathing, she peeked over the counter and out the window. Someone was there. A young woman dressed in camouflaged fatigues, wielding a giant gun.

Barrett peeked, too.

Then they ducked out of sight.

Silently, Violet picked up the frying pan and motioned outside.

Barrett shook his head and gestured. He pointed to the windows, then pointed at him and her and mouthed the words, "She might be like us."

Violet didn't understand.

Like us?

Barrett motioned for her to stay where she was. Remaining low to the ground, he crept to the other window. He peeked out, then ducked. He held up two fingers and hitched his thumb over his shoulder.

There were three of them.

Violet could hear them creeping closer, closing in.

They had the house surrounded.

Three against two.

Like us.

Her mind zipped to the device they'd left in Milwaukee. The one with all the blinking dots.

Like us.

She swallowed.

If it was true, then she and Barrett were trapped.

They couldn't get out.

They couldn't overpower them.

They might not even be able to hide. Violet and Barrett could hear heartbeats, and right now, hers was careening out of control. Even so, hiding was the safest option. Unfortunately, Violet could only think of one place to go, and that made her palms slick with sweat.

Her attention darted to the closet door. With her jaw set, she motioned for Barrett to follow. Quickly. Silently. They left Father behind and crawled into the front closet.

"They'll find us in here," Barrett whispered, so soft it was barely audible.

The sound that followed was much louder.

The device Barrett left on the kitchen table pinged.

Violet quickly parted the coats. She removed a panel from the wall, exposing the secret door behind. They hurried inside. She pushed back the coats. She slid the panel into place as the pinging stopped. She shut the door and she pulled Barrett down the pitch-black staircase. Deeper and deeper into the very bad room.

Floorboards creaked above.

Violet covered her mouth. She could smell Barrett's nervous sweat beside her as three pairs of footsteps moved into the kitchen.

"Did he pass out?" a woman asked.

"I think he was knocked out," another answered. "Look at the bump on his head."

"We need to search this place from top to bottom," a male voice said. "Pater said they'd be here."

Pater?

The sound returned—a tinny, recurring *ping*.

All three pairs of boots clomped to the table. Violet's entire body squeezed as tight as a clam. Barrett wrapped his arm around her shoulder.

The device continued to chime.

"What is it?" one of them asked.

"Some sort of gadget," another said.

"Should we open it?"

"No," the male replied. "We don't know what will happen if we do."

The pinging stopped.

Silence fell.

Violet waited for them to use their superhuman hearing, to identify the two heartbeats pounding wildly beneath them. But the moment didn't come. Which meant the three up above couldn't be superhuman. Barrett seemed to realize the same thing, for he relaxed ever so slightly beside her.

"Let's search the rest of the house."

The footsteps dispersed.

One approached the closet.

The door opened.

Metal hangers scraped against the metal pole.

"There are two backpacks up here," a female shouted. "And a stack of books."

The closet door closed.

Violet exhaled.

So did Barrett.

But then the gadget began chiming for a third time and her stomach squeezed. The footsteps congregated once again. They seemed to be huddled around the kitchen table, like the gadget might do something other than ping. When it stopped, the male said, "Wherever they are, it isn't here."

"What are we supposed to do?"

A moment of silent consideration followed the question.

And then, "You two bring *him* to the blockhouse."

"Do you want us to bring that, too?"

"That stays here. For all we know, it's some sort of tracker. We can't risk giving our location away. Contact Pater, find out what he wants us to do with him. I'll stay here and keep watch. They left their stuff. If I had to guess, they're coming back."

"And if they do? How are you possibly going to fight two of them?"

"I don't plan to fight at all." A gun cocked. "My aim is sharp. I'll snipe them both before they even know I'm here."

———

Violet pulled the string.

A halo of light shone from a bare bulb hanging from the ceiling.

Above them, the house was empty.

Father had been dragged away.

The women had taken him to the Blockhouse, wherever that was. The man was waiting in the woods outside, watching for their return.

Down below, Barrett pivoted in a slow circle. What had once been a sterile and neatly organized torture chamber had morphed into a disaster zone. It was as though Father had torn the room apart in a rage and left it all to rot. Papers and graphs and crumpled notes mottled the floor, and yet, this wasn't what grabbed Barrett's attention. That belonged to the terrible, awful machine running around the perimeter of the room. By the time he completed one full revolution, his eyes were as round as saucers.

"Violet," he finally said, "this is a freaking particle accelerator."

She didn't know the machine had a name. She only knew Father had built it and used it often, hoping to bring her powers out of hiding.

He spotted the chair in the center with its mishmash of electrodes and steel cuffs. His face lost all color. With his mouth pinched, he bent over to pick up a framed award that had been smashed on the ground. "He's a biophysicist?"

She nodded.

He looked through the ruined notes and graphs, then pulled

open a filing cabinet where Father kept his journals. Meticulous recordings of all the work he had done. Barrett removed one and flipped through its pages, his eyes turning into saucers all over again. He looked around, spotted a rucksack hanging on the far wall, and shoved the journals inside, all while whisper-explaining everything Eden had told him when they communicated on the gadget he'd left upstairs. The city of Minneapolis was on lockdown. The three people who showed up in army fatigues might not be superhuman, like them. But they had guns. Big guns. And they seemed very eager to use them.

"We need to get to Stevens Square. Do you have any idea where that is?"

She shook her head, then pulled the rolled-up map from her back pocket.

"That won't help us. We need a map of the city."

She opened another filing cabinet. She rummaged inside and found an atlas at the bottom.

Barrett nodded excitedly. He brought the map beneath the hanging lightbulb and flipped to the twin cities of Minneapolis and St. Paul. He jabbed a spot on the edge. "Right now, we're here." He moved his finger diagonally across the paper. "We need to get here. But we have to stay far away from here." He circled an area that was downtown Minneapolis, then looked up the length of the rickety staircase. "I don't know how I feel about going up there."

They didn't need to.

Violet gave his shirt sleeve a tug, then brought him beneath the stairs, where Father had dug an escape tunnel that led far into the woods.

20

Eden strode back to the newsroom with spark plugs in her veins. Her parents were okay. Barrett and Violet were okay. At least they had been fifteen minutes ago. Most fascinating of all, Violet didn't have a Queen Bee. Which meant she couldn't be controlled.

After their call dropped, Eden tried three times to reach him. All three pings had gone ominously unanswered. Eden didn't like it. What had made that crashing noise? And why wasn't Barrett pinging her back?

She stepped into the newsroom, noting the change in mood. Not more than an hour ago, the atmosphere had felt energized, caffeinated. Now, a palpable heaviness had crept in, like gravity doubling down. Perhaps the severity of the situation was finally setting in. The picture Chuck Perez was painting had certainly grown more dire. The sick were dying in droves.

Eden searched for Dayne. He was no longer at the round tables. He wasn't at the newswire or standing at any of the desks. The glass doors in the back swooshed open. As a woman exited, Eden caught sight of him.

She marched through the somber chaos and barged inside—a

corner office with large windows and a stately desk cluttered with papers, behind which sat Dayne rubbing his temples. When he looked up, his expression had changed as drastically as the atmosphere.

"I thought you were going to the boardroom," he said.

"I was. But then I got a call." She held up the gadget he'd given her and stepped further inside. "Barrett got in touch with me. He and Violet were at her father's house. I told them they weren't safe and needed to leave. Then our call dropped."

Dayne sat up straighter, like this last bit was interesting news.

"I sent them to Stevens Square. I told Barrett I'd send a message ahead of them so the people there would know they're coming. Do you think they'll let them in?"

Dayne's face fell. "I don't know."

"Can we check?"

"I'm afraid we can't."

"Why not?"

"The community in Stevens Square has gone radio silent. They haven't answered any communication for the past twenty minutes."

"What's their normal response time?"

"Thirty seconds."

The answer punched her in the gut. She'd sent Barrett and Violet to Stevens Square, and now Stevens Square had gone incommunicado. "What does this mean?"

"I'm not sure. It could be the government has shut down all forms of communication coming in and out of the city. Maybe that's why your call with Barrett dropped."

"You think the government can shut down illegal forms of communication?"

"It's possible."

But not probable. She could see it on his face. She could hear it in his voice. Eden tried to ignore both. She tried to hold on to hope. Communication had been shut down because of the toxin.

The community in Stevens Square was fine. So were Barrett and Violet. The crash she'd heard before the call dropped was nothing but a patch of static.

The glass doors opened.

The same lady who exited earlier popped her head in now. "One of our correspondents is on his way to Stevens Square."

Dayne came forward in his chair. "You were able to get a hold of him?"

"On the first try."

And just like that, her hope popped like the delicate soap bubble it was.

———

Eden knocked on the closed door of the boardroom, her blood zinging with adrenaline. Whatever meeting they'd been having was well underway.

The door swung open.

A familiar face stood on the other side. A petite woman in a tailored, black business suit with a lily-white, lace-trimmed camisole visible beneath her jacket. Lark Shangguan. Not the avatar. Not a hologram. But real and in the flesh, standing in the boardroom of the IDA's east tower.

"How did you get here?" Eden asked

Ignoring the question, Lark looked past her, out into the hall-way. "Where's Dayne?"

"In the newsroom. Something's happening in—"

"Minneapolis. We know." Surprisingly, Lark didn't slam the door in her face. She walked away. She took a seat at the long conference table where nine pairs of eyes beheld Eden as she stood in the doorway. Every person was an original member of the Resistance. Francesca. Jericho. The six survivors from Bunker Three. And Asher, with his eyebrow cocked. "Can we help you?"

"Dayne is stuck in the newsroom. He asked me to come on his behalf."

"How very thoughtful. And unnecessary. We're perfectly capable of filling Dayne in when he's no longer stuck. Which means you can scurry yourself along." He twiddled his fingers like they were tiny feet scampering away.

The air in Eden's lungs went hot. She squared her shoulders and glared. If he wanted her to *scurry along*, he would have to get off his butt and make her. He made no move to do so.

Lark plucked a piece of paper from the table and slipped on a pair of black-framed readers. Beside her, Francesca frowned at the opened door. Her short hair was clean but un-styled. She and the six survivors wore the same basic outfit as Eden—sweatpants and crewneck sweatshirts—as though they'd been mass produced in an assembly line. Meanwhile, Jericho sat at the head of the table looking much more original in a ribbed, mustard turtleneck and a pair of black slacks.

A spread of food had been arranged in the center of the table —bagels, half sandwiches, fruits, and vegetables. Along with a white porcelain carafe, a pitcher of water, and a stack of cups, beside which lay a copy of *Concordia Times* and a scattered pile of papers. The television was on mute as it covered the situation in Minneapolis. Ticker tape scrolled across the bottom of the screen, calling it a terrorist attack. The unidentified toxin seemed to be isolated to the central business district but the entire metropolis was on lockdown as the death toll continued to mount.

"Is Brahm behind this?" Eden asked.

"His name is written all over it," Lark replied.

Eden took a tentative step inside. "What's he trying to accomplish?"

"The same thing he's always trying to accomplish. Create catastrophe and spread fear. Give it a day or two, and he will undoubtedly step in as the hero."

Eden glanced at the television. "Why Minneapolis?"

To this, Lark had no answer.

Nor did anybody else.

Francesca drummed the table with two fingers. "Do we think

this is it—the Great Winnowing Brahm's been prophesying about?"

"The Great Winnowing?" Eden asked. She licked her bottom lip and darted a glance at Asher. So far, he hadn't grabbed her by the hair and tossed her out into the hallway. Instead, he sat with his elbow propped on an armrest, rubbing his chin like he found her continued presence puzzling.

"It's one of Brahm's more prevalent prophecies," Lark said. "The last step before he can usher in his utopia. We're not clear on the *how* or the *when*. But we are fairly certain it will involve a lot of death."

Francesca scrubbed her face. "We need to get our hands on that stupid book."

Eden took another step, close enough now to set her tablet on the table. "What book?"

"Sanctus Liber," Lark said.

Eden's brow furrowed. That was Latin for *Holy Book*.

"The Monarch's sacred writings." Lark rolled her eyes. "It contains every prophecy penned by Brahm throughout the years. He wrote about The Attack when we were in boarding school. The moment that first nuclear slug hit, his followers became that much more fanatic."

Eden frowned. "Why?"

"They saw it as proof that he was, indeed, prophetic."

"But they were his own predictions. He was making them come true."

"We didn't know that at the time." Lark looked up from her paper and pulled off her reading glasses. "Oswin believes in a hierarchy of knowledge. The more loyal you prove yourself to be, the more privy you become to the darker aspects of his ideology. As well as the lengths to which he will go to carry out that ideology. The problem is, by the time you get to that point, you're so indoctrinated you don't realize how extreme your beliefs have become."

"It's like boiling a frog," Jericho said.

"You can't actually do that," Eden replied.

Everyone looked at her. She could feel their attention, Asher's most acutely.

"They'll jump out of the pot once the water reaches a certain point." Erik had told her so, along with several other popularly held but false beliefs. He loved debunking a good myth.

Asher snorted. "Well then. I guess frogs are more intelligent than his followers."

Eden shifted. "Why do you want this book?"

"It contains his prophecies," Francesca said.

"Which he makes come true," Asher added.

They both looked at her like she was dumb.

"So this book will tell you what he plans to do next."

"Your skills of deduction are unparalleled."

The heat in her lungs intensified, but she lifted her chin and ignored Asher's mockery. Instead, she addressed her question to Lark, who had yet to look at her like she was soap scum on grout. "Where does he keep it?"

"We're not sure, but we suspect his catacombs."

"His catacombs?" Her mind went immediately to the empire of death, the catacombs in Paris. Surely these weren't the same ones.

"It's where the Great Mothers are entombed."

Eden pulled out the chair in front of her tablet and took a tentative seat, like the slower she moved, the less likely anyone would be to make her leave.

Lark selected half a blueberry bagel from the tray. "Before we captured the asset, he would stand in the catacombs and read from Sanctus Liber every Thursday night. These recitations would be broadcasted live at Swarm's weekly meetings."

Eden recalled the gatherings the Brysons had hosted. Along with the first time Amir Kashif went off script—on a Thursday evening, visiting the Aigners in Baltimore. She pictured brainwashed groups of people staring at a hologram of the asset standing in some consecrated crypt as he read from Oswin

Brahm's *sacred writings*. It gave her massive heebie-jeebies. "Is this where the soldiers live—in Brahm's catacombs?"

Asher leaned back in his chair and folded his hands behind his head. "We don't think they live *in* them. But we do believe they were raised in the general vicinity."

"Which is where?" Eden asked.

"That's what we've been trying to figure out," Francesca said.

"Amir doesn't know?"

Lark tore off a bite-sized chunk of her bagel. "Brahm keeps everything to do with the *Electus* incredibly close to his chest. He hasn't fully trusted his followers since the destruction of his test group."

The heat in Eden's lungs zipped into her ears. So blatantly, she wished she hadn't pulled her hair back. What if Asher noticed the incriminating blush? She swallowed nervously and, with her elbow on the table, casually covered her left ear from his view.

"Only his innermost circle is privy to their location," Lark continued. "Amir has never been part of that circle. He has to keep his ear to the ground. Anytime he gets wind of a potential location, I do recon. So far, I've completed nine missions. Each one has been a bust."

"And now we have to pause our work in order to do this." Francesca held up her tablet with a sneer.

Eden's ears went hotter.

"I found another one." A highlighter squeaked against a printed sheet. A survivor from Bunker Three—a tall Black woman named Nairobi—capped the yellow marker.

At Eden's look of confusion, Jericho explained, "We're cross-referencing names from the database Amir gave us with our list of known Swarm Members."

"These are all of his followers?" Eden asked.

He plucked a grape from the cluster cupped in his palm. "The ones we know of."

"Can I have a look?"

"Be our guest," Lark said.

Eden gathered the sheets into a stack and began scanning the names, her attention snagging on several she recognized. Nicholas Marks, deceased. Isabella, Gage, and Clay Bryson. Also deceased. She came across individuals with last names that matched the ones on the back of the pamphlet. She came across people in government, like the Police Chief of Chicago. She came across celebrities, like Star—the A-list pop-artist with millions of rabid fans. Eden and Cassian had shared an elevator with her on their way to the Prosperity Ball.

The list was disturbingly long.

The name Nairobi had just highlighted was a guard at the decommissioned military prison in which Cassian was being held. It made the sparse contents in Eden's stomach churn. "What's stopping Oswin Brahm from killing them in prison?"

"His pride," Francesca spat.

"If the man has a weakness," Lark said, "it's his proclivity for a good show. He's been hunting Pru for years. He's not going to put all that time and energy to waste by having her and her followers killed in the dark. That's never been his style."

"Dear old Ozzy won't be satisfied with merely killing his enemies," Asher said, his sneer matching Francesca's. "He'll want people to cheer while he kills them."

The sentiment put a chill in Eden's bones. She'd seen it before. Footage of the global celebration that broke out after Karik Volkova's public execution. There had been spontaneous parades. Dancing in the streets. Restaurants uncorking their best bottles of champagne and serving glasses on the house. All for a man who was one of Oswin's disciples. How much more would he want to see the death of his enemies celebrated?

On the television, Chuck Perez continued to cover the unfolding story as the ticker tape scrolled. Surprise, surprise. Interitus had officially taken credit for the toxin. Eden's lip curled. Frame a thing the right way and no matter how egregious, onlookers wouldn't object. Onlookers might even cheer.

Brahm had proven himself to be an expert framer. He had his hand on the control button of information. He was shaping the narrative, and the public was buying it—hook, line, and sinker.

Just like *she* had for so long.

But now her eyes were open and she could never unsee the things she'd seen these last few months. She could never go back to the old paradigm, where illegal was bad and Oswin Brahm was good. Her understanding of the world had been irrevocably altered the moment Dr. Norton told her the truth in his basement kitchenette, and ever since, she'd been thrust deeper and deeper into a world with infinitely expanding shades of gray.

As if to prove the point, two of the survivors from Bunker Three excused themselves. It was time to administer another dose.

With a shiver, Eden did her best to push the memory of the asset's tortured screams out of her mind. She despised what they were doing to him, but there was nothing she could do about it at the moment. Her concern for Cassian and her parents and Barrett and Violet were so all-consuming, this stranger of a boy and his maltreatment would have to wait.

She picked up her tablet. She moved through the names—frustrated that she had to check her speed so as not to rouse suspicion. Annoyed every time she pretended to cross-reference names on the list of known Swarm members as if the whole thing wasn't already imprinted in her mind. She offered an advantage, but she had to hide it lest she ended up on the receiving end of those doses.

She swiped to the next person on her list.

Manuel Van Cooper, a naval construction mechanic stationed in Annapolis. The *only* construction mechanic stationed in Annapolis. She ran him through the plug-in and feigned a quick look through the stack of papers, already knowing he wasn't there. Once his information loaded, she began wading through it. When she reached the third screen of intel, she saw something she had yet to see.

A flag.

"I've got one," she said, coming forward in her chair. She turned the tablet around to show Asher.

He snatched it from her hands.

Francesca pointed. "Those links are yours."

His eyes remained fixed on the screen as he tapped and typed. Then he stopped and grinned. "He's a gambler."

Eden's thoughts flitted to Mordecai. "On the Underground?"

"Illegal gambling dens. They're popular on the Highway."

The Highway.

His precious.

Asher went back to work, clicking and tapping and swiping while Francesca watched over his shoulder. Then she jabbed her finger at the screen. "Look right there," she said.

Asher turned the tablet around so the others could see.

He'd hacked inside a password protected hospital database. A photograph of Manuel Van Cooper's elderly mother filled the screen. Beneath it, a long list of diagnoses, prescriptions, and some pretty astronomical medical bills. "Looks like his job as a naval construction mechanic isn't cutting it. So Mr. Van Cooper has taken to gambling. He doesn't have a single checkmark by his name."

"What does that mean?" Eden asked.

"Our guy, Van Cooper, is a man of integrity."

"He honors his bets," Lark clarified.

"How is this supposed to help us?" Jericho asked. It was a reasonable question. Manuel Van Cooper was a construction mechanic in Annapolis. How would they use his penchant for gambling to help them pull off a prison break?

"He has access to military vehicles," Asher said.

"*Transfer* vehicles," Lark added.

They all looked at one another.

"We're going to blackmail him," Eden finally said. Issue an ultimatum. Help them with the prison break and his illegal activities would remain under wraps. Refuse, and he would have to add an arrest and lawyer fees to the astronomical medical bills.

Asher took a deep breath, as though considering. "I don't think blackmail is the right approach for a guy like Manny." He turned his queen over, running her up and down his knuckles. "I think this calls for an old-fashioned hustle."

21

They crouched on the outskirts of Stevens Square with eyes on the place Eden had told them to go—an abandoned hospital where a community of illegal residents lived.

But the hospital wasn't abandoned.

Big, scary vehicles were everywhere. Men and women in uniform swarmed the grounds, dragging people toward the trucks, shoving them inside. A girl twisted free. She ran toward her mother, who was being dragged in the opposite direction. A man in uniform pulled out his gun and shot her in the back.

She fell to the ground and didn't move.

The mother screamed and screamed, and Violet felt a scream, too. It was growing in size, hurling up her throat. Barrett must have sensed it, because he cupped his hand over her mouth and pulled her down into the tall weeds.

Her heart punched her sternum—wild, hysteric thumps.

Barrett put his finger to his lips, urging her with his warm brown eyes to stay quiet. But another gunshot exploded and a flock of birds flew and more people screamed.

Violet clapped her palms over her ears. Barrett's hand shifted like he was going to move it away, but she grabbed hold of it and

135

held on tight with her eyes squeezed shut. They stayed that way until the big scary vehicles drove away. Every single one.

Barrett peeked over the weeds to watch them go. When they were gone, he looked at the abandoned hospital, where five bodies lay on the ground. He seemed to wrestle with something inside. An internal battle Violet couldn't see or hear as seconds stretched into minutes. Until finally, his expression hardened with resolve and he whispered determinedly, "I have to check on them."

Violet's pounding heart lurched into her throat. What if the vehicles came back? What if officers were hiding inside? What if they took Barrett? But she couldn't get the words out and he was already gone, scurrying like a mouse with his eyes on the sky.

Violet didn't exhale until he returned, looking sadder than she'd ever seen him. "They're dead," he said, shaking his head, fisting his hair. "I don't think that girl was older than twelve."

Two squirrels scrabbled up a tree.

Barrett jumped at the sound, then shook his head harder and plopped his rear in the dirt. "Those vehicles belonged to the RRA."

Violet didn't know what that meant.

Barrett set his elbows on his knees. "The country's Resident Registration Agency. They're in charge of governing citizenship, registration, and documentation." He huffed, his mouth grim. "And now, I guess, raiding illegal communities and shooting runners in the back. Even when those runners are kids."

Violet stared at the tire grooves they'd left behind. This was supposed to be a safe space, a place to hide until they could escape Minneapolis.

Barrett rubbed the back of his head and spoke Violet's mind. "What in the world are we supposed to do now?"

Cleo hobbled inside their suite on a pair of crutches, looking more like herself with her snakebite lip piercings returned to her bottom lip. Now that they weren't out in public trying to hide their identity, there was no reason for her not to wear them. She stopped with a huff, one of her long braids caught between her armpit and the crutch pad. She disentangled it—looking as annoyed with her impediment as Eden's father had been with his. She released a low, impressed whistle as she took in their new living quarters.

Eden shut the door, eager to talk.

But Cleo held up her hand. "We should check for bugs," she whispered. "This suite could be wired. My room at Kaiser could have been wired. The thought didn't occur to me until we were leaving—a total lapse in judgment. I blame the concussion."

Eden didn't think Cleo's room had been wired. She didn't think this suite was wired. But she had to admit, Cleo's suspicions had a track record of validity, even when Eden thought they were absurd. She entertained her injured friend with a quick but thorough sweep.

No bugs were found.

Cleo took the thick tome that was Oswin Brahm's biography from the coffee table and settled herself on the couch with her bad leg propped on an ottoman.

"I definitely need to read this," she said, running her finger down the spine. She opened the book and flipped through the pages, shaking her head all the while. "America's superhero is actually the villain."

Eden grabbed a pillow and sat beside her. "Do you think he planned for his wife to die in The Attack?"

"It makes him more sympathetic, having lost someone, too. More relatable to the public he's trying to woo."

A nauseating lump rolled up Eden's throat.

Cleo snapped the biography shut and set it aside. "Tell me everything."

Eden dove in. She told Cleo about her conversation with

Barrett. She told Cleo about the playbook, Sanctus Liber, and how the Resistance had been working to locate it. Several times, Cleo had to ask Eden to slow down. Cleo was clever—probably even brilliant—but her mind couldn't process information at the same speed as Eden's or Barrett's.

When she finished, Cleo said, "It's a shame we don't have the device."

At first, Eden thought Cleo was referring to the device in Eden's pocket—the one she used to communicate with Barrett. But then her thoughts turned to another device—the one they'd left with Jack Forrester. The one with at least twenty-eight blinking dots. By now, probably more.

"IP addresses," Eden muttered.

"They don't give exact locations, but they do provide a general vicinity." Cleo leaned back, looking from the pristine white kitchen to the sliding glass doors that led to a balcony. Outside, the sky was dark. Another day had come and gone. Another day with Cassian locked in a prison cell.

With every passing hour, she felt more and more like a carved pumpkin. Gutted. Hollowed out. Increasingly desperate. In the quiet moments, when she had nothing to distract her, she caught herself praying, bargaining, making promises. But to who —God? Her family had never been particularly religious. Did she believe in such a being? Some all-powerful, benevolent creator? And if she did, what did such a being think of her—a mortal who had been tampered with, corrupted by a man who had murdered millions. A super freak, as Cleo called her, designed to bring forth some twisted Utopia. The ends didn't justify the means, and yet with every passing hour, Eden felt more inclined to justify anything if it meant helping Cassian.

"It's hard to stomach," Cleo said, as though reading Eden's mind. But when she continued, her words weren't about Cass. "The people here are living like royalty. Meanwhile, in Chicago …" She shook her head. "Inequity is inescapable. Even off the grid."

Eden agreed, but she was too preoccupied to linger on the injustice. Her parents and the Foresters and Dr. Norton had their hands on a device that might very well point to the elusive location the Resistance had been looking for. And Eden had found a target. She told Cleo about Manuel Van Cooper, a construction mechanic for the navy. She told her about the gambling dens and Asher's plan.

"He wants to take all Manuel Van Cooper's money," Eden said. "Then offer to cancel his debt in return for a favor."

"What's the favor?" Cleo asked.

"Do something to the vehicles transporting the prisoners." Eden set her elbows on her knees and clasped her hands. Her left leg bounced. "I need to be a part of this."

"Then make it dumb not to bring you."

"How?"

"You're an exceptional poker player."

"I've never played a hand in my life."

"Then learn. You have every advantage in the world, Six. You can compute all the odds with your freaky photographic memory. Measure your opponent's heart rate and breathing pattern. Calculate the exact dilation of their pupils, for crying out loud. Give yourself an hour to study the game and I have no doubt you could stroll in to the next world series poker tournament and win the whole thing."

"You don't think that would rouse suspicion?"

"You don't need to be one of Brahm's super freaks to be a poker prodigy. There have been and will continue to be plenty of prodigies that have nothing to do with a psychotic genius inserting nanobots into embryos. Look at Asher." Cleo made a face, like someone had broached the topic of vomit at the dinner table. "He doesn't have any nanobots helping *him*, and yet he created The Amber Highway at sixteen."

Eden considered this, her nerves frayed and frazzled. Keeping her secret was taking a toll. Paranoia was beginning to cloud her judgement. She thought about her mug shot and Cassian's picture in the war room. The Resistance had set their sights on Cassian, but that didn't mean they couldn't shift their focus to her. One wrong step could land her right beside the asset, where she'd be no help to Cass at all.

"Tell me more about this newsroom," Cleo said, rubbing her hands excitedly.

America Underground would be leaking the location tomorrow, all while the country was spinning into panic. Nobody could say whether Minneapolis was an isolated attack. Concordia was currently zeroing in on Barrett Barr and Violet Winter, who'd entered the city right before the toxin was released. Further proof that the teenagers were members of Interitus. The death toll had reached sixty-seven, eight of whom were first responders. Hospitals were overflowing. Which had Cleo thinking about her mother and Eden thinking about her own.

According to Barrett, she'd been crying; her father had looked ready to faint. The thought of them grieving the loss of their daughter when they'd already grieved the loss of their son shredded Eden's insides. Her brain was being split in too many directions. She removed the gadget from her pocket. "I wish we could use this to contact them."

Cleo nodded in frustrated agreement. Dr. Beverly Randall-Ransom wasn't on The Amber Highway. Neither were Eden's parents. There was no code to plug in that would send Dr. Norton a notification. Which meant it was impossible. But Cleo sat up, her eyes brightening. "We could contact Mona."

Mona.

Something fluttered in her belly.

Dayne would know how to reach Mona.

Once they reached her, Mona could contact Dr. Beverly Randall-Ransom, who would know how to send word to Eden's parents.

Her desire to put them out of misery swirled into an acute longing impossible to resist. They sat with the possibility for a moment, then made their way to the newsroom. By the time they reached the elevator, Cleo had gone waxy. She'd been released from Kaiser with strict orders to rest with her leg up, not traipse by foot all the way to the IDA in the dark. Despite the pallor of her skin, her eyes danced. She was about to step inside the command center of the country's largest, most illicit newspaper. This was her Disneyland.

The elevator doors slid open.

It wasn't nearly as busy as it had been earlier in the day. More than half the desks were empty. Phones were no longer ringing. Computer keys, no longer clacking. Even so, Cleo's face stretched long with wonder, like a kid on Christmas morning.

Dayne sat at one of the round tables in the back, conferring with two others, one of whom gave him a nudge and pointed in their direction. He looked over his shoulder—his hair a mess, his eyes bloodshot—and smiled in surprise.

"They let you out," he said, walking toward them. He had a five o'clock shadow. His breath smelled like stale coffee. He looked like a man who hadn't taken a single break all day. Eden wondered if he was staying so feverishly busy because he cared this deeply about the cause, or because he wanted to avoid thinking about the Millers. Probably a combination of both.

"I think they were getting annoyed with my complaints," Cleo replied.

Dayne chuckled.

Eden pounced with a question. "Have you heard from your correspondent?"

He frowned. "We haven't been able to get in touch with him."

"All day?"

He shook his head.

The ominous feeling in Eden's gut expanded as Cleo leaned heavily on her crutches and surveyed the room—physically weak, but mentally stimulated. "This place is amazing."

Dayne's frown turned upside down. He stood taller, his chest puffing at the compliment. The two of them had hit it off at the Miller's, slipping into the role of doting mentor and admiring mentee. It seemed their rapport would continue here. "Once you're fully recovered, I'll have to find you a desk."

"Really?"

"With writing chops like yours? Only a world-class idiot would keep you away." He gave her a paternal smile. "We're slowing down here. Mostly set for tomorrow's edition. I was just about to find Jericho." A bitter edge crept into his voice as he said the name. Apparently, forgiveness wasn't one of Dayne's strengths. "See what I missed in the boardroom."

Eden filled him in. Then she removed the gadget from her pocket. "Can we use this to get in touch with someone in Chicago?"

He scratched his stubbled cheek.

Eden braced herself for his reticence. Contacting Violet's father was one thing. He had willingly submitted his contact information to *America Underground*. Trying to contact Mona so she could get in touch with Cleo's mother was something else altogether. Dr. Beverly Randall-Ransom wasn't on the highway, and she was undoubtedly—as Asher so snidely pointed out— being monitored. The move was too risky.

But his disapproval didn't come. Maybe suppressed grief was making him reckless. Maybe it was Jericho's betrayal. Or maybe Dayne Johnson was a natural-born risk-taker, and twenty-one years of living as a wanted insurrectionist made him even more so.

Whatever the case, he waved at them to follow—past the round tables, through the glass doors and into his office. He sat down at the desk and pulled up the contact information for every off-the-grid community across the nation. Then he took Eden's gadget and plugged in the proper code for Chicago.

22

Cassian stood beneath the lukewarm spray of the shower. A half wall of cement afforded the only privacy he would have from the pair of gun-wielding guards standing watch, one of whom sported a crooked nose and a purple bruise beneath each eye.

Time had turned into an enigma. Since there weren't any clocks or windows in this hellhole—at least none Cass had access to—he had to measure it in meals and facial hair. His existence had diminished into something very small. There had been no more interrogations. No more sightings of Prudence Dvorak. No more Lady Justice. No more doctor. No more excursions down dark hallways so the guard with the limp could demand answers to questions Cass only partially understood. It was just him and a six by nine cell. This shower area, which he'd been to twice. The camera-lined corridor that stretched between. And a rotation of the same four guards.

Cass stuck his head beneath the stream and dragged his hands down his face. To keep the despair at bay, he'd spent his waking hours doing sit-ups and one-armed push-ups. He kept his thoughts active and intentional. If his mind was a vehicle, he couldn't be a passenger. He put himself in the driver's seat, taking every opportunity to observe and calculate and memorize.

He cased his own cell, scrutinizing every square inch, searching for something—anything—that might lend itself to an escape. In the corridors, he counted cameras and doors and steps. He peered down perpendicular hallways, hoping to glimpse where they might lead. He knew the approximate heights, weights, and ages of all four of his guards.

The one with the broken nose was left-handed and had a bum knee. The blonde was a compulsive knuckle cracker. He popped them regularly and often, unless his shift overlapped with the guard who shaved his head. There was no knuckle-cracking when Baldie was around, just the rattle and crunch of the Tums he chewed like candy. Then there was the guard with the freckles, who wore a wedding band and smelled like ladies' perfume—so far, two different kinds.

Cass ran scenarios through his mind, plotting getaways and escapes, none of them feasible. When that grew tiresome, he turned his attention to the puzzle pieces he and Eden had been gathering before they followed that tunnel and he landed here. Francesca Burnoli led them to Willow Bryson. Willow Bryson led them to the Bryson's safe. There, they'd found a pamphlet and a photograph of Isabella Bryson's sister, Lillian Kashif. Lillian led them to her surviving son, Amir. And Amir led them to Washington, DC, where Prudence Dvorak had pressed the blade of her knife against Cleo's neck.

"Did you come for the asset?"

Cass glanced at the guard with the black eyes.

"Where are they keeping him?" he'd asked.

Was *him* the asset? If so, then didn't that mean the guard worked for the Monarch? Cass thought about the raid. The bombs and the gunfire and what happened to Cleo? Now that he knew the government didn't have Eden, this was the question that would pounce unexpectedly. Whenever it did, he heaved it from his mind, along with a myriad of others. Then he would drift into a fitful sleep, where his subconscious shoved him out of the driver's seat. It took the wheel, taunting him with a disturbing mixture of euphoric dreams and sickening nightmares.

Kissing Eden in the Miller's kitchen.

His mother, pushing him into the closet.

Kissing Eden in the Miller's basement.

His father with the baseball bat.

Kissing Eden in Lou's ring.

The crack of bone and the spray of blood.

Kissing Eden in Beverly's driveway.

The roar of the crowd as his chest heaved and his opponent lay at his feet, open-eyed and unseeing.

"You gave your money to the widow."

Cass shut off the water with an aggressive twist of the knob. He dried himself with a thin towel and dressed in his jumpsuit. The broken-nosed guard cuffed him gruffly. Then he pulled his walkie-talkie from his belt, the bruise beneath his left eye twitching as he pushed the button. "Prisoner two is ready. Over."

There was a squawk.

"Bring him to the interrogation room," Lady Justice replied. "Over."

Cass perked up. He hadn't seen her since she visited his cell with the doctor and he warned her to tread carefully.

"Copy that," the guard replied. He returned the walkie-talkie to his belt and grabbed Cass by the wrists. "Time for a little field trip."

As they went, Cass counted his steps.

From the shower area to the first camera.

From the first camera to the second.

From the second to the third.

He observed the configuration of the lights. The shape of the cell doors and the position of their handles until they reached the door at the end of the corridor where he'd first been interrogated.

The door slid open.

And none of it mattered. Despite the push-ups, the sit-ups, the methodical thinking, the active cataloguing of information—all of it an attempt to stave off madness—Cassian Gray experienced his first hallucination.

For there, sitting in a chair with his elbows on the table, was a demon.

A real live monster.

The very one that had killed his mother.

————

The hallucination came like a grenade, blowing every box containing his darkest memories to shrapnel. They burst in a violent blast and in its wake, those memories had nowhere to hide.

His father's angry voice. His mother's muffled cries. The bruises on her arms. The bruises on his own. A storm-tossed lake. His mother's unrelenting grip as she held his hand, as she cut the engine, as she led them to the stern of the boat, as she told him they had to jump. The shock and terror of the cold, swirling water enveloping him.

Eight years of peace.

Then the crash of a door. That angry voice shaking the walls once again. The tremble in his mother's hands as she pushed him into a closet. The tremble in her voice as she told him to stay. The turning of a bolt. The thwack of the bat. The expanding pool of blood on the floor. His fists pounding on the door. His shoulder barreling into the wood. Her blank, unseeing eyes. Then the crack of his own bones as the demon turned the bat on him.

Cass stared at the monster. No longer wild-eyed. No longer wielding a bat. But sitting at the table dressed in a tailored suit, his dark, neatly trimmed hair peppered with silver and his bloodshot eyes brimming with tears.

Cass lost all reason. He forgot about his cuffed wrists. He forgot about his injured shoulder. He forgot about the guards with the guns. Like a bull seeing the flap of a matador's cape, he charged.

The monster's eyes grew wide—the black of his pupils expanding until his irises were nothing more than the thinnest of golden-brown rings as he hastened to his feet and stumbled backward.

The guards reacted, too. They tried tackling Cass, but they couldn't bring him down. They could only shove him into the wall. The knuckle-cracker dug his forearm into Cassian's throat, his lips moving with words Cass couldn't hear. Not with blood pounding in his ears and fire blazing in his lungs. Cass shoved the knuckle-cracker away.

A loud pop filled the room.

Excruciating pain shot through Cassian's body like angry wasps in his veins. His muscles seized. His legs convulsed. He collapsed to the floor. The guard with the broken nose knelt hard on his neck and pressed the barrel of his gun into Cassian's forehead.

The door flew open and slammed against the wall.

"Enough!" Lady Justice commanded as she strode inside with eyes ablaze.

The guard removed his knee from Cassian's neck, but the gun remained.

"You had no authority to tase him," she reprimanded.

The knuckle-cracker spluttered. "But he—he was going to—"

"What, exactly? His hands are cuffed behind his back."

The knuckle-cracker looked incredulously at his counterpart's bruised eyes. His crooked nose. There was a lot Cassian could do with his hands cuffed behind his back. But the woman didn't wait for an answer. She grabbed Cass beneath one arm. The guard with the broken nose grabbed him beneath his other. Together, they pulled him to his feet and shoved him into a chair.

The woman cinched a taser cuff to his ankle. "If you don't want that to happen again, don't move." She snapped her fingers at the monster, who stood with his back pressed against the far wall. "Sit."

He did so quickly, obediently.

Cass glared—his chest heaving, his nostrils flared. The man across from him wasn't a reflection in a mirror or a lookalike in the ring. He wasn't a memory or a nightmare. He was real. In the flesh. Whole and healthy and neatly dressed.

"We'll give you some privacy," the woman said.

The monster's face drained of color. "You're leaving?"

"If he moves, he'll be tased. The second time is no less painful and even more debilitating." The door closed behind them with a boom.

Privacy was an illusion.

Cass had only to glance from the two-way mirror on the wall to the mounted camera in the corner to understand that this interaction was being watched and recorded. For what purpose, he didn't know. Rage so consumed his mind and body, he couldn't even make an educated guess. "What are you doing here?"

"I—I couldn't ..."

"You couldn't *what*?"

"I couldn't believe my eyes. When I saw you on the news. When I realized it was you. I—I knew it wasn't true. I knew it couldn't be true. My son is not a terrorist."

"I am not your son." He delivered the words with such unwavering animosity, such low and ominous warning, the monster flinched.

It was gasoline on fire.

Because monsters didn't flinch. Monsters didn't obey women

like contrite school boys. Monsters didn't feel or fear. Nor did they clasp their hands imploringly like this one was doing right now. "Listen, Cassian, you have to cooperate with these people. If you don't, you will be executed. The date is already set. They plan to announce it to the public tomorrow evening."

Cass stared incredulously. Was this a joke? A set-up? An attempt to throw him so far off balance he'd accidentally give them a morsel of information that might lead to Eden?

The monster leaned forward, his forearms flat on the table, his fingers spread wide, a gold band glinting on the ring finger of his left hand. "If you know something, if you have any information at all, tell them and they will let you go. There's no reason for you to sacrifice your life for a group of people who wouldn't return the favor. There's no reason for you to die."

"Says the man who beat me with a baseball bat and left me for dead."

Another flinch, followed by a cagey glance at the mirror. "I— I'm not that person anymore."

"Go to hell."

"I already did!" The monster pounded the table with an angry, familiar fist. And despite everything—Cassian's strength and training and the anger he donned like an impenetrable shield, the pit in his stomach filled with the fear of a pre-pubescent boy.

"You want me to go to hell," he said. "But I was already in hell. For years." The monster dragged his hands down his face. He sat with bowed shoulders, as though some terrible, invisible weight rested upon them. "But I got out. You can, too. Just tell them what they want and they will strike a deal."

"Why do you care?"

"Because. I want a second chance. I want to make things right."

Make things right? Was he kidding? Was he delusional?

"Please. Tell me what to do and I'll do it."

"Bring my mother back from the grave."

His body sank. His arms dangled pathetically by his sides. "You have no idea how much I wish I could undo what I did." The monster clutched the silk knot of his tie. "I loved her. I loved her so much, I couldn't think straight. When I thought you were both dead, when I thought you had drowned, I nearly died from the grief. I tried to drink it away. For years. Then I found out you were alive. *She* was alive. She took you away from me. She took herself away from me."

"For our protection."

"I know that now. But I didn't then." He buried his face in his hands. "God forgive me, I didn't know. I was out of my mind. When Mona found me. When she told me—"

The name came like a sharp ping in his brain. Like the bursting of a blood vessel. Spots danced in his eyes. "What did you say?" Cass interrupted.

The monster stopped his pathetic blubbering and looked up from his hands. "I was out of my mind. I—"

"Who found you?"

"A—a woman. Her name was Mona. She told me you were alive."

"Liar."

The monster blinked several times, as though truly confused by the accusation. "I'm not lying. She found me in Colorado. She told me you were alive. I didn't believe her, of course. Until she showed me a photograph. She gave me your location in exchange for money."

And just like that, a second grenade detonated.

His mother's friend.

His mother's betrayer.

The woman who'd found Cass after his mother was dead, after his father nearly beat him to death. The woman who had taken him to Beverly's like she cared. That woman had led the monster to their doorstep.

She had a lot of mouths to feed.

It was true back then. It was still true today. And he'd brought Eden to the Damen Silos. Mona had known they were going to Bethesda. There was a bounty on their heads—an increasingly large and lucrative bounty. And now he was in here and Eden was out there with no idea that Mona was a monster, too.

23

A high-pitched pinging sound dragged Eden awake. She opened one eye, groggy from the late night, and wiped drool from the corner of her mouth before realizing where the pinging was coming from. The gadget on her bedside table! She jerked upright and snatched it off the nightstand.

The incoming code wasn't from Barrett. It was from Mona, who they'd been trying to reach last night to no avail. Eden kicked the comforter off her legs and hurried across the hall into Cleo's room. She flipped on the light.

The mountain of blankets on the bed mumbled an incoherent objection. The pair of them had stayed up past two, playing round after round of Texas Hold 'Em with the deck of cards they'd retrieved from The Landing's concierge. Eden plopped down on the bed and gave the mountain of blankets a shake as she accepted the call.

A holographic projection appeared.

She expected a miniature hologram of an old woman with a grumpy face and sagging jowls. Instead, it was the young, skinny teen who'd greeted Cassian and Eden when they first arrived at the Silos. The same young teen who'd fetched their supplies before they left on their train trek east. Mona's gopher, munching on one of the largest, shiniest apples Eden had ever seen.

Cleo peeked out from her cave, registered what was going on, and hurled herself upright. "Twig!" she exclaimed, before cupping her forehead like one staving off a bout of dizziness. Apparently, she'd lurched upright too fast.

The kid's eyes went round. "Cleo?"

She pressed herself close to Eden, nearly cheek-to-cheek so the kid called Twig could see her in the projection.

His eyes went rounder. "You're alive!"

"And kicking," Cleo said. "Where's Mona?"

Twig shrugged. "Usually when she leaves, it's to stock up on provisions, but we have more than usual at the moment." As if to prove his point, he bit into the flesh of his apple, spraying holographic flecks of juice through the air.

"You can thank my Tesla for that," Cleo said.

And Cassian's bike. Mona would have traded both in for cash by now. Eden was glad the people living in the Silos had plenty of food. Although, considering what was happening in Minneapolis and the impossibility of knowing how it might affect communities such as this one, they would do well to maintain their current rations.

"When is she due back?" Cleo asked.

"She didn't say." Twig took another bite and talked around the mouthful. "She's been gone an awful lot, so she put me in charge of communication."

"That's a pretty big job for a kid," Cleo said.

"Who you calling a kid?" Twig wiped his mouth with the back of his hand. "She knows she can trust me better than anyone."

Cleo sat up straighter, hugging an armful of comforter to her chest. "Well, good, because we need you to pass a very important message to her as soon as she returns."

He wedged the apple between his teeth and picked up a pencil and one of Mona's sticky notes.

"I need Mona to call me. I'm hoping she can pass a message along to my mom, and my mom can pass a message along to Eden's parents." Cleo gave him the code that would allow Mona to contact them.

When Twig finished recording, he removed the apple and said, "*America Underground*, huh?"

The statement caught Eden off guard. She wasn't aware the code linked them directly to Alexandria. It made her feel queasy as Cleo and Twig finished their back-and-forth.

He took another big bite of his apple and offered them both a salute before Cleo signed off and disconnected.

She asked for her crutches.

Eden handed them over. "You think it's okay he knows our location?"

"Twig?" Cleo scooted to the edge of the bed and hobbled to her feet. "I'm not worried. He has no reason to share it with anyone but Mona."

Eden bit the inside of her cheek, wishing she felt reassured.

"Let's grab some breakfast," Cleo said, crutch-walking to the door. "Then we'll head to the boardroom and convince the council that you are their ace in the hole."

———

Lady Justice brought Cass to his cell with the taser pressed against his spine like a warning. He didn't fight. He didn't count his steps or study the keypads or calculate the time it would take to incapacitate the woman and disappear down one of the darkened hallways. His mind was a smoking field of ruin and wreckage—a war zone in the aftermath of a battle. The death count yet unknown.

Mona.

She'd pretended to care about his mother, about him. And yet, she was the one who had betrayed them. Had she planned it from the beginning? Had she deceptively gained his mother's trust, weaseled her way into his mother's confidence, intending to sell them out? Or had she carried out the betrayal on a whim, in exchange for money that would feed all the mouths she needed to feed? Did it matter?

They reached his cell.

The woman in the suit opened the door.

Cass shuffled inside. Dazed. Stunned. Sick.

The woman unlocked his cuffs.

He sat down on the bench and rubbed his wrists. Eden was out there. Mona was out there. Eden's parents were out there. He tried to remember if they'd mentioned anything about Dr. Norton and Milwaukee in front of the old woman. He couldn't recall, but that didn't mean they hadn't. The unknown of it turned his gut to rot. Authorities were offering a bounty to anyone who might point them in a helpful direction. Mona had only to point them to Eden's parents. If authorities threatened them, Eden would turn herself in. Of this, Cass was certain. And if the government got Eden, they would destroy her. Of this, he was also certain.

"Your father looks a lot like the man you killed in the ring," Lady Justice said.

Cass closed his eyes, wishing he could stuff the memory away, but there was no place to stuff it. The boxes had been blown to pieces.

"What did he do to warrant such hatred?"

"He killed my mother." The rot in his stomach churned. He looked up at the woman standing in the doorway, studying him with her head slightly cocked. He looked at the pin on the lapel of her suit coat. "Does that matter to you? Does your vow to protect the innocent extend to those living *off* the grid, or are they outside your jurisdiction?"

"People who step off the grid remove themselves from anyone's jurisdiction."

"She stepped off the grid to save my life."

The woman's face paled. The change was slight. But it was there all the same.

Cass rested his head against the wall behind him.

Voila. Tout au mieux.

His mother's voice.

Eden's voice.

They circled into a sword that pierced his soul.

As much as he ached for those words to be true, they weren't.

It wasn't *all better*.

It couldn't be all better.

Not with him in here.

And Eden out there. With Mona and his father and the government and the Monarch.

"I looked into your accusations," the woman said.

He lifted his head and stared back at her—listlessly, hopelessly.

She cast a paranoid glance over her shoulder and stepped further into his cell. "You were right," she whispered. "A lot of things don't add up."

———

"I'm really good at poker," Eden blurted as the door began to close.

"I'm better," Asher replied.

Cleo used her crutch like a doorstop. "Wanna bet on that?"

The taunt snagged his attention. He looked from the end of Cleo's crutch to the challenging gleam in her eye. Behind him, Lark, Francesca, Jericho, and the young woman named Nairobi watched from the conference table.

Cleo raised her eyebrows, one lower than the other because of the glued-together gash over her right eye. "Or is the high and mighty Gollum afraid to lose in front of his buddies?"

He narrowed his eyes.

She crutch-stepped past him, inviting herself into the boardroom. She leaned her crutches against the table, plunked her satchel next to Asher's queen, and took an empty seat. She removed a deck of cards and shuffled.

"What do you possibly have to wager that's of any value?" Asher asked.

"Have a seat and I'll tell you."

He stared at her for a beat, then sat in the seat to Cleo's left. He crossed his ankle over his opposite knee—his large body occupying every inch of space the chair had to offer. Cleo handed the deck to Lark and asked her to take a look. This was a standard deck. There were no tricks up their sleeves. Whoever won would do so fair and square. Once Lark completed her examination, Cleo gathered the cards into a pile and shuffled once more. "If Eden wins, she gets to join the hustle."

"And the prison break," Eden added, taking a seat across from Asher.

Francesca scoffed.

Cleo kept going. "If Asher wins—"

"*When* I win," he cut in with an eye roll.

Cleo responded with an eye roll of her own. "Both of us are banned from setting foot in this boardroom ever again."

Eden choked.

Cleo tapped the cards against the table. "We'll stay out of your business and let you do your work."

The corners of Asher's half-opened mouth curled upward like this was too good to be true. Everyone else exchanged looks while Francesca shook her head vehemently. "Uh-uh. No way."

"Oh, come on, Fran," he said. "I've got this. I've more than got this. If we take the bet, you don't have to worry about them crashing our meetings anymore."

Eden had to bite the inside of her cheek to keep from reacting. He really had no idea what he was getting himself into.

Asher looked at the others, giving them the opportunity to object. When nobody did, he turned to Cleo with a Cheshire grin and stuck out his hand. "You're on."

Cleo shook it.

With a huff, Francesca pushed back in her chair and folded her arms like a kid on the playground who wanted to play kickball, but was overruled in favor of four-square.

Cleo removed a sandwich bag filled with Skittles and Whoppers from her satchel. The concierge—as resourceful as it was—had no poker chips on hand. They had to get creative.

She launched into the rules. They would play Manny's game of choice, Texas Hold 'Em. She would deal ten hands. Whoever had the most candies after the tenth game would be considered the superior player.

Asher and Eden agreed and the competition began.

Subject 006 versus Gollum.

The creator of the Amber Highway versus one of the Monarch's super freaks.

It wasn't a trick deck. But it wasn't a fair fight, either.

Eden pretended to focus. She even pretended to make a few minor misjudgments. Even so, by the time the last hand was being dealt, Asher had a meager three Whoppers and two Skittles. Eden had a whole pile. And any hope that he might make a comeback shriveled and died as soon as she turned up a full house. Francesca went bone white. Eden raked in the last of Asher's candy as he leaned back in his seat looking like a man with some serious indigestion.

Cleo smiled triumphantly.

They had hustled the hustler.

24

sher honored his bet. They got right to work and neither Cleo nor Eden were kicked out of the boardroom. Francesca was mutinous. The others, resigned. And Asher, surprisingly well mannered. Instead of increasing his hostility, besting him in poker seemed to earn Eden *and* Cleo his grudging respect.

He was dubbing their scheme the Halloween Hustle. According to him, tomorrow night was the biggest, busiest gambling night of the year. Every high roller worth his or her salt would log in to partake in the holiday festivities.

For the past three years, Manuel Van Cooper spent the night partaking at The Cage, the triple black diamond of gambling dens. Only those with the highest scores and the best track records were allowed in. Of those, only a small percentage reached Big Betty, a special table in the back. Earn your seat there, and you'd no longer have to pay for admission. The Cage would pay *you*. Last year, Manny earned his seat and made out like a bandit. This year, they knew he'd be looking to do the same.

Asher would take on the identity of King George, who'd earned his seat at the table the same year The Cage debuted, and was known for raking in money like the supposed tyrant after which he was named. He had hot nights and cold nights, much more of the former than the latter. When he was hot, he was unbeatable. Last year, he'd been cold. Hence, the impressive pot of cryptocurrency Manny had taken to the bank. The two would gun for one another. They just needed to ensure the actual King George wasn't in attendance. Jericho made a call to Harlan, who made a call to the FBI, which led to a tip-off. By tomorrow morning, someone on the king's bankroll would send him a warning.

Lie low. Go dark. For a week, at least.

Halloween was tomorrow, which meant Asher would be good to go. He went to work creating a newly minted avatar for Eden with forged credentials.

"Who do you want to be?" he asked, his fingers poised over his laptop. They'd been at it for several hours now, and he had yet to say a single condescending thing.

Eden's mind rewound to the previous Halloween in San Diego with Erik, before her world and her understanding of that world had been flipped on its head. Erik had gone as Einstein. She, Marie Curie—a scientist from France so famous she was enshrined at the Pantheon. Two of the greatest minds of their time, a Halloween power couple.

"Madame Curie," she suggested.

Asher ran a search. The username was up for grabs. He went to work creating her identity—an up-and-comer with a clean track record and an upward trending score. Just high enough to legitimize her presence. King George would bet big, driving up the stakes. He would keep Manuel Van Cooper on his toes, whetting his appetite with signs of a potential cold streak. Madame Curie would work her way to Big Betty. By the time she arrived, the pot would be big enough to pay off the debt Van Cooper's mother had wracked up in medical bills. He wouldn't be able to walk away. But he wouldn't win. Neither would King George. Victory would belong to the newcomer, putting Manuel Van Cooper at Eden Pruitt's mercy.

They went over the plan.

Again and again.

Until a knock sounded on the door and a lady from the newsroom peeked inside. "Dayne wanted me to pass along a message. The location of the prisoners has been successfully leaked."

"Excellent," Lark said, clicking the end of her pen. "I'll get in touch with Amir, make sure his ears are perked. We'll want to know as soon as that leak hits the NSA's radar."

The lady left.

Nairobi stretched her arms tall toward the ceiling and yawned.

"It's late," Jericho said, checking his watch. "If we want to grab dinner, we'll have to go now before the commissary closes."

Their meeting was officially adjourned.

Eden stayed behind to go at Cleo's pace. By the time they arrived, Francesca was already seated at a table with Nairobi and Jericho, slouched over her tray as she followed Eden and Cleo with her good eye.

Eden helped her friend get situated at a table on the opposite end of the commissary, then collected their food—meatloaf, corn, and mashed potatoes, all of which had been languishing beneath a warmer.

Cleo made a face as Eden handed her a tray and a can of generic soda. "Still no word from Mona?" Cleo asked, leaning close.

Eden checked the gadget in her pocket just to be sure, then shook her head and took a bite of her mashed potatoes.

Cleo cracked open her drink. "So weird," she said. "It's not like Mona to be gone all day. You'd think she would have returned our call by now."

"What are you two whispering about?"

The sudden sound of Asher's voice was so jarring, Eden nearly choked on her potatoes. She and Cleo broke apart.

He stood towering above them with no tray, just a large bag of Xtra Hot Takis and a bottle of Mountain Dew.

Cleo set her can on the table with a click. "About how horrible you are at poker."

The giant actually smiled. "Mind if I sit?"

"It's a free country," Cleo said. "At least, it used to be."

He parked his Mountain Dew, pulled out a chair, and tore open his bag of Takis. Across the commissary, Francesca glared with such intensity, Eden could feel it like a hot laser beam on the side of her face.

"What's her deal?" Cleo asked, nodding at the girl with the glass eye.

Asher shoved his hand into the bag. "Seriously?"

Cleo rolled her eyes. "Look. We get it. We shut down your emergency alert system and led the military to your doorstep, but you don't see Jericho and Lark looking at us like they might sneak into our suite in the middle of the night and suffocate us with our pillows."

"Jericho and Lark never lived in DC. And Fran is prickly by nature. She takes awhile to warm up to anyone, let alone two people responsible for the deaths of almost everyone she knows."

His words made Eden want to burrow into the ground and never come out again. She swirled her mashed potatoes with her fork, her appetite obliterated.

Asher leaned back in his chair, lifting the front legs off the ground. "I'd like to know where you learned to play poker like that," he said to Eden.

Color rose in her cheeks.

Cleo swallowed a bite of meatloaf and scoffed. "I know this might be a mind blowing concept, but just because you're some sort of cyber wunderkind doesn't make you superior at everything."

"That's an interesting theory." He popped a Taki into his mouth and studied Eden as he chewed. Interesting, perhaps. But he obviously didn't subscribe to it.

She suspected her face was turning an incriminating shade of tomato. She cleared her throat. "My dad's always been obsessed with the World Series of Poker. I started playing with him when I was four."

"Right. Your dad." He brought his chair down. "The guy in the CIA. You know, funny thing. I looked him up on our lunch break and there's no record of him being in the CIA."

Eden's underarms broke into a sweat.

"Haven't you ever heard of witness protection?" Cleo intertwined her fingers above her tray, her tone and expression as combative as Asher's had ever been. "A person so intricately wrapped up with Karik Volkova's downfall has a giant target on his back. Any decent father is going to ensure his family doesn't live the rest of their lives in constant danger."

Asher ate a few more Takis looking mostly unconvinced.

"What about you?" Eden blurted, desperate to distract him.

"What about me?"

"Why are *you* so good at poker?"

"I'm obviously not good at poker."

"Okay, then. Why are you such a cyber genius? According to Cleo, you created the Amber Highway at sixteen. How does that happen?"

He shrugged. "Boredom. A lifetime of neglect. The strong and persistent desire to stick it to my old man."

"Is he a government official or something?"

Asher chuckled like Eden had just told a funny joke. "He hates anything he can't control. I always made a point to be one of those things. Then I created the Amber Highway, which can't be controlled by anyone. Not even me."

Cleo scooped a bite of corn. "Why the daddy issues, Ash?"

He lowered his eyebrows. So far, Eden had only ever heard Francesca call him Ash, and they'd known each other for years. "There are so many whys, where do I even start?"

"With the main one."

"He killed my mother."

Cleo and Eden's attention collided. Asher's father killed his mother? This was Cassian's story. *Cassian*. The mere thought of his name pierced her like a sword. She needed to get him out. She would do whatever it would take.

"How?" Cleo asked.

Eden coughed. "Cleo!"

She held up her palms. "What?"

Asher rested the bag of Takis in his lap and twisted open the Mountain Dew. "Didn't your mom ever teach you manners?"

"Powerful women don't typically get to where they are by prioritizing politeness."

Asher tipped his Mountain Dew in concession. Or maybe approval.

Eden wasn't sure she agreed. Dr. Beverly Randall-Ransom had been perfectly polite and accommodating when she welcomed Eden into her home.

"How'd you become part of the Resistance?" Eden asked, eager to move along. She didn't want to dwell on Asher's *daddy* issues. Not when they were so similar to Cassian's.

He took a long, lazy drink, his eyes trained on hers, as if deciding whether to answer.

"Did they recruit you or something?" she pressed. Eden had to imagine the creator of the Amber Highway would be a hot commodity to such a ragtag rebellion.

"I like to say we found one another. Our purposes aligned."

"You knew about the Monarch?"

"Oh, yeah." His expression darkened. "His whole corrupt empire. I'm very eager to tear it down."

Cleo lifted her soda. "To aligned purposes."

"To Oswin Brahm's demise." He tapped his bottle against her can. "May it be as agonizing as he deserves."

That night, in the privacy of their suite, Eden continued to study the ins and outs of the game. She learned and memorized strategy from the very best poker players throughout history. She learned and memorized everything she could about their target—Manuel Van Cooper. All of it was a welcome distraction from the dagger in her heart that was Cassian's absence. But when her head hit the pillow of her too-soft king-sized bed, he stood front and center in her dreams. Like Asher in a chair, there was no space he didn't occupy.

The next morning—on Halloween Day—Eden and Cleo still hadn't heard a peep from Mona. Cleo tried reaching out a few more times, but not even Twig responded to their pings. They could do nothing but assume he'd delivered the message. Mona had found a way to send that message to Cleo's mom, and now —hopefully—that message was en route to Eden's parents.

After breakfast, they headed to the boardroom and there met a conference table full of somber faces.

Eden's heart plummeted. "What's wrong?"

Even as she asked it, she knew. Amir must have figured out the truth. He must have sent a warning and now everyone here knew, too. It's what she'd been bracing for, her existence in Alexandria marked with pins and needles. The Monarch knew who Eden was. The government had to know who Eden was. Amir worked for that government. Which meant it was only a matter of time until the Resistance discovered who Eden was. They must have finally figured it out.

She took a step back, her muscles tensing. She would not be poisoned. She would not be shoved into a refrigerator where she would lose her autonomy.

"The community in Minneapolis is gone," Francesca said, without even a hint of animosity in her tone.

The tension in Eden's body leaked away. So did the blood in her face. "What do you mean, *it's gone?*"

"They're not there," Lark replied, her arms aquiver with repressed fury.

"Dayne sent another one of his correspondents earlier this morning," Asher said. "When the correspondent arrived, the place was completely cleaned out."

Cleo sank into the nearest chair.

Jericho scratched his goatee. "There wasn't a trace of life anywhere."

Eden's heart thumped. She'd sent Barrett and Violet there. She thought it would be a safe place to take refuge until the National Guard moved out of the city. But if that off-the-grid community was gone, then where were Barrett and Violet?

"What about Chicago?" Cleo asked.

"What *about* Chicago?" Francesca replied.

Beside her, Asher peered suspiciously.

"If the community in Minneapolis is gone, maybe other communities like it are gone, too."

"Dayne sent correspondents to Minneapolis because Minneapolis went silent," Asher said. "He has no reason to check on Chicago."

Eden and Cleo exchanged an uneasy glance. Chicago had also gone silent.

"This has to be related to the toxin," Jericho said. "The National Guard sweeps in. The city goes on lockdown. Suddenly, the community there is gone?"

Eden tried to wrap her mind around it. An entire community like this one. AWOL. "What do we think happened to them?"

"The Great Winnowing," Lark spat, her voice a simmer.

"So that means … they're all dead?"

Lark didn't answer.

Nobody did.

Never had the absence of words spoken such volumes.

25

The world was silent. Not just quiet, but a complete absence of sound as Eden stood on an empty street corner, staring at herself in the reflection of a storefront window. Or rather, staring at her avatar, Madame Curie—the younger version, with her honey brown hair pulled into a frizzy updo. She wore a black pioneer dress—full-length and high-collared with buttons and bell sleeves. Beneath, a pair of Victorian lace-up boots.

She reached inside the front pocket of her frock and wrapped her hand around three golden coins, each one embedded with a unique code. With a deep breath, she took a step toward the door, where a holographic coin floated above the handle. She removed its twin and slotted it into place.

The street disappeared.

So did the door.

The absence of noise, too. The unnatural silence was replaced by the frantic beat of techno music and the deep throbbing of a bass. Eden was standing on the edge of a dance floor. A strobe light flashed upon a gyrating mass of avatars ranging from strange to frightening, their movements frozen in blinking snippets of light. Nearby, a giant tigress of a woman, complete with a tiger's tail, twerked on the bar to whistles and catcalls.

It was a Halloween party unbound by physics and nature. None of it was real. And yet, it felt real, which made the bizarreness even more bizarre—this living, breathing virtual reality that pulsed with manic energy.

"Welcome to Club Mirage," someone shouted, a figure standing beside her. Neither male nor female. Not even human, but a mythical creature with talons and feathers. "And happy Halloween!"

Here she was, standing inside the biggest nightclub in the metaverse on one of the biggest nights of the year, second only to New Year's Eve. It was fully immersive and fully legal, except for one small thing. Club Mirage had a parasite. That parasite was The Cage. Only gamblers with a high enough ranking knew how to get there. Thanks to Asher, Madame Curie was in the know.

Eden skirted around the sweating, shimmying mass toward the back doors. She let herself out into an empty courtyard. The night air felt cool. The music thumped through the walls as she walked toward a garden maze, all the way to a neglected bench in a forgotten corner overgrown by weeds. She sat in the center of the bench, and there—to her left, ingrained in the wood—was the outline of an amber lotus leaf. Eden traced it with her pointer finger and another holographic coin appeared, floating in the air like a tiny, circular ghost. Just like before, she pulled its match from her pocket, slotted it into place, and the music went away.

The garden, too.

She was still sitting on the bench, but the bench was on a stage in a silent theater, spotlighted beneath a bright glow that turned everything beyond the light's reach into black nothingness. There were no props, other than the bench she sat on and a freestanding door several feet away, inside the spotlight's halo. Standing in front of it was another avatar. This one seven feet tall, whose silver skin was patterned with scales. It stood with its hands clasped, staring into the middle distance like it couldn't see Eden nearby.

Only when she stood did the towering creature notice her, its eyes as silver as its skin.

She cleared her throat. "I'm here to play."

Her voice echoed like it would inside a cavernous, empty hall.

The creature beckoned her closer.

When she came, red laser beams shot out from its silver eyes—its retinas a scanner, collecting her virtual ID. According to Asher, her true identity didn't matter. She could be a ninety-five-year-old peeping Tom for all anyone cared. She could have ten more avatars waiting in the wings for a variety of illicit purposes. What mattered was Madame Currie's track record—her ability to play and pay up when she lost. Thanks to Asher, that was solid.

The red lasers blinked green.

Her virtual ID had been approved.

The creature opened the door with its large, scaly hand and a brand-new world opened before her. A scene straight from the Bellagio. A world with its own distinct noises. The chiming of slot machines. The chatter of spinning roulettes. The rolling of dice. The shuffling of cards. The clinking of chips. The twittering hum of multiple conversations unfolding at once, interrupted by the sporadic shouts of celebration and ire.

Eden walked past blackjack tables manned with dealers—more androgynous than Francesca—dressed as fancy vampires in black tuxedos. According to Asher, these were not humans. They were avatar bots, owned and operated by The Cage. She kept walking until she reached the special wing where the high rollers played. There, all the way in the back, on a raised dais, closed in by golden stanchions and red velvet rope, was the Mecca of all gambling tables—Big Betty.

The dealer stood at the table distributing cards to two participants.

Captain Jack Sparrow and King George. The latter sat in a regal robe and crown, stacking and restacking his chips, letting them fall through his fingers with a staccato click-click-click. Tonight, he was planning to lose more than he would win, thanks to the deep pockets of Harlan Wallace. Word needed to spread. The Royal Brute of Great Britain was cold. If Manuel Van Cooper wasn't already planning on visiting Big Betty, they hoped the rumors would entice him.

As if sensing her stare, King George made eye contact.

Eden looked away as someone brushed past her.

It was the man of the hour.

In real life, Manuel Van Cooper was short in stature, with a thin nose and a neatly trimmed mustache. His friends called him Manny. Here in The Cage, Manuel Van Cooper was a green alien with an eyepatch and a goofy propeller hat. Fellow gamblers called him Void.

He made a beeline for Big Betty while Eden made herself comfortable at a beginner's table. She calculated probabilities with ease at every stage of the game. She studied the dilation of her opponent's eyes as they looked at their cards, as they looked at the board. She knew exactly when to fold, when to call, when to raise.

When her pot doubled, she moved to the next table.

Then the next.

Then the next.

Until she drew the attention of the pit boss—who wasn't just a vampire, but Count Dracula. With his eyes upon hers, he stepped onto the dais and unclipped one of the red velvet ropes. Eden had officially been invited in.

By then, the pirate was gone.

He'd been replaced by an avatar with beefy shoulders, a thick neck, a black tie, a black fedora, and black sunglasses. He was sandwiched between King George and the green alien named Void.

Eden took a seat at the end of the table.

The blood-sucking dealer gave her an impassive nod and slid King George the dealer chip. "Welcome to the table, Madame Curie. May Lady Luck be on your side."

"She sure hasn't been on mine," Agent 007 muttered.

Eden threw in the small blind.

Big Betty required a minimum bet of one thousand. Eden put down half. To her left, Void doubled, according to the rules of the game. And they were off. Eden sat back—calling but not folding—getting a handle on the flow, searching for Void's tell, studying the correlation between the dilation of his eyes to the cards in his hand. Three hands later, her pot and the King's were roughly the same. Void's was bigger. The agent's, considerably smaller.

He cashed out.

The dealer wished him a happy Halloween. "Play some tricks. Or snag some treats."

With a vulgar reply, Agent 007 stalked away. Now it was just the three of them—Eden, Asher, and Manuel Van Cooper hiding behind their avatars.

"Maybe now the tide will change." King George dropped his chips through his fingers. "Luck can't last all night."

He directed the comment at Void.

He ignored Madame Currie like she posed no threat at all.

Eden flew under the radar, carefully observing as Void and King George passed chips across the table—a back-and-forth dance neither looked ready to quit. Especially not Void, who came out the victor more times than not. Asher was playing the part well, goading Void with a theatrical performance, one marked with a convincing combination of frustration and moxie.

The dealer slid the button to Eden and shuffled the deck.

Void tossed in the small blind.

King George doubled with the big.

The dealer dealt the hole—two cards to each of them. Before Eden looked at her own, she made a point of studying her target. The eye not hidden beneath an eye patch definitely dilated. She looked down at her cards and saw the ten of hearts and the ace of diamonds.

Eden called.

Void pursed his lips, then said with a shrug, "Let's make this interesting." He doubled the big blind, folded his arms, and leaned back in his chair in a clear, almost obnoxious nonverbal dare.

King George studied his opponent for a long moment, then threw in his chips.

Eden did the same.

The dealer burned a card, then placed three face-up.

The king of diamonds.

The eight of spades.

The ace of clubs.

Void called.

King George raised.

Eden matched, carefully maintaining a casual grip on her cards.

Void slid his chips into the pot.

The dealer burned another card and flipped over the fourth on the board. The ace of hearts. Her heart raced. Her palms grew sweaty. She exhibited none of these signs, however, as all three of them checked.

Another card burned.

The fifth and final card flipped.

The ten of diamonds.

Eden studied Void. The twitch of his upper lip, the noticeable dilation of his unpatched eye. He had something good. But in this game of probabilities, she had something better.

It was time to send her message.

She brought her fingers to her stack of chips and moved the one on top back and forth ever so slightly. King George was primed, waiting for the signal.

Void started with a raise.

The King countered with a raise of his own.

Eden called.

All eyes went to the alien.

His long, ET-like pointer finger tapped the table, then he raised again.

King George studied Void from beneath his crown. He scratched his earlobe in a mindless manner that wasn't actually mindless at all, but a tell Manny should have picked up on. The King was about to bluff. He let go of his ear, then scooted the rest of his chips into the pot.

The Royal Brute of Great Britain was all in.

His chips had dwindled significantly, but he still had more than Eden and Manny. He was King George, after all—notoriously rich with money to burn. And this was The Amber Highway—unregulated, illegal. Which meant the old-fashioned rules of all-in didn't apply. If they were going to remain in this hand, they would have to match the King. Neither of them had the chips to do it.

King George leaned back in his seat, his attention turning to Eden.

She got more chips from the dealer and went in.

Manny was up.

If he folded, he would be out a lot of money.

Was it enough to secure his help?

Void tap, tap, tapped the table.

With a rub of his chin, he got more chips. He went all in, too.

Void showed his cards.

Two pair—aces and kings.

With a curse, the King showed his.

Another two pair—aces and eights.

The alien grinned like the Cheshire Cat, his unpatched eye brimming with triumph. Until Madame Curie showed her hand.

Two tens and three aces.

A Full House.

His face fell—fast and hard—as her overhead score went through the roof. King George burst into hearty laughter, then asked the dealer for more chips. Void stood from his chair like his soul had been sucked from his body.

Guilt twisted Eden's gut.

She didn't enjoy hustling this man, but Cassian needed all the help he could get. Manny could help them. Before he could get far, she cashed out and followed him past the Blackjack tables, past the roulette and the slot machines.

"You can get your money back," she whispered in his ear.

He stopped.

She handed him the third coin from her pocket with a code to a private, encrypted chat room. Then she pulled off her specialized headset. Across the table, Asher was pulling off his.

"Did it work?" Francesca asked.

With a wicked grin, Asher launched into the tale. He gave them all a detailed rundown as Eden clutched the matching coin —a real, live coin—in her palm. Like Asher's chess piece, it would light up as soon as Manny made the call. She unclenched her hand, willing the coin to blink.

Jericho lifted his water glass in cheers when two things happened simultaneously.

The coin flashed.

And a loud klaxon alarm wailed.

26

The power went out. Darkness filled the boardroom as the loud, haunting siren wailed like the world was coming to an end.

A thundering boom rattled the walls.

Eden lurched to her feet.

So did everyone else.

"Basement," Jericho commanded, snatching the container of headsets.

Eden pocketed the coin—the *blinking* coin—and joined the others in the hallway, where emergency lights flashed and the siren keened.

Cleo hobbled on her crutches.

Eden stepped toward her, prepared to carry her still-injured friend to the basement like she'd carried her to the White House Bunker, suspicion be damned. Asher beat her to it. He shoved his laptop against Eden's chest and swept Cleo into his arms like she weighed nothing at all.

Together, they burst into the stairwell and hurled themselves downward.

Eden imagined the commotion in the west tower. Dayne Johnson shouting in the newsroom, ordering his late-night staff to save as much as possible before evacuating to safety. She imagined the panic in The Landing as the siren's blare yanked Alexandrians from their beds. Eden took up the rear, right on Asher's heels, ready to use her body as a shield to protect Cleo should a bomb detonate on top of them.

In front, Jericho opened a hatch in the floor. He lowered a ladder into the rudimentary bomb shelter below. They climbed down, one by one, and when Eden reached the cement floor, her jaw unhinged. They weren't alone. A familiar young man with blonde hair lay unconscious in the far corner, his ankles and wrists bound.

The asset!

Jericho came down last, shutting the hatch over his head.

Asher set Cleo on her feet with surprising gentleness. He grabbed his laptop from Eden, who continued to stare—open-mouthed—at the asset. He strode to a desk on one side of the room and opened the computer.

"We need eyes on the sky," Lark said.

Asher seemed two steps ahead of her, his fingers dancing in that choreographed way they did whenever he was working with technology.

The desk had its own intercom. Beside it, there were pallets of water and boxes of protein bars, along with a few bedrolls, blankets, and pillows.

The room was long and rectangular, made of concrete. Hairline fractures ran up the walls. The steady plink-plink of a leaking pipe sounded somewhere nearby. The bunker didn't look like it would hold up against a direct hit. If a bomb fell on the IDA, everyone would die.

Except Eden.

And the asset in the far corner.

She thought he was in a refrigerator. Apparently, he'd been moved. And now, he wasn't moving at all. If not for his shallow breathing, Eden might think him already dead.

Another blast resounded—so loud, Eden's shoulders

scrunched toward her ears. She expected the ceiling to rattle. Bits of debris to fall. She expected the others to duck and shout.

But Cleo only cocked her head. "It sounds far away."

"They have to be missing us," Lark agreed.

Asher's laptop brightened with a green radar on which several dots blinked.

"They hit the Westin," he said. "And the Wyndham."

Jericho pointed at the screen. "And the Masonic Temple."

Francesca exhaled. Loudly.

Cleo limped closer.

The radar flashed and a moment later, the bunker filled with another loud blast, like the delay of thunder after a lightning strike. Eden heard this blast at a volume nobody else could hear. That much had become clear, and she had poised herself to calculate the distance. Indeed, the explosions weren't nearby. They were two and a half miles south.

"Why are they dropping bombs *there*?" Cleo asked.

"It's our dummy location," Jericho answered. "Given the nature of our work, we didn't think it wise to divulge our true coordinates. Nobody knows our exact location except for the people here. If someone wants to join us, I meet them at the airport." He looked up at the ceiling. "Somehow, the government got wind of our false coordinates."

"Someone sold us out." Francesca whipped around, her face a picture of mutiny aimed directly at Eden and Cleo.

"Give it a rest." Cleo stood with her hand propped against the wall. Her crutches had been abandoned in the boardroom. "What happened in DC was a misunderstanding."

"A misunderstanding?" Francesca snarled.

"We thought you were Interitus. You thought we were Swarm. We didn't purposefully sabotage you then, and we certainly didn't do it now."

"Well, someone did!" Francesca shot back.

"Or," Jericho said—his deep voice measured and calm as he

stepped in between them. "The government confiscated a map when they cleared out the community in Minneapolis."

At this, Francesca looked slightly mollified.

But not Eden.

A slow dawning horror had crept through her body. It started in her toes and crawled up her legs. Mona knew they had gone to Bethesda. Suddenly, the government was in Bethesda. And now, thanks to Eden and Cleo, Mona knew they were in Alexandria. Suddenly, the government was in Alexandria. The horror seeped into her abdomen. Was Mona the sell out? Was Francesca right? Were they responsible for this?

She looked at Cleo, trying to read her thoughts. Was she drawing the same conclusion? But Cleo wasn't looking back. Her eyes were on the screen of Asher's laptop, where a legion of blips smaller than the jets circled on the radar. "Are those—?"

"Thermal drones," Asher said.

Thermal drones.

Eden's throat closed.

"We should be fine," he continued.

"How?" Eden choked. The thought of surviving another raid —of standing amongst more death and destruction—made her blood run cold. "Thermal drones won't fall for a dummy location."

On a map, such a location might provide a convenient decoy. But nobody was actually *in* that location. The drones wouldn't register any warmth. Any body heat. That was all here, in their actual location. She imagined the drones reaching the IDA. She imagined their radars lighting up with red.

"We set up clusters of mock heat in each of the hotels that were just bombed," Jericho said. "And these buildings are cloaked."

At the confused look on Eden's face, he elaborated. "High density black silicon. It traps the light and makes any warm object beneath invisible to infrared detectors. We have it covering The Landing, Kaiser, and both IDA towers."

"Stealth mode," Cleo whispered.

Relief came like a broom. It swept away Eden's horror. She wouldn't be standing amongst the dead again. She wouldn't be responsible for more catastrophe. Not today. Even so, she stood there feeling immensely sobered. She and Cleo never should have contacted Mona. Asher told them not to; they should have listened. Suddenly and belatedly, it occurred to her they were in the middle of a war, and she was letting emotion and sentiment cloud her judgment. Not anymore. Doing so put innocent lives in jeopardy. Doing so also hindered their progress. She couldn't work on breaking Cass out of prison when they were stuck down here.

She reached inside her pocket and pulled out the coin.

The blinking had stopped.

She'd missed Manny's call, and she couldn't call him back. Manny didn't have a physical coin; he had a virtual coin—one he could only access when he was in the metaverse. Which meant the ball was in Manny's court. They would have to wait for him to try again. But what if Manny didn't try again?

She glared at the radar, cursing the jets. The bombs. The drones. The timing. *Mona*. Had this air raid not happened, she'd be in the metaverse right now. Instead, she was in this dank, depressing bunker with an unblinking coin and the unconscious asset. She could feel Cassian slipping through her fingers.

Jericho bent over the intercom and pressed a white button on the panel. "Citizens of Alexandria," he announced, "our city is being attacked two miles south. Everyone is to remain in their respective bunkers until further notice. Try to get some sleep. This is going to be a long night."

He let go of the button and flipped a heavy-duty switch set against the concrete wall in front of him.

The wail of the alarm overhead went quiet.

In the eerie silence that followed, another bomb exploded.

27

I t was a long night, indeed. In close quarters, away from Cleo's antibiotics and her pain medicine. Eden helped her get situated on a bedroll. Her restlessness was just beginning to ease—a blessed sleep creeping closer and closer—when the asset needed another dose.

The survivors from Bunker Three had taken over this duty, administering the poison in four-hour intervals—a fact Eden had pushed out of her mind. But she couldn't push it out of her mind now. Not as Asher left to retrieve a vial from a portable deep freeze in the basement overhead.

When he returned, her heart was galloping beneath her sternum. She didn't want to be here. She didn't want to see this. She certainly didn't want to hear it. She squeezed her eyes and looked away. But nothing could block out the young man's screams. Cleo grabbed her hand and held on tight. It was horrific. Worse than she remembered. A gut-wrenching, blood-curdling wail as everyone in the bunker turned away, as if doing so would negate their own culpability. They were treating this young man like he wasn't human, and in so doing, they were dehumanizing themselves. The whole affair seemed to damage the soul of everyone involved. Even Asher. She could see it in

180

the grimace he tried to hide and the small twitch in his left eyelid.

When the worst was over, Cleo let go of Eden's hand. But sleep refused to come. They lay on their bedrolls, listening as Asher fiddled on his laptop, examining what he could of the asset's network. But there were only so many times a person could circle a fortress from the outside. Asher wanted in, but he couldn't get in. He failed over and over again until frustration won and he slammed his computer shut.

Beside her, Cleo's pulse quickened.

Eden could practically hear her thoughts.

Jack Forrester knew how to get in, so why couldn't Asher?

Eden rubbed her temple, where mysterious bouts of pain came and went for no rhyme or reason. Sometimes, once a day. Sometimes, twice. Sometimes, if she was lucky, not at all. Her system needed updates. With those updates, perhaps her system wouldn't have been so easy to breach.

At seven the next morning, the trucks came. Soldiers combed the area, searching through the rubble—for survivors, for human remains. Would they widen their search when they found neither? Despite all the meticulous planning—decoy heat sensors and black silicon cloaks—would they still be found?

All they could do was wait.

And administer another dose.

At two in the afternoon, Eden's coin blinked for the second time.

She showed Asher. They had headsets. Jericho had brought them with. But Asher shook his head. For the time being, the only system in operation was their emergency system. Responding to Manny's summons would require more than their emergency system, and that was a risk they couldn't take. Not when the soldiers were still combing the area.

Two hours later, the soldiers cleared out.

The trucks drove away.

But the drones remained, circling the smoky sky like birds of prey.

Not until the last one flew away did Jericho restore the power and call for an immediate, mandatory assembly in the auditorium. When all was said and done, they'd spent twenty-six hours in the bunker and administered five doses.

Eden helped Cleo to the elevator, hating herself for being part of it.

Francesca and the others opted for the stairs. As soon as the door to the stairwell shut behind them, Eden shared her Mona theory.

Halfway through, Cleo began shaking her head. "No way. It couldn't have been."

"She knows we're in Alexandria. Before that, she knew we were in Bethesda. And according to Twig, they have more rations than usual."

"Because she traded in my Tesla."

"That was weeks ago." Eden pushed the elevator button. "You know how hard food is to come by for these communities right now. You think Chicago has plenty because of your Tesla?"

Cleo's head shaking only grew more resolute. She was determined to hold on to her denial, and Eden didn't have the heart to pry it away. She helped her friend to their living quarters. Cleo was too exhausted to attend the mandatory meeting—a testament to her exhaustion. She didn't like to miss anything.

After Cleo took her medicine and climbed into bed, Eden poured herself a glass of water and turned on the TV. Concordia National was in the middle of a special alert broadcast. The United States government had carried out a second air strike on Interitus. This time, in Alexandria. If the government knew the air strike was a failure, Concordia didn't let on. Perhaps listeners needed encouragement more than truth, given the distressing situation evolving in Minneapolis. Once symptoms of toxin exposure developed, there was no way to stop the progression. And the progression—thus far—resulted in one hundred percent fatality. It was a terrifying statistic. One that kept people compliant and in their homes.

With a heavy sigh, Eden pulled the unblinking coin from her pocket.

The news coverage turned to Chairwoman Kendra Cruz, sitting behind her stately desk with her hands folded, her posture straight. Considering these recent events, they must push forward with all expediency. They needed to send a strong message to all terrorists hiding within their borders. They would begin with the eight they had in captivity. An execution date had been set by America's Board. The prisoners would be put to death on the twentieth of November.

It was less than three weeks away.

O n Eden's way to the assembly, the coin began blinking. Her jog turned into a run. She slipped inside the auditorium, her face flushed. Jericho stood on the stage, speaking to an attentive audience. Eden scanned the crowd, searching for the back of Asher's head, which was never too hard to find given his size. She spotted him in the front row next to the aisle and hurried forward in a stooped manner so as not to draw attention. Francesca sat on his left. Lark sat beside Francesca.

Eden opened her hand.

The coin blinked in her palm.

Without a word, the four of them left. Once inside the boardroom, Eden put on a headset. Asher got to work, and in no time at all, Eden was standing in a small room, dressed in a black frock and lace-up boots. She was Madame Curie once again, and there, at a lone table in the center of the white room, sat the green alien named Void sans the propeller hat. That, apparently, had been his Halloween costume.

The second he looked up and saw her, his shoulders sank

with relief. "I was beginning to think you weren't going to show."

Eden sat in the chair across from him. "We were held up."

"Who is *we*?"

In all the hurry to get here, to meet with Manny before he gave up altogether, she hadn't considered the questions he might ask. Or the answers she would give to those questions. From what she had learned about Manny, she didn't think he would be an accomplice to terrorists. Not even for his chronically ill mother.

Besides, there were other ways for Manny to collect money. Like going to the authorities. If she told Manny the truth about her identity, would he run to the government to strike a deal? If he gave them the right information, would they pay his mother's medical bills and ignore the fact that he'd been attempting to do so by frequenting illegal gambling dens? Whatever information she gave him now could be passed along to America's Board. Which meant she had to tread carefully.

He stared at her—this green alien named Void with his long hands clenched into fists, awaiting her response.

"*We* are a group of people trying to stop really awful things from happening." Lark called it The Great Winnowing. If that was what this was, it wouldn't stop with Minneapolis. Which city would be next? How many more people would die if Oswin Brahm had his way? "We are hoping you will help us."

Manny scratched his green, bald head. "I don't know who you think I am, but I can assure you, I'm in no position to help anyone."

"You're a military mechanic in Annapolis."

"How do you know that?"

"I work with Gollum."

His unpatched eye went buggy.

"We know you're trying to take care of your mother, which means you are a good son. A good person. You do honest work, but it isn't enough to keep up with the medical bills. So you use your skills as a cardsharp to supplement your income. Which means you're not above breaking the law."

Manny squirmed.

"So long as it's for a noble cause." Eden set her elbows on the table and leaned forward. "On November the twentieth, eight innocent lives are going to be taken."

"The prisoners?"

She nodded.

"They're not innocent. They're terrorists."

"The media is lying, Manny. The government you work for is lying." It was a hard pill to swallow, especially coming from an avatar who had conned him out of a mind-boggling chunk of change. Still, Eden pressed on. "They want you to believe the prisoners are members of Interitus, but think about it, Manny. The prisoners were little kids during The Attack. Some were babies. I promise they had nothing to do with the bombing in Chicago. They certainly aren't responsible for the toxin in Minneapolis."

"Then who is?"

"Oswin Brahm." She didn't pause. She didn't waver. She didn't even take a breath. She said it with a straight face and a matter-of-fact tone.

Manny blinked. Then he laughed.

"It's the truth. Whether or not you believe it. Oswin Brahm is exterminating real live people. Innocent people. He's starting with illegal residents. An entire community has already been wiped out in Minneapolis."

Manny's grandmother was an immigrant. She came the legal way, before The Attack. But plenty of her people hadn't come legally. They'd fled Central America to save their lives and the lives of their children. They snuck across the border and they settled in the United States. Did Manny look down on such people? Were they nothing more than gum beneath the country's shoe? Or were they his countrymen? His kin? As thoroughly as Eden had investigated Manny, that remained a question mark.

She had no idea how he felt about illegal residents. She had no idea how he felt about the borders closing. Not when she'd been reading about him on a tablet screen, and not now, as she sat across from his avatar.

"The people in that community were not vermin or cancer or reprobates, no matter what Concordia is leading the public to believe. They were families. Mothers and children. Elderly. People like you and me, just trying to live. Now they're gone, and Oswin Brahm won't stop. He will continue until every community like it is eliminated." All while the public looks the other way. Just like Eden had done last night when the asset was being tortured. Her stomach twisted. Her sense of urgency grew. "Once he has eliminated illegal residents, he will find a new target. He will keep going until the only people remaining are those who have pledged their undying allegiance to him."

Manny stared at her—the pupil of his visible eye dilated, his breathing faster than usual.

Eden waited. There was nothing more she could say. Manny would either believe her, or he wouldn't.

"Let's say this is true," he finally conceded. "How could I help you?"

"The prisoners are going to be transferred."

"When?" Manny asked.

"We don't have the date yet, but we expect the transfer to happen soon. Certainly before the fifteenth. When that happens, we need the transport vehicles to fail."

Understanding dawned. She could see it moving up Manny's face like the slow rise of the sun. "And I have access to those vehicles."

"If you do this for us," Eden said, "the debt you accrued last night will be erased. If you do your part successfully, you will have more money in your pocket than you will know what to do with. Not to mention, you will save eight innocent lives."

Manny tapped one long, green finger against the table and chewed his bottom lip.

Eden didn't break eye contact. She willed Manny to see the honesty in her gaze. She willed Manny to believe her.

"Can I have some time to think about this?" he asked.

"How much?"

"A day. Maybe two."

She wanted to say no. He couldn't have a day or two. Cassian was locked up in prison. His execution date was quickly approaching. The transfer was going to happen sooner rather than later. They needed to plan and organize and solidify.

But what choice did she have?

They needed Manny.

And Manny needed time.

She nodded at the coin by his hand. "You know how to reach us."

He nodded back.

"Manny," she said, leaning over the table. "If you're going to look for the truth, do so carefully."

For if Manuel Van Cooper ended up with a bullet through his head, their plans would be dead in the water.

28

Eighteen wheels spun beneath Violet, creating a soothing highway lullaby that dulled the worst of her hunger. Over the past nine days, she'd readjusted herself to the feeling—an old acquaintance that gnawed and gnawed at her stomach, carving a pit so deep it might never be satiated. They'd spent the first five days trapped inside the city, which had been surrounded by the National Guard. They stayed far from down-town, sticking to shady backstreets and rundown districts. They had nothing but the clothes on their backs and a rucksack full of Father's journals.

Violet survived on her nanobots and Barrett's stories, which he told through chattering teeth. At night, when they huddled together to keep warm, Barrett worked through what they'd witnessed in Stevens Square. Especially the twelve-year-old girl.

"She bled out by the time I got to her," he would say. "Maybe if I hadn't waited so long …" This part, he would leave dangling. And Violet would take his hand and squeeze like maybe she could take some of his sadness away.

On day three, Barrett's hunger became so unbearable, he stopped turning his nose up at the dumpsters. But even those were light fare thanks to a city-wide lockdown that put restaurants in limbo. On day four, she came across a filthy blanket and a moldy parka shoved inside a gutter behind a pawn shop. The discovery had felt like hitting the jackpot. On day six, the National Guard cleared out, which left them with their next problem to address.

Crossing state lines.

Their faces had been plastered all over Concordia News. 18-year-old Barrett Barr was a murderer and a terrorist. The girl with him was his off-the grid accomplice. They couldn't be seen. Which meant they'd spent two more days hiking north through Minnesota backwoods, all the way to a state park at the tip of Lake Superior. They hitched a ride on the side of a barge like a couple ticks. Ever since, they'd been zigzagging through Wisconsin on a slew of semi-trailers in an attempt to get to the only place they could think of going.

Dr. Norton's cabin in Milwaukee.

Tricky business, as they were never sure where the semi would take them when they hopped on. If they were lucky, the trailer was hauling food and drink. If they weren't, well, at least they were protected from the elements.

Currently, they were traveling along 39 South from Stevens Point to Madison in the back of a trailer carrying pallets of novelty sodas. They'd squeezed over the top of them, all the way to the front, making enough space to ride comfortably while hidden from view. Barrett sat across from her with Father's ruck-sack between his knees, thumbing through a journal and sipping from a sherbet orange can labeled Mandy Squeeze.

Violet put pieces of Mother's camera back together, trying to fix it like she'd fixed the busted device with all those blinking dots. But the refurbished Canon refused to be fixed. Thanks to her fall from the rafters, the screen was cracked, and they'd left the black cord that brought the camera back to life behind. She'd lost Mother all over again. The bruise this left on her heart felt more unbearable than the hunger.

She slumped against the aluminum wall inside the trailer, her ear picking up bits and pieces from the radio inside the semi's cab. Last week, there'd been an air strike in Alexandria. The military had dropped bombs on another cell of terrorists, which Violet now knew to be code for the good guys. Since then, there'd been nonstop talk about the upcoming execution, wherein all eight prisoners—Cassian included—would be put to death without trial. The date was only one week away.

Across from her, Barrett sat up straighter, his attention intent upon the page he was reading. She sat up straight, too. Had he finally found an answer? Was it about her missing Queen Bee?

She waited for him to finish. When he did, he looked up with eyes that had gone painfully soft. She waited again for him to speak. That wait never took very long. But he seemed momentarily stumped for words, which wasn't like him at all.

She leaned closer.

His attention dipped again to the page. He scratched his nose. Then he said, "She didn't leave you."

Violet's brow furrowed.

"Your mom," he continued. "She didn't leave."

His words made no sense. If Mother never left, then why had Violet stopped seeing her? Where was she?

He worried his bottom lip between his teeth, then handed her the journal.

She hesitated.

These were Father's words.

Did she really want to hold them?

Barrett held the leather-bound booklet aloft, waiting for her to decide.

She finally took it like one might take a dirty sock. Or a rattle snake.

His handwriting was cramped and slanted and as she read, her hand fluttered to her mouth. Barrett scooted beside her.

He had found a confession.

A rambling, guilt-ridden confession, the ink splotched with tears.

Barrett was right. Mother hadn't left. Mother loved Violet too much to leave. So Father did what he had to do. He couldn't let her stand in the way any longer. He needed to draw out Violet's powers, and that would involve a level of pain Mother wasn't strong enough to witness. So he took Mother's life and he buried her in the meadow she loved.

The last line tolled like a haunting bell.

I killed her, he wrote. *For the sake of the world.*

———

Jericho handed Eden earplugs like they might actually block out the loud ringing of gunshots. She put them in because that's what everyone else had done on this cold, wet afternoon three days before the big day, when they would either succeed or fail at breaking Cassian out of captivity.

While the sky misted, a somber contest unfolded, one that would determine who had the best aim. Almost a full week had passed since bombs fell two and a half miles south of the Potomac Yard. In all that time, she'd received no word from Barrett and Violet. Nor had she seen anything on Concordia News concerning their potential whereabouts. Concordia News was too busy covering the upcoming execution of eight domestic terrorists.

Public anticipation was palpable. Excitement ran like a current through the air. Eden felt it all the way here, in Alexandria. She wanted to call them all monsters—evil wrapped in human skin. How could they be okay with an execution without trial? But she knew they weren't monsters. Most of them were regular, decent people. If her own world hadn't been upended, she would be a part of those people. Her parents, too. They would see the faces of the prisoners on the evening news and they would sleep better at night knowing those prisoners were behind bars. Their days numbered.

This unnerved her considerably. She preferred evil. It came

with clear-cut lines and boundaries, with the good guys on one side and the bad guys on the other. And if the bad guys were evil? Well then, their lives didn't matter. The good guys were justified in using any means necessary to defeat them. But such was not the case. For starters, who decided which side was good?

The line shuffled forward. Eden took up the rear, right behind Asher. Travel arrangements to their ambush site had been made. They would leave in two days and they had room for eight people. Everyone agreed, the eight best marksmen would go.

All the obvious people had come to give it their best. Along with two Alexandrians whom Jericho had personally invited—the only Alexandrians with any experience in weaponry. Cleo and Dayne were absent, opting instead to work in the news-room. There was no reason for either to stand outside getting wet. Despite being a wanted insurrectionist, Dayne had never shot a gun in his life. And Cleo, who was still walking with a noticeable limp, was in no condition to be part of the team.

Up ahead, Jericho handed the gun to Francesca. Each person got ten rounds to hit a target exactly one-hundred fifty yards away. Lark had gone first. As someone who'd spent the last three decades perfecting her shot, she was a shoo-in for the top eight. Progress was slow; the target had to be changed after every participant. The gun, reloaded.

By the time Asher's turn came, water was dripping from his tight curls. He dragged the back of his arm across his forehead and got in his stance. Lark, Jericho, Francesca, and three survivors from Bunker Three had secured their spot in the top eight. Surprisingly, Francesca had come in second. Impressive for someone with only one functioning eye. A fourth survivor from Bunker Three was holding the seventh place spot, and Nairobi was currently in eighth.

Asher lifted the gun and peered through one narrowed eye.

"I hate to do this to you, Robes," he said to Nairobi. "But you're gonna have to say goodbye to the top eight."

He fired his ten rounds in quick succession. Jericho replaced the target while Asher reloaded the gun, and sure enough, he had edged Nairobi out of eighth place by one shot. He grinned a cocky grin and offered the gun to Eden.

She hesitated.

"I forgot. The girl with the nine lives is afraid of firearms." He looked down at her with one eyebrow cocked. "Are you sure you want to participate?"

Eden recalled Francesca's scathing words when they were stuck underground in Washington, DC. *You expect her to properly inject the asset when she can't even take a gun?* She *had* properly injected the asset, as much as she regretted doing so. Eden shoved her fear down and took the weapon.

"Just because I don't like guns doesn't mean I can't shoot them." She got into position, her muddied boots slightly wider than shoulder width. She squinted through the drizzle to take her aim, which was more lethal than Lark's. But she only needed to come in eighth.

She fired ten rounds.

Jericho whistled.

Lark actually grinned. She took the gun from Eden and gave Asher's shoulder a clap. "First poker. Now shooting. I think she has your number."

Asher peered at her with a hint of familiar suspicion. "Let me guess, your CIA father taught you how to shoot?"

Eden removed her ear plugs. "I told you I had skills that would come in handy."

Way more than any of them realized, which was becoming a point of mounting frustration. Her mind and body could run one hundred miles per hour, but she was forcing them to go fifty.

Asher shrugged. "It's better if I stay here anyway. Manage the technical side of our mission."

"Which puts you," Jericho said to Nairobi, "in Annapolis with Manny."

"I'm happy to go," she said, just as Eden spotted Cleo limping across the grounds with her eyes ablaze and a book in hand.

Asher noticed, too. He bent toward Eden's ear and asked under his breath, "Is she coming for me or you?"

Eden didn't think it was her. Cleo typically reserved that level of annoyance for him. Sure enough, she marched straight up to Asher, stopping just short of poking him in the chest with an accusatory finger. "You are a liar."

He took a step back. "Whoa."

"I've been working on an op-ed piece for Dayne. A tell-all about America's supposed hero." She held up the book. It was Oswin Brahm's biography.

"You can't publish something like that," Francesca objected.

"I know," Cleo said. "We're not running it without authorization. It's just something we want to have at the ready when the time comes." She turned to Asher, her head tipped back so she could look him in the eye. "I'm a thorough reporter. I take care with research. So I've been looking into you."

"Me?"

"All of you." She swept her hand to include Lark, Jericho, and Francesca. "The leaders of the Resistance. The people who knew Brahm's true colors first. Almost everyone on the council has a personal vendetta against the man. Emmett owned a tavern in Washington, DC, that was blown to bits in The Attack. Lark was manipulated into recruiting innocent girls, one of whom was Harlan's late granddaughter. Brahm killed Amir's mother. He forced Dvorak into pregnancy and tried to kill her, too. Members of Swarm gouged out Francesca's eye. Which leaves you." She tossed a glance at Jericho. "And you," she said, returning her glare to Asher. "Just now, I was sharing my progress with Dayne when he casually tells me your mother died in The Attack. He overheard Nairobi mentioning it the other day."

Nairobi ducked sheepishly.

Cleo finished her tirade. "You told us she was killed by your dad."

Asher looked down at her with an expression like *yeah, so?*

Cleo gaped. "That's a really messed up thing to lie about."

"It wasn't a lie."

Confusion struck Eden between the eyes. By the looks of it, it struck Cleo, too. "So, Nairobi was lying?"

"No," Asher said.

"Your mom died in The Attack?"

"Yes."

"Then Oswin Brahm killed her."

He raised his eyebrows and kept them lifted as understanding dawned. With her mouth hanging open, Eden looked around and observed that this wasn't a shock to anyone else.

Francesca stepped forward, right beside Asher. "Brahm has no idea we have an ace up our sleeve."

Asher smiled dispassionately. "As someone who lived under his roof for fourteen miserable years, I know a lot of his secrets."

———

Cleo's cubicle could barely accommodate three regular sized people. Eden was above average in height for a woman. Asher was six foot six. Yet somehow, Cleo managed to squeeze all three of them inside. Technically, Eden didn't need to be here. Cleo was perfectly capable of conducting this interview on her own. But Eden was teeming with curiosity, and when she invited herself along, neither Cleo nor Asher objected.

Eden and Asher sat on stools—Eden further in the corner, Asher more in the middle, looking surly while Cleo opened to a fresh page in her notebook and clicked her pen. When she looked up, she did so expectantly.

Asher crossed his arms. "What's the point of this? It's not like you can run anything."

"Your father has a whole team of recruiters."

"I know."

"You don't think eventually we'll use all this," she gestured around her, indicating the newsroom in which they sat, "to do some recruitment of our own? We'd be fools not to, and when that day comes, I want to run a piece so convincing and incriminating that whoever reads it will want Oswin Brahm to rot."

Her words hit an agreeable chord. Asher's expression softened.

Cleo tapped the thick biography beside her notebook. "According to this, Oswin's son is dead."

"And named Felix," Eden said. After Oswin's father, the police officer who lost his life in a riot.

"Asher was my mother's surname," he said. "When I found out he murdered her, I decided I didn't want to be Felix anymore."

"Why does this say you died of an overdose when you were fourteen?" Cleo asked, giving the biography another tap with the end of her pen.

"Do you think he would have just let me leave?"

"So you faked your death," Cleo said.

"I uncovered his plans and worked with them." Asher sat with his wet boots flat on the ground, his long legs splayed. "He started portraying me as a troubled kid when I decided to fight back. I think I was twelve. He spun a specific narrative, ensuring he could dismiss my accusations as nonsense if I ever shared his secrets with the world. By the time I turned fourteen, I'd gotten too big for corporal punishment."

Corporal punishment.

AKA, physical abuse.

Eden thought about Francesca's glass eye. That awful room

in the Bryson's basement. *Ad Astra Per Aspera*. Through hardship to the stars. Gage and Isabella Bryson had adopted the Monarch's ideology, and their foster children had paid the price. How much higher of a price had Asher paid as the Monarch's son?

He'd been so harsh when they first met. Survival 101, he called it. Be cutthroat or die. Those were the choices. Apparently, Asher had spent his life being cutthroat.

"He decided I was beyond rehabilitation. No amount could set me on the right path. Lucky for me, I bugged his office and caught wind of his plans. An overdose would fit the narrative. He planned to have one of his minions shoot me up in my sleep. He'd play up the grief, use it to gain more sympathy from the public. Convincing him that his minion was successful was one of my more brilliant accomplishments. It required a lot of moving pieces, but I managed to pull it off."

Eden swallowed the sick rising up her throat. Despite every-thing—knowing how many millions of people Oswin had killed, his wife included—the idea of him plotting the death of his own son made her blood run cold.

Cleo looked up from her notes, her expression pinched—as though trying to hold back the sympathy Asher obviously didn't want. "Was he always abusive?"

"I don't remember a time when he wasn't." Asher shrugged like it wasn't a big deal. But it was a big deal. A horrible, awful, giant deal. "Thankfully, he was gone more often than not. If I had to guess, I have his precious army to thank for that."

"You really don't know where they are?"

"I was never invited. I only knew that whenever he came back, he was always eager to make up for lost time."

He said it in such a way that made his meaning clear. Oswin Brahm's idea of making up for lost time didn't involve playing a game of catch with his son.

29

D r. Norton's cabin in the woods looked like a page from a fairy tale. Through the chilly evening, past fir trees and pine trees dusted with frost, golden light shone from its windows. A smoke stack rose into the star-strewn sky. After so many days of fear and hunger, it created such a warm, inviting picture, Violet nearly ran.

For the first time since Father's truck rumbled up the gravel drive and the vase broke apart in an explosion of glass, she took a proper breath. Beside her, Barrett scrutinized their surroundings. When he was satisfied nobody had followed them, they crept out from behind the bushes and made their way past Dr. Norton's truck and the Forrester's car to the front door.

Concordia Nightly played inside.

Violet could smell meat and spices.

Her mouth watered.

Barrett knocked.

The television went silent.

There was scuffling and whispering. The flutter of a drape. Then the door swung open and Dr. Norton stood on the other side.

His mouth fell open at the sight of them. Dirty and travel

worn, with Barrett wrapped in the filthy blanket and Violet swimming inside the moldy parka. He quickly ushered them inside, into the cozy warmth where a large pot of soup bubbled on the stove and thick slices of bread steamed atop a baking sheet. It was a meal much too big for one man to eat. But of course, despite the empty living room, he wasn't alone.

The moment Dr. Norton spoke their names—Barrett and *Jane*—the others hurried up the stairs. At first, only their heads appeared. Then the rest of them came. Despite Violet's filth, despite her very obvious need of a shower and clean clothes, Eden's mother wrapped her in a tight, fierce, trembling hug.

Ellery stared.

Violet couldn't stop eyeing the food.

"Eden's alive," Barrett said, wasting no time.

Alexander took an aggressive step forward. "How do you know?"

"We spoke with her," Barrett said.

At his words, Ruth Pruitt nearly fainted.

Alexander had to wrap his arm around her waist to keep her upright. He pulled her to his chest and hugged her with the same ferocity she had hugged Violet. Only he didn't let go. Her shoulders shook as she cried.

"Come sit down," Dr. Norton said. "You both look hungry."

Neither objected.

Violet's stomach was a cavernous abyss.

It rumbled and grumbled as Annette fetched them blankets made of thick, soft fleece and Dr. Norton served them heaping bowls of taco soup with hefty slices of warm bread. Annette took the moldy parka and the dirty blanket with a wrinkled nose and carried them outside. Violet grabbed the spoon and began shoveling the soup into her mouth, uncaring of its scalding heat. Dr. Norton tried to warn her, but she kept going until her bowl was empty and the bread was gone and Barrett had told them half the story.

He'd spoken with Eden through an illegal channel called The

Amber Highway. Oswin Brahm was the Monarch. The blinking dots represented his army of superhuman soldiers. Eden, Cassian, and Cleo had stumbled upon a group of people in Washington, DC, who called themselves the Resistance and were working to fight against Brahm. It was true that Cassian was in prison, but Eden and Cleo were alive.

The doctor refilled Violet's bowl and gave her another thick slice of bread as Barrett continued.

They had gone to her father's house in Minneapolis in search of answers. They *did* have an altercation at the border, but they didn't kill anyone. Jane's real name was Violet. That's what she wanted to be called. Three of Brahm's soldiers showed up and took Father away. But Barrett had gotten his journals. A whole stack of them. So far, he'd found nothing about Violet's Queen Bee but he'd only read through the journals once, and was positive another read through would prove fruitful. The toxin was real. An off-the-grid community in Minneapolis had been raided by the RRA. And now here they were, back where they'd begun. As he told it, he made it sound exciting. Like he and Violet had gone on a grand adventure. Perhaps they had.

When Barrett finished, Jack ran his fingers through his hair. Ruth and Alexander sat holding hands on the couch. Annette was chewing her nails into nubs. Dr. Norton leaned against the counter with one ankle crossed over the other, finger-combed his silver mustache. Ellery kept her eyes trained on Violet as she tore off a hunk of bread with her teeth.

"Is there a way for us to contact Eden through this illegal highway?" Ruth asked.

"I don't know." Barrett stirred his soup. "Violet's father had some sort of special gadget. So did Eden. It acted like a kind of phone? But we left it behind when we ran. Do you have anything like that?"

Dr. Norton shook his head.

Jack paced. "If Oswin Brahm knew where to find the two of

you in Minneapolis, then he'll know where to find our home in Milwaukee."

"Is there anything there that will lead them here?" Annette's question came in a strangled whisper. Her attention kept darting from whoever was talking to her daughter.

"No, but the guy strikes me as someone who knows how to find people. He obviously knows about Eden and Barrett and … *Violet*. Which means he also knows about Elle."

Annette's fingers returned to her mouth.

Ruth patted her back.

Ellery looked the opposite of afraid. She flipped her auburn hair over her shoulder and lifted her chin. "All the more reason to activate me. At least then, if they come, I can defend myself."

Jack and Annette ignored her.

"We need to get out of Milwaukee," Jack said.

Violet slumped in her chair.

She didn't want to leave. Not again. Not so soon. Maybe they would go and she could stay. She could climb into her bed down the hall, burrow beneath the thick comforter, and dream about Mother. Who hadn't left. Who never left. She'd been murdered by Father.

"We could go to Chicago," Barrett suggested.

Everyone looked at him.

"There's an off-the-grid community there. They live in the Damen Silos."

"The what?" Jack asked.

"The Damen Silos. They're located in an abandoned shipping yard in Pilsen."

"How do you know this?"

"It's where Eden and Cassian went when they left." He fiddled sheepishly with his half-eaten slice of bread. Alexander and Ruth had been so desperate for Eden's location. They had begged and pleaded with Cleo. All the while, Barrett had played dumb, like he was no wiser than them. "There was some girl with a glass eye who knew something about the Monarch. They went to the Damen Silos to speak with a woman named Mona, who knew the girl with the glass eye. I'm assuming they'll have the gadget we need to get a hold of her."

Violet dug into her third bowl while the group planned their exit. Dr. Norton was on-the-grid. According to the government, he was an upstanding retired military doctor with no priors, no red flags, not even a parking ticket. He was also the registered owner of a military-style truck. All of them could easily fit into the back of it. The only problem? They would have to cross another state line. The truck would be searched. If that happened, they couldn't be found.

As they began discussing secret hatches, Violet left her broken camera on the table and made her way to the bathroom. She turned the shower all the way to hot, and as the steam rose, she stared at herself in the mirror. Her ink black hair was oily and matted. She brushed overlong, choppy bangs from her face, which was streaked with dirt and grime. Her eyes were large and oval and dark. Her cheekbones, high. Her mouth, small. Her chin, pointed. With her stomach heavy with food, she studied each feature, searching for Mother.

Beautiful.

Weak?

Dead.

Buried in the meadow.

No matter how hard she stared, Violet could only find fragments and traces. Like a teasing glitter of light on a spiderweb. She wanted to capture the whole thing, but there was nothing substantial to grab.

Steam clouded the mirror.

Mother's face was gone.

Violet resigned herself to never seeing it again as she stripped off her dirty clothes and stepped beneath the scalding spray.

———

Eden clenched her teeth. If she released them, they would chatter. Not because the room was chilly—the room wasn't even real—but because her nerves had reached a fever pitch.

Tomorrow was the night.

If all went according to plan, she would be reunited with Cassian. Her heart physically ached at the possibility. With every passing day, her thoughts became all the more consumed. She spent each night replaying his words, his touch, every moment they'd spent together. Then she'd wake up the next morning with nerves more frayed than the day before. Because what if this didn't work? What if their carefully laid plans went sideways?

The knots in her stomach wrenched tighter. She couldn't think about the plan going sideways. The prospect of failure was too terrifying. Too overwhelming. Too debilitating. She couldn't give it any space. She shoved that possibility aside and focused on the three-dimensional holographic map hovering over the circular table. She was sitting in the war room along with every other person involved in the prison break. They were together virtually, separated physically.

Manny was in Annapolis. Nairobi was with him. Amir and Emmett were in Bethesda. Harlan, somewhere in Colorado. Cleo, Dayne, and Asher remained in Alexandria. Eden, Francesca, Jericho, Lark, and four others from Bunker Three were in a safe house in Chesapeake. The eight of them had arrived at the safe house inside steel shipping tanks marked hazardous, lined with black silicon, supposedly on their way to the Port of Virginia. The truck was stopped twice. Each tank was scanned before the driver was sent on his merry way.

Eden took a deep breath and focused on Asher, who was walking them through their carefully choreographed plan. According to Amir, the prisoners would be loaded into a high-security transport vehicle and taken five hours south, to an undisclosed location outside the small town of South Mills,

North Carolina. Nairobi would be stationed on a moped outside the prison grounds, watching for the convoy, reporting to Asher as soon as it left. A portion of the route would wind along the edge of Great Dismal Swamp—a state park and wildlife refuge. This was where the ambush would unfold.

There would be four vehicles in the convoy. Manuel Van Cooper was going to mount tracking devices to each vehicle's fuel injection system. The devices came with a remote, which was currently in Jericho's possession. Push the right button, and the trackers would emit a small EMP that would temporarily stun, and thus disable the vehicles.

Which led to the trickiest bit of their plan—the dead zone.

This had occupied the bulk of their attention, as it involved the greatest potential for error. The zone was made possible by an illegal device called an Atax. They were only sold on the black market, and could absorb radio frequencies, block tracking systems, and jam signals within a given radius. They'd spent several days alone figuring out ways to increase that radius. Currently, they were discussing what to do should surveillance drones come into play. They couldn't have one flying into their dead zone. As soon as its signal dropped, the red flags would wave.

Asher studied the holographic map, twirling his queen around his thumb. "If this dead zone is the square we want, and a drone is threatening that square, then we need to lure the drone away."

Cleo's attention dropped to his revolving chess piece. "With a sacrifice."

He clicked his tongue and shot her a wink, their gaze connecting and holding. "Precisely."

Francesca looked between them with a scowl. "And who is going to be this sacrifice, exactly?"

"We don't need a *who*," Cleo said. "We already have a *what*."

Asher brought a handful of holographic vehicles into play like game pieces on a board. Each one was a newly minted, all-terrain Faraday Force—the crown jewel of off-roading. Thanks to Harlan, they had four of them.

"There are eight of you. If all goes according to plan, we'll have eight more before the night is through. We can fit six into a vehicle."

"That's a tight squeeze," Francesca said.

"Eden will sit on Cassian's lap," Cleo replied with an impish grin.

Heat pooled in Eden's ears.

"They will expect this road to be deserted." Asher slid one of the Faraday Forces into a quadrant northwest of the dead zone. "We put this vehicle here and have it self-start at a specified time."

"Creating a signal," Cleo said.

"They'll send their drones to check it out," Asher continued. "Just as their convoy is hitting the dead zone."

They continued their run-through.

Once the convoy came to a stop, the drivers would radio for help. But without a signal, none of those messages would go through. The group in Chesapeake would be lying in wait, surrounding the convoy on all sides. Much to Lark's chagrin, their guns would not be loaded with bullets. They would be loaded with tranquilizer. They needed the guards' retinas and fingerprints to carry out their plans and none of them were sure whether dead retinas and dead fingerprints would work.

They would tranquilize the guards the moment they stepped out of their vehicles. By the time they freed the prisoners, the vehicles will have had sufficient time to recover. They would re-program the convoy to resume its course toward South Mills. When the convoy arrived, the tranquilizer would wear off and the prisoners would be secure in their Chesapeake safe house, waiting to stuff themselves into steel shipping containers so they could make their way to Alexandria.

All of it was too neat.

Too tidy.

If Eden understood anything by now, it was how rarely plans went off without a hitch.

Hence their backup. Hi-tech, black-market explosives. The same weight and shape as a grenade. With pins like a grenade, too. Only, unlike their predecessor, a pulled pin didn't have to mean detonation. One could hold on to the button indefinitely to keep the blast at bay. Everyone taking part in the ambush would be armed with several.

The bombs were a last resort, for emergency use only. They didn't want anything or anyone to explode. The goal was stealth. They didn't want to draw attention. An explosion most certainly would.

Eden wiped her virtual hands along her virtual pants and clamped her teeth tighter, her nerves quadrupling.

Tomorrow was the night.

If this worked—and it *had* to work—Cassian would be free. She would be in his arms.

30

They tromped through dense brush with semi-automatics strapped around their shoulders, their breaths escaping in puffs of white. They were phantoms in the night, marching in a single-file line with black helmets and black fatigues and black army boots and black tactical vests, each one loaded with an encrypted satellite radio, high-tech explosives, and night-vision goggles.

Eden didn't need the night vision goggles. She could see everything perfectly fine without them. She could hear everything, too. The heartbeats of her comrades. The rhythm of their breathing. Every broken twig. Every rustling leaf. Every slithering, crawling, flying creature in the dark as they high-stepped their way to the ambush site.

All eight of them were miked, connected via radio to Nairobi, who was lying in wait outside the prison yard in Annapolis, and Asher, with his team in Alexandria. They had turned the IDA boardroom into a control center. They were monitoring the tracking devices Manny had placed on each of the prison vehicles.

"The gates are opening," Nairobi said. "Bird in the sky. Over."

A drone.

Eden's nerves solidified into a brick.

"Just one?" Asher asked.

"Affirmative," Nairobi replied.

She gave him her exact coordinates. Eden could hear the tapping of computer keys. Her palms went sweaty as she gripped her semi-automatic and continued her trek through the wildlife refuge.

"There are only three vehicles. Over."

Eden stopped.

So did the tapping. "Where's the fourth?"

"It's still in the prison yard," Cleo replied in the background.

The brick in Eden's stomach doubled in size. There were supposed to be four prison vehicles. This was what Amir had reported, and this was what Manny had confirmed. He'd planted EMPs inside all four. So why were there only three?

"What do you want me to do?" Nairobi asked.

"Stay in position," Asher answered. "Wait for the fourth."

Nairobi was supposed to tail the convoy from a safe distance. Improvisation this early in the game didn't bode well. Eden and the others continued forward. Her mind was abuzz. Did someone discover the tracker? They were almost there now. She could sense the change in the environment ahead. The break of trees. The belt of highway. Were they—the ambush team— walking straight into an ambush?

"Three of the vehicles are en route," Asher said. "ETA, four hours, two minutes."

It all came down to this.

In four hours and two minutes, their carefully laid plans would either succeed or fail.

Eden stretched her cold, numb fingers as they reached the edge of the tree line. In front of them, Highway Seventeen stretched from north to south. There wasn't a car in sight. Asher began directing Jericho, who made quick work of planting the Atax on the east side of the road. They traveled a predetermined route to verify the radius of the dead zone. Then they waited on the perimeter, just outside the zone, to maintain communication.

There was no sign of the fourth vehicle.

Nairobi remained in place, watching should it appear.

Asher monitored the convoy through the drone.

Lark identified the tree she would scale when it was time to move into position, which wouldn't happen until t-minus twenty minutes. They wanted to mitigate loss of communication for as long as possible. As soon as they moved into the dead zone, they would lose all contact with Asher and Nairobi.

Eden took deep, slow breaths and settled in for the wait as the chatter across their comms continued.

————

Cass waded through the warm pool toward a woman floating face-down in its center. Her hair undulated in the water like pale strands of gossamer. The honey blonde color made his heart thump. Dread stretched like a yawn as he reached out to take her arm. She flopped face-up—her blank, unseeing eyes a familiar mixture of blue and gray and green.

He shook his head.

No.

It wasn't possible.

She couldn't die.

He clutched her shoulders.

Her head lolled, her wet hair streaked with red. *Blood* red.

He spun in a circle.

The pool was filled with blood.

"I pulled out the monsters," Mona said, perched on the edge with her feet submerged. "I pulled them out for you."

The yawning dread turned into a horror that tore up his throat and shot forth in a guttural cry. He charged across the ring.

The monster shouted, "I didn't kill her!"

Cass swung. Again and again. Wildly. Recklessly. Blindly as the monster cowered with his hands over his head.

"It wasn't me, I swear!"

"Who was it, then?" Cass roared.

"It was you, son. You killed her."

His rage combusted into a consuming fire that burned and burned and burned as he tackled the monster to the ground and pummeled him. He landed blow after blow until the bell rang and the crowd cheered and the referee dragged him away from the dead man lying in a puddle of crimson.

Then Eden was there, clutching the dead man to her chest.

She was alive. She was hugging the man. Rocking him back and forth as she cried and screamed. The man wasn't the monster. The man was Eden's dad.

With a long, sharp gasp, Cass bolted upright.

His cell was dark.

His heart crashed in his ears. Cold sweat trickled down his spine.

It was a nightmare.

Eden wasn't dead.

He hadn't killed her father.

But you did kill someone's father.

He shut his eyes, wishing he could block out the accusation. But the accusation was true. He *had* killed someone's father. He dug his fingers into his hair. He squeezed his head as though he might squeeze away the truth.

I lost my mind.

The monster's words clung to him. No matter how many push-ups and dips he did in his cell. No matter how furiously he scrubbed when he showered, those words refused to go. Because they were also true. Cass had lost his mind, too. In a fit of rage, he had killed an innocent man.

Which made him no different from the monster.

His cell door swung open. The small space flooded with

light. A guard marched inside. Not the one with the bum knee. Not the one who cracked his knuckles. Not the one with the rattling Tums. Not the one who smelled like a different perfume every morning. This guard was new. He didn't make eye contact or explain his sudden, intrusive presence. He simply pulled Cass to his feet, cuffed his hands behind his back, and pushed him out into the corridor, where a second guard waited, as unfamiliar as the first.

They led him away.

Not toward the showers or the interrogation room.

"Where are you taking me?" Cass asked.

Neither answered. They just pushed him forward. Up a set of stairs. Through a wider corridor and out into the night. Fresh air. He inhaled deeply. It felt like the first drink of water after a day spent in the desert. Up above, swollen clouds roiled in a jet black sky. A few paces in front of him, several vehicles idled, their rear lights glowing red as exhaust escaped in puffs of white that dispersed with a gust of biting wind.

A door slammed.

Beneath the lights of the prison yard, a woman strode in his direction. Lady Justice. Only she wasn't wearing her usual attire. No business suit. No blazer with a brooch. Instead, she wore khaki slacks and a navy rain jacket with yellow lettering, clearly labeling her an employee of the United States government. Cass hadn't seen her in days. Maybe weeks. He'd lost all sense of time. Their last interaction had been after the visit from his father, when she confessed things didn't add up—an admission that had clearly agitated her. Ever since, he'd wondered about her safety. He'd wondered if nosing around had numbered her days. But here she was, speaking into a walkie-talkie as drops of rain began falling from the bruised sky.

"Get them into the truck," she commanded.

Them.

He looked over his shoulder and squinted through the thickening rain.

Prudence Dvorak was being pushed toward him, flanked by one guard instead of two. He surveyed the surrounding grounds, but his sight refused to extend beyond the prison lights. He had no way of knowing what kind of security waited ahead.

The rain fell harder.

Cold drops drummed against the tops of the vehicles as a guard shoved Cass into the back of a van. The guard pushed him onto a bench, where his ankles were shackled and bolted to the floor. Dvorak was pushed inside after him, her ankles shackled and bolted, too. Then the guard left, and it was just them, sitting across from one another. Her dark eyes were alert, her hair rumpled from sleep.

Outside, doors slammed shut.

A cacophony of voices mingled with the chattering rain.

"Where are you going?" a male voice called.

"I will ride in the back," Lady Justice replied.

"With the prisoners?"

She stepped into view, framed inside the opened doors, her navy blue rain jacket wet. Her copper hair, too. A male guard stepped beside her, watching dubiously as she climbed aboard. This obviously wasn't protocol.

"You heard the command. These two require the highest level of security. We can't have any funny business." She sat on the bench beside Dvorak and cocked her rifle. "Now if you please, officer, take your position behind the wheel."

31

Time passed like a snail as the night sounds chorused. The peeping of frogs. The chirping of crickets. The yipping of coyotes somewhere in the distance. Interspersed with the occasional lonely hoot of an owl.

Eden began to shiver.

"ETA, thirty minutes," Asher said.

And then, "The fourth vehicle is on the move."

The observation came from Dayne, his voice recognizable in the background.

It was quickly followed by Nairobi's and the pitter-patter of rain through her walkie-talkie. "Gates are opening. Fourth vehicle is leaving the yard."

Eden stopped breathing.

"What do you want me to do?" Nairobi asked.

"Tail it," Asher commanded. "Make sure to stay out of sight."

Eden forced herself to inhale. She could do nothing about the fourth vehicle. She could only focus on the task at hand. A task that was now only twenty-four minutes away.

"Fourth vehicle is merging onto Highway 450, due west," Cleo said.

"I'm on it," Nairobi replied.

Asher prepared for the diversion.

With twenty-two minutes to go, he gave his throat a clear. "Sending the signal in three … two … one."

Eden squeezed her eyes.

Please work, please work, please work …

"Bullseye," Asher said.

The bird in the sky had received an incoming command. A moment later, away it flew. Toward the Faraday Force parked on an access road that should have been deserted.

Jericho snapped his fingers and waved them into the dead zone. "Team is moving into position. Over."

He remained where he was, outsize the dead zone, with the remote that would detonate the EMPs. Eden and Francesca crawled on their bellies beneath a large bush. Two of the survivors from Bunker Three did the same thirty-five yards south. Between them, Lark crossed the road, slung her gun over her back, and scaled a tall tree with the nimbleness of a tightrope walker. The remaining two crossed as well and spread out beneath a copse of bushes.

Eden propped the semi-automatic on the ground in front of her. She aimed it at the road and curled her finger around the trigger, doing her best to block out the flashback. She was not on the roof of The Sapphire. She was not being controlled by the enemy. She was not aiming her gun at her mother or Cassian. She was in her full and right mind as she detected the rumble of engines, as she calculated their distance and speed.

Her heart thudded violently beneath her ribcage, punching a bruise against her sternum. Beside her, Francesca's heart did the same. Any second, the three vehicles would crest the hill. Did Manny do his job? Had he set up the EMPs correctly?

Beams of light cut through the dark.

Across the highway, Jericho had the remote. He would detonate the EMPs in five … four … three … two …

Ping.

Ping.

Ping.

They came like rapid fire, one after the other. A sound Eden was positive only she could hear; Francesca had no reaction at all. Her catch of breath didn't come until the headlights went dark and the convoy came to a sluggish stop right inside the dead zone.

Eden gaped, her body flooding with disbelief.

The EMPs had worked.

She closed her eyes and shoved every ounce of attention into her ears, focusing on the convoy and the heartbeats within. There were two in the front seat of the lead vehicle, a military grade SUV. There were two in the front seat of the rear vehicle, another military grade SUV. There were two in the front seat of the middle vehicle, a prison van. Along with several heartbeats in the back.

Her own leapt.

Those heartbeats belonged to the prisoners.

One of whom was Cassian.

He was here.

Not more than twenty yards away.

The drivers attempted to dispatch for help, but they had no signal. They attempted to radio one another, but they couldn't get through. The driver side door of the lead vehicle opened. A uniformed man behind the wheel was just placing his left boot onto the cement when the sharp hiss of a dart sliced through the air.

It met its mark with a dull thump.

The man toppled from his seat onto the road.

The passenger-side door opened. A second uniformed man slipped out into the night and crouched behind his vehicle with his gun ready. Out of sight to Lark in the tree, but visible to Eden on her belly.

She peered through the scope of her rifle, took aim, and pulled the trigger.

Another sharp hiss.

Another dull thump.

The guard collapsed.

The driver of the middle vehicle must have seen, because he tried dispatching for help once again, this time with a quaver in his voice. He didn't know what was going on. The men in the rear vehicle couldn't see anything. The night was a cloak. Their guns, too silent. The rear driver stepped out with his elbow draped over the top of his door. "Is anyone getting a—?"

Hiss.

Thump.

Collapse.

The passenger door flew open.

Eden aimed and pulled.

Hiss.

Thump.

Collapse.

The driver of the middle vehicle tried starting the van while his comrade kept calling for help. Neither worked. Soon, the surveillance drone would return. Which meant they only had a brief window of time before the government knew something had gone awry. Eden willed the door to open. For the uniformed guards to step out of their vehicle so she could shoot them. But neither man budged.

"Cover me," she whispered as she began army crawling forward.

"What are you doing?" Francesca hissed.

Eden didn't stop to answer. It was eight against two. And they were running out of time. When she was out from beneath the bush, she pushed to her feet and ran. The doors of the middle vehicle flew open. A series of loud pops chased her heels. A spray of bullets blasted the concrete in her wake as she dove behind the lead vehicle.

Darts sliced through the air from several directions, all of them missing their mark as both guards rolled beneath the van.

Belly down, with her elbows on the concrete, Eden aimed her semi-automatic between the tires and fired two decisive rounds.

Hiss.

Thump.

Hiss.

Thump.

The night went silent.

All six guards were down.

"Disable the Atax!" Lark shouted, quickly climbing down from her perch as Jericho sprinted toward the device he'd planted beside the highway.

Moments later, Asher's voice came to life in Eden's ear as the others crawled from their hiding spots. "Surveillance drone is four minutes away," he said, his tone more urgent than Eden had ever heard.

"Move!" Jericho shouted.

She pushed to her feet and ran to the back hatch of the prison van, where several hearts were beating fast and hard. She wanted to force the door open. Bust the lock with her bare hands. Instead, she waited while Francesca and another dragged the unconscious driver around to the back. Francesca lifted his hand and pressed his thumb against the screen pad.

The lock disengaged.

Eden threw the doors open.

And there were the heartbeats. Only six. Bound and gagged and wide-eyed with terror. Dvorak wasn't among them. Neither was Cassian.

The ground disappeared beneath Eden's feet. She was falling, falling, falling while some distant part of her brain noted the blinking device planted in the middle of the prisoners. A blinking device that had just been triggered by opening the door. A blinking device that counted down the seconds from nine to eight.

"It's a bomb!" Francesca shouted.

"Abort!" another screamed.

And suddenly, Eden was running.

She was sprinting as fast and as far away as she could when a fiery blast lifted her off her feet and hurled her into the trees. She landed with breathtaking pain. It pierced through her side, sucking the oxygen from her lungs. Her ears rang—a loud, high-pitched keen that blocked out all other sound as she coughed and blinked and tried making sense of her surroundings. In every direction, fire blazed in scattered piles of debris. She cried out for help, only to cough some more. She rolled onto her side, her hand moving to something large and sharp protruding from her rib cage. She'd been completely impaled by a sword-like piece of metal.

The world spun as she wrapped her hands around one end. Bracing herself, she yanked the metal free. Blood poured from the wound. But then it stopped. The wound closed. The ringing dulled.

Someone nearby screamed.

Eden crawled forward and came upon a man in uniform.

She had no idea how he was conscious. Not just because of the tranquilizer she thought she'd hit him with, but because he was missing half his body. There was nothing at all where his legs should be.

Nausea swelled.

The world kept spinning.

The man kept screaming, his bone-white face smudged with ash. He grabbed onto Eden's hand, a wild panic thrashing in his eyes, and cried out for his mother. He begged for his life. He told Eden he didn't want to die. *Please. He didn't want to die. He didn't want to die!* With every terror-soaked plea, Eden held onto him tighter. As though her grip might keep the worst of his fear at bay. With smoke and fire all around, she stayed by his side until his eyes went glassy and blank. Only then did she remove her hand from his, and only then did she notice the ring on his pinkie finger. A ring in the shape of a Monarch butterfly.

Somewhere close, Lark shouted her name.

Eden pried the ring off his pinkie with shaking hands and forced herself to her feet. Jericho and Lark lumbered into view, supporting an unconscious Francesca. The skin on her face had melted. The hair on one side of her head had been singed all the way to her scalp.

They called for the others.

But nobody called back.

Eden tried searching for them.

She found only one, worse off than the guard.

"We need to get out of here," Jericho rasped. "*Now.*"

Lark had sustained an injury to her leg.

Eden took her spot to support Francesca. She could have carried the girl on her own. Instead, Jericho supported half of Francesca's weight as they ran through the trees and over fallen logs. They didn't stop until they reached the vehicles. They placed Francesca in the back of one. Eden climbed beside her. Lark slid into the passenger seat with a grimace. Jericho jumped behind the wheel, started the engine, and slammed on the gas.

Francesca moaned.

Lark yanked the dead earpiece from her ear and snatched the walkie-talkie from the console. "Asher, do you copy? Asher, can you hear me?"

His voice returned in a chop of static.

Lark pressed the button. "Mission failure. Prisoners dead. Dvorak is MIA."

So was Cassian. He was MIA right alongside Dvorak.

More static crackled from the radio.

Along with several loud squawks.

Snippets and snatches broke through—Asher's voice, Nairobi's voice—as Jericho zoomed over rough terrain, jostling them so aggressively, Eden felt like her brain was being scrambled. Beside her, Francesca released another moan.

"Approaching a bridge." The clear statement came from Nairobi. She was still tailing the fourth vehicle.

It was followed by Asher's staticky reply.

Their Faraday Force rocketed onto an access road. The trees cleared. The reception, too. Eden could finally hear what Asher was saying.

Stop the vehicle.

The command was followed by the rev of a moped.

The patter of rain.

The crunching of weeds beneath wheels.

And then, a loud blast.

A second explosion.

Nairobi shouted, "They went over the bridge! I repeat, the fourth vehicle went over the bridge!"

<h1 style="text-align:center">32</h1>

ommotion sounded in Eden's ear as Jericho gunned it —the roar of the engine, the crunch of gravel, the pounding of hearts.

"I need confirmation now," Asher commanded. "Who was in that van?"

"We're working on it."

Dayne's voice.

Cleo's voice.

Lark's voice.

Jericho's voice.

All of them swirled into a turbulent clamor.

"What happened?"

"They planted a bomb with the prisoners. It triggered as soon as we opened the door."

Jericho turned the vehicle without braking. Eden braced herself. Francesca flopped and moaned. One side of her face was covered in angry, red blisters.

"We played right into their hands," Asher said. "They won the match."

"We didn't lose pieces, Asher!" Lark yelled. The Faraday

Force hit a dip at full speed and went momentarily airborne. "We lost people."

Six prisoners.

Along with four survivors from Bunker Three.

And that guard.

Eden closed her fingers around the butterfly ring. He'd called for his mother in the end. Not the Monarch. Not his *pater*. But his mom. That's who he had wanted in his final moments.

The chatter continued.

People made phone calls.

They shouted out snippets of information.

Eden sat in the back with Francesca, every muscle in her body tightly clenched. The fourth vehicle had gone over a bridge. It had plunged into the Potomac after avoiding the high-tech explosive Nairobi had detonated in an attempt to stop it. But what did it matter? Who cared, really? Nobody was in that van. The van was just a van. Cassian was in Annapolis. He was still in the decommissioned military prison. For whatever reason, they decided not to transfer him.

Asher issued more directives—commanding Jericho where to go, how quickly they needed to get there, what they needed to do once they arrived. Francesca moaned again. Lark shouted at Asher like this was his fault. Like he was the one causing Francesca pain. Like he was the one who'd planted the bomb.

"Fran needs medical attention!"

"We need to carry through with the plan," Asher shot back. "Harlan's guy is on standby to get rid of the vehicles."

Vehicle.

There was only one.

Because there were only four of them.

Not sixteen.

Four.

"The semi-truck is arriving in five minutes."

"I'm telling you, Asher, she will die in that steel tank!"

"If you don't go now, all of you will die. They'll have the

entire area on lockdown within the hour. None of you will get out."

Jericho sped through another turn, the back tires running over a curb. He whipped the Faraday Force into the empty parking lot of a sleeping warehouse and pulled to a skidding stop. Eden helped Jericho get Francesca out of the back seat. They carried her through the dark as she whimpered incoherently. They climbed onto the loading dock and set Francesca down when an incoming message came. One that had been delayed. It was from Amir.

Cleo read it aloud in the background. "Prudence and Gray are not with others. Transfer to Sterling. Route 495, due west."

The chattering stopped.

Everything went silent as the message plowed into Eden like a freight train at full speed.

No.

No, no, no.

It was a mistake. A fake. A lie.

Cassian wasn't in that van.

Eden brought her hands to her neck.

Something was choking her.

Strangling her.

She couldn't breathe.

Nor could she think or feel or function.

Jericho kicked a crate and shouted a great war cry of a shout.

Eden's knees buckled.

She pictured the vehicle falling. Plummeting into the river. Sinking to the bottom. She imagined the van filling with water. Cassian trapped inside. His lungs screaming for oxygen like hers were screaming for oxygen. She squeezed her eyes tight, but the images kept coming. They pummeled her, one after the other. He was locked in the back of a prison van and that van was at the bottom of the Potomac River. He wasn't superhuman. He didn't have microscopic robots running through his veins, enabling his brain to go without oxygen. Nobody did. Except for her. And

Barrett. And Violet. And the ninety-four weaponized freaks that completed Oswin Brahm's army.

Her eyes burned.

A cavern opened inside her chest, and in its center, a horrendous homesickness. A black hole that sucked up every newton of gravity and piled it upon her shoulders.

Somehow, beneath that weight, her breath returned. Oxygen keeping her alive.

But Eden didn't want to be alive.

She didn't want to do this anymore.

She didn't want to fight in this war, this sinking ship with no lifeboats. She didn't want to be on this loading dock with these strangers. She didn't want to be in her own body. She wanted to close her eyes and go to sleep and never wake up again. She wanted Cassian alive. She wanted her parents by her side. But she couldn't go to sleep and she couldn't wake up. This wasn't a nightmare.

Cassian was dead. He'd drowned in the Potomac.

Pain tore through her gut—a torment her nanobots could not fix. Agony so overwhelming that for one wild, unhinged moment, she considered removing an explosive from her vest, holding it to her body, and pulling the pin. A self-destruct function she could carry out all on her own. A self-destruct function that would obliterate the ache.

But she couldn't pull the pin.

Not when Cleo was still alive. Not when Erik and her parents and millions of innocent people, oblivious to the war raging around them, were still alive. She pictured Cassian's boot flying at her face in a perfectly executed roundhouse kick, refusing to let her shrink. Refusing to let her flee.

Be a weapon, he'd told her. *And use it against him.*

Moments—memories—flashed through her mind like fleeting vignettes. Cassian, holding up his hands in the back of an alley. Cassian, fighting two grown men in a parking garage. Cassian, in the quiet intimacy of Dr. Beverly Randall-Ransom's kitchen, inviting her to trace the lines of his tattoo. Cassian, unbearably handsome in his tuxedo as he led her onto the dance floor. Cassian, diving from behind a brick wall to save her mother. Cassian, carrying her father down sixty-six flights of stairs. Cassian, on top of the Damen Silos, the morning sunrise painting his silhouette a rose gold as he told her about his mother.

Voila, tout au mieux.

Training with him at Lou's.

Kissing him at Lou's.

Every blissful, intoxicating moment they shared at Elmer and Eloise Miller's.

Never again would his dark-fringed golden eyes meet hers across a room, simmering with strength and fierceness and steadiness and desire. Never again would she feel his strong arms wrapped around her waist, pulling her into a hug. Never again would she hear the deep rumble of his voice as she lay against his warm, solid chest. Never again would he challenge her. Protect her. Comfort her. Provoke her. This hardened, dangerous stranger who invited her onto the back of his bike and didn't run away when he found out what she was.

Outwardly, she sat with the rest of them. Francesca, unconscious. Jericho and Lark, numb. Eden didn't move or blink or speak. Not when Harlan's guy came and drove away with the Faraday Force. Not when the semi-truck arrived. Not as she climbed into the steel container. A coffin with an oxygen tank.

But inwardly?

She screamed.

She screamed and she screamed and she screamed as she turned off her comm and let darkness enfold her.

33

Rain pounded the roof of the van.

Cassian peered at the two women on the bench across from him—Dvorak, dressed in a jumpsuit similar to his own, and the lady brandishing an assault rifle—as the engine rumbled to life and the van began to move. She was obviously going against protocol. Employees of the United States government didn't ride in the back of a prison van with supposed terrorists, even if those terrorists were unarmed and bound by steel.

Dvorak side-eyed Lady Justice with a heavy dose of suspicion. She side-eyed Cass, too, like maybe he and this government employee were in on this breach of protocol together. "Where are you taking us?"

"Your location was compromised," Lady Justice replied. "As your impending execution has become the solace of our nation, all necessary measures are being taken to ensure you remain secure." Her lip curled slightly when she spoke, as though these *necessary measures* displeased her.

"Why is it just us?" Dvorak asked. "Where are the other prisoners?"

The curl in her lip grew more pronounced. "They are being taken to a different location."

The brakes squealed as the van came to a slow stop.

Cass strained to hear through the pattering of raindrops and caught the faintest sound of mechanical gates opening. They were leaving the prison yard. His fingers twitched behind his back. He shifted his feet, the chains around his ankles rattling. Those chains were bolted to the floor. If he had Eden's strength, he could pull the bolt up like a weed. He could incapacitate the woman in the navy blue rain jacket, pry open the van doors, and jump to his freedom. As it stood, he didn't have Eden's strength. Especially not after so many days locked up in a six by nine cell.

"We seem to be in the throes of a chess match," the woman answered. "The government of the United States versus Interitus. The Board has concluded that six of our prisoners are nothing more than pawns in this terrorist regime."

Pawns were expendable.

Judging by the sudden pallor of Dvorak's face, she was thinking the same thing.

"Two are rooks." The woman crooked her eyebrow at them. "Or perhaps the queen and king."

"There is no terrorist regime," Dvorak said. "And *you* are a pawn. The United States government is an entire line of them."

The woman's mouth tightened.

Cass studied her, wondering who she believed—Dvorak or the government's rhetoric. She knew things weren't adding up. She'd admitted as much when she escorted Cass to his cell all those days ago. What was less clear was whether she continued pulling on the string. For all he knew, she decided to drop it. To shove the inconsistencies away. Human propensity for denial was strong. Confronting this level of corruption and deception required a response. Ignoring it could destroy a person's conscience, so long as they had a conscience to destroy. He searched for her brooch, but it wasn't pinned to her navy blue windbreaker. Was the piece of jewelry only for business suits, or did she decide to give it up?

For an extended period, they drove in tense silence—the rain relentless on the roof. The woman's mouth was set in a frown, her brow troubled. Until finally, she broke the quiet. "Two months ago, an officer with the Chicago Police Department was found dead. He was on duty during the break-in at SafePad."

Cassian sat straighter. She hadn't stopped; she'd kept pulling on the string.

"Officials ruled it a suicide," she continued. "According to the autopsy report, the officer shot himself in the temple. According to initial reports—*redacted* reports—the bullet that killed him entered the center of his forehead."

Cass's eyes remained fixed on hers.

The woman stared back at him, unblinking. "The Bryson's case can hardly be called a case at all. It's riddled with discrepancies. And an officer on scene mentioned a very disquieting room in their basement."

"You've been busy," Cass said.

"I've been unsettled," she replied. There was a bite in each word. Her attention shifted to Dvorak, who was watching the lopsided exchange with a look of keen interest. "As Karik Volkova's successor, and the new leader of Interitus, you've been at the top of the FBI's most wanted list for years. And yet you sit here and say Interitus doesn't exist."

One corner of Dvorak's mouth curled upward. "The rabbit hole is deep and dark."

"Where does it lead?" Lady Justice asked.

Cass leaned forward, as hungry for answers as the woman with the assault rifle. He knew, in a general sense, where the rabbit hole led. At the end, they would find the man who sat at the top. The man who was pulling the strings. The architect behind Eden's design. The one they had gone to Washington, DC, to find. His followers called him the Monarch. Dvorak had scathingly referred to him as *Pater*. *Who* this was, Cass had no idea. The raid in DC had interrupted this particular revelation.

Dvorak didn't answer right away. Instead, she studied the woman and Cass as though measuring their worth. As though calculating what and how much to disclose. "You wouldn't believe me if I told you," Dvorak finally said.

"Try me," the woman replied.

"Oswin Brahm," Dvorak shot back, without taking so much as a breath.

Silence came in the wake of that name.

Bloated with disbelief.

Ripe with incredulity.

This was the last person he expected. And yet somehow, as the name settled, the absurdity of it lost its edge. He pictured the man with all his money and fame and privilege, as handsome as Cassian's own father. Sometimes, the worst monsters came in the most polished packages.

"Oswin Brahm," the woman repeated.

Dvorak nodded.

The woman's eyes flashed. Apparently for her, the absurdity remained as sharp as ever.

"Interitus is a sham," Dvorak continued. "Karik Volkova was a puppet. Oswin Brahm, his puppeteer."

"You want me to believe that Oswin Brahm was the mastermind behind The Attack?"

"I don't care what you believe. I'm simply stating the truth."

The woman smiled a mirthless smile. An angry, aggressive smile. "Oswin Brahm's first wife died in The Attack."

"Disturbing, isn't it?"

"Afterward, he poured millions of his own money into this country."

Another nod.

"The public considers him a national hero. So does the Board."

"He's positioned himself well," Dvorak said.

The woman's hostile smile slid away. So did most of her coloring. She opened her mouth—as if to ask another question—when a deafening blast tore through the air. The van swerved violently. Gravity hurled Cass off the bench as tires screeched against pavement. The woman slammed into the van doors. Metal crunched. Dvorak screamed. For one disorienting moment, Cass was thrust into the air. The woman hit the roof.

They were rolling.

They were falling.

The van hit something solid.

Cass's head cracked against the bench.

The world went black and silent.

———

Sound disappeared.

For a second. For a minute. For an hour. Cass had no idea. He only knew that when he roused, he did so to the sound of gushing water and a frigid wetness that soaked through his jumpsuit.

The shock of it jolted him upright.

An interior emergency light cast an ominous glow on the unconscious woman and a bleeding Dvorak, her legs submerged.

Water was flooding inside the van.

And they were trapped.

Cass kicked his boots against the bench. Dvorak joined him. As the woman groaned, they banged harder.

She opened her eyes—whether from the freezing water soaking through her khaki slacks or the noise they were creating, Cass didn't know. She groaned a second time. Blinked once. Twice. Then looked around, her disorientation morphing into horror.

She fumbled inside her pockets and removed a set of keys. By the time she found the right one, she had to hold her breath and go underwater to unlock him. Then she moved to Dvorak while the water continued to pour, filling the van at an alarming rate. Cass pushed against the doors. When that didn't work, he barreled into the doors—twelve years old all over again, trapped in a closet, his mother being pummeled to death outside. He gritted his teeth and barreled again. And again. Dvorak and the woman joined him. Together, they heaved and kicked.

But the doors refused to budge.

The water was up to their necks.

The woman was screaming, pounding, panicking.

Cass climbed onto the bench and told her to breathe—deep breaths in, deep breaths out. "Once the inside is filled, the pressure will stabilize and we should be able to open the doors."

The woman nodded.

So did Dvorak.

He placed his palms flat against the van's roof, then his cheek. He took one last, long breath and plunged beneath the water. The sound went quiet. Muffled. They swam to the doors and, with what strength remained, gave one last heave.

The doors gave way.

He pushed through the opening and swam.

All was dark and cold as he kicked his legs and paddled his arms.

His lungs screamed.

His boots were like leaden weights pulling him downward.

But he kept kicking. He kept paddling.

Up, up, up until he crested the surface with a loud gasp. Rain fell against his face as he swam to the shore, as he dragged himself onto the rocks. Dvorak and the woman followed—coughing, spluttering. Then collapsing beside him.

They were free.

He was free.

He had escaped from the back of a prison van submerged at the bottom of a river in the dead of a rain-soaked night. The woman shielded her eyes from the downpour and peered across the tumult toward the opposite bank. "Do you see the driver? Did he get out?"

Cass looked up at the bridge from which they had plummeted, its guardrail a twisted snarl of metal. And beyond that, fire and smoke billowed into the weeping sky. His mind spun. His blood pounded with adrenaline. Someone had set off a bomb. Who and why?

The woman took a lurching step toward the river.

Cass grabbed her arm.

"He might be trapped down there," the woman said, yanking free.

"If he is, there's nothing you can do to help him."

The woman shouted a curse, blood and rain dripping down her face, then she ran her hands down her cheeks. She took several deep breaths, puffs of white mixing with the rain. Finally, she nodded at the road above. "That's 495, where the Potomac runs east to west." She set her hands on her hips and nodded over Cassian's shoulder, into the trees behind him. "That way is north."

The Potomac River.

495.

They weren't far from Washington, DC.

"I need to go up the road. I need to get help." She swiped at a lock of copper hair plastered to her cheek. "If the guard is dead, then I am the only witness. I will tell them I escaped out the passenger side window at the front of the van where I was supposed to be sitting."

"Why are you helping us?" Dvorak asked.

"I took an oath to protect the innocent. He insisted I was failing on the job." She jabbed her finger toward Cass. "He pointed me to evidence, and to my immense chagrin, it supported his claim. I went into this profession to uphold justice, not aid in corruption."

Dvorak's stare bore into the side of Cassian's face as he squinted through the rain. "What if the driver got out?"

"He will tell them I was in the back and I will tell them I was knocked unconscious. You two got my keys and escaped. By some miracle, so did I."

"They won't believe that," he said.

"I don't have another choice!"

"Come with us."

The woman shook her head. "I have a daughter. She's four. If I go with you, I lose her."

"If you stay, you're going to end up like the Brysons."

"It's a risk I have to take. Now go. Hurry." She removed the semi-automatic, which was still strapped around her body. She pushed it against Cassian's chest. "Once they find out your bodies aren't in that van, these woods will be crawling with dogs."

34

vorak's teeth chattered.

Cass clenched his jaw to keep himself from doing the same.

They were soaking wet. The rain was relentless. The cold had seeped into the marrow of his bones, but he kept moving. Soon, authorities would dive beneath the icy depths of that river and find an empty van where the prisoners ought to be. It was imperative that they get somewhere safe before that happened.

Dvorak had tunnel vision.

Bethesda.

They needed to get to Bethesda. They needed to speak with Amir Kashif, an employee of the NSA. Not a follower of the Monarch, as he and Eden and Cleo had suspected, but a spy. According to Dvorak, Amir would have answers. He would know how many survived the air raid in Washington, DC. He would know what was left of the Resistance—for this was what they were. He would know what happened to the other prisoners, the *pawns* that had been taken to a separate location ahead of them.

They trudged thirteen miles northwest, through woods and fields, along back roads. All the while, Dvorak gave him answers. She filled in the holes that had plagued him since he was captured and imprisoned. He suspected her willingness to divulge was largely due to the distraction talking provided. It seemed to keep the worst of her teeth chattering at bay.

Oswin Brahm was the Monarch.

This, he now knew.

Swarm was the name Dvorak and Amir had given his followers. Dvorak and everyone else in Washington, DC, existed to fight Swarm and stop Oswin Brahm, who was only just getting started. The Attack. The bombing of his own hotel. These were only a prelude to the main event, which she called The Great Winnowing. Genocide on steroids. One that would—if left unchecked—extend to all four corners of the earth.

When he asked her how Brahm could carry something of this magnitude out, Dvorak reminded him of the man's power and influence. Swarm was not small. He had an impressive number of people on his side, many of whom wielded a chilling level of power and influence on their own. Then she told Cass about his army. *The Electus.*

The phrase hurled him back in time, when he and Eden and Cleo were underneath Washington, DC. Before an alarm started blaring and all hell broke loose. Dvorak had just told them that Karik Volkova—the most infamous terrorist of all time—was nothing more than a puppet. But if that were true, then who had created the group of weaponized humans? Eden had asked the question. Upon doing so, Dvorak's attention had snapped in her direction.

"You know about the Electus?"

Now, Dvorak told him the Electus was Brahm's army. But six hardly made an army, especially when two of those six had already been destroyed. It didn't add up. Until the wheels of his mind turned a bit further and the ninety-three names on the pamphlet swam to the surface. Martyrs for the cause. Dead mothers and their dead babies. But what if the obituaries had lied? What if those babies weren't dead?

Goosebumps crawled across his skin. Goosebumps that had nothing to do with the cold. Those babies weren't dead. They were alive. They were Oswin Brahm's soldiers, and according to Dvorak, the Resistance was set on destroying them. They currently had one in their possession. Or at least, they did before the raid. They called him *the asset*. Whether he remained in their possession, Prudence didn't know.

As she filled him in, Cass tried not to panic. Did she suspect Eden was also one of Brahm's soldiers? Did Lady Justice try to strike the same deal with Dvorak as she'd tried to strike with him? If so, did Dvorak put the pieces together?

By the time they reached the outskirts of Bethesda, the rain had finally stopped. The sky was lightening. She was unwilling to go to Amir's house. He could not be compromised. He was crucial to their cause. So instead, they crept through the shadows of an alley in complete silence. It ran next to a street Eden had once stood upon, when Amir Kashif had gone off script. When he'd deviated from his normal routine and made a pit stop before heading to the diner. Eden had called it a private drinking lounge.

They reached a back door.

The outline of a small lotus leaf had been etched into the upper right corner.

The Amber Highway.

Dvorak was just lifting her hand to knock when the door flew open.

An old man on the other side jumped.

So did Dvorak.

"Saints alive," the man exclaimed in a thick Irish brogue, setting his gnarled hand over his chest. "Yer not dead!"

He stuck his head out from the door. He peered past them, down the length of the alley, then ushered them inside like a twitchy ferret, pulling the whiskers of his grizzled beard.

Without words to distract her, Dvorak's teeth had resumed their chattering.

"Yer frozen to the bone." The man waved at them to follow. He hobbled down the length of a hallway—his gait stilted with a pronounced limp. "The whole thing is on the news. They think yer at the bottom of the Potomac."

They stepped into a backroom where a fire crackled in the grate. There was a sofa and a sitting chair and a desk in the corner. Along with a television playing Concordia News. A female reporter stood inside the screen wearing a bulky rain jacket. Behind her, a slew of emergency vehicles flashed their emergency lights. "Amanda Hawkins escaped the icy waters, but so far, there has been no sign of her counterpart."

Amanda Hawkins.

Lady Justice had a name.

"The van transporting two of the prisoners plummeted off the bridge after a bomb detonated on the road ahead of them. Divers are currently on the scene, but the conditions of the river have delayed the recovery mission."

"The driver must not have made it," Cass said to nobody in particular—relief washing over him. If the driver was dead, then authorities would have no reason to doubt Amanda Hawkins' story. She escaped out the passenger side window of the prison van. Once authorities discovered the prisoners had also escaped, Amanda Hawkins would plead confusion. She had no idea how they managed it. The prisoners had been properly secured when they left the prison yard. Maybe Amanda Hawkins and her four-year-old daughter wouldn't end up like the Brysons and Yukio and the security guards at SafePad.

"How in the blazes did you escape?" the man asked, pulling a folded stack of gray woolen blankets from a closet. He tossed one to Cass. He handed another to Dvorak.

She wrapped it around herself and moved as close to the grate as she could without catching fire. "He managed to get Amanda H-hawkins on our side." She gave her head a begrudging tip toward Cass. "I n-need to know everything, Emmett. Wh-what was supposed to go down tonight?"

"They've been working on a prison break. They were supposed to ambush the transport vehicles and get all eight of ye to Alexandria."

"Alexandria."

"It's the new headquarters. We've joined forces with *America Underground*."

"Who's left, Emmett? How many survived the raid?"

He scratched his bony chest, one corner of his mouth pulling down uncomfortably.

"Rip off the Band-Aid," Dvorak said.

"Fran and Asher are alive. At least, they were before the prison break went sideways. There were six more survivors, along with Eden Pruitt and Cleo Ransom."

Cass sank into a nearby armchair and took—what felt like—his first proper breath since an explosion knocked him unconscious in Washington, DC. He'd known Eden was alive and not in the government's custody. Otherwise Amanda Hawkins wouldn't have offered him freedom for information on Eden's whereabouts. But hearing it confirmed, along with Cleo's survival, filled him with such swift and acute relief, his throat went tight and hot.

Cleo and Eden were alive. They were together. In Alexandria, where they'd been planning a prison break. In juxtaposition to Cass's relief was Dvorak's horror. It remained steadfast, even when Emmett assured her the asset was still in their possession. So few had survived. And they had no idea what had happened to the six prisoners from whom they'd been separated. Emmett was just as clueless as they were. He only knew what was on the news—two prisoners and a guard were believed to be dead at the bottom of Potomac after a bomb exploded on the road and the prison van skidded off the bridge. Emmett had been trying to get in touch with Amir, with headquarters in Alexandria, but everyone had gone silent.

He hobbled to the desk in the far corner of the room and grabbed his phone. He dialed a number and put the call on speaker. It rang and rang and rang. Emmett shook his head and hung up. "I was just on my way to his house to see why he wasn't answering."

Emmett was talking about Amir.

He had been on his way out when Cass and Dvorak arrived.

"You should go," Dvorak said, her expression tight with worry. "Let him know I'm okay. Tell him we need to speak as soon as possible."

Emmett nodded. "I'll leave me phone here. That way, he'll have a way to reach ya if he's home and able to call. In the meantime, you can change into some dry clothes and make yerself some coffee. Get warm. Sit tight. We'll be in touch as soon as we're able."

35

Cass ran his hand along his smooth jaw, courtesy of the disposable razor in Emmett's linen closet. He stopped in the doorway and took a drink of his coffee. In the room in front of him, Dvorak sat cross-legged on the couch. She was dressed in dry, oversized clothes with a mug cupped between her palms. A ribbon of steam curled into the air. She stared into the crackling fire, flames dancing in her dark, glassy eyes. To the public, she was a terrorist who had carried on Karik Volkova's legacy. An evil criminal deserving of execution without a trial. But in this moment, she looked vulnerable and young. A few stands of silver hair—bold and bright against black—the only sign of her age.

The television was dark and quiet. Before taking Emmett up on his offer of dry clothes and hot coffee, they'd been unable to tear themselves away from Concordia National News. But then the news started to repeat itself. The recovery mission was on hold until river conditions improved. Prudence Dvorak and Cassian Ransom were believed to be dead, but death couldn't be confirmed until divers pulled their bodies from the back of the prison van. As far as the other prisoners—the six that had also been transferred—Concordia mentioned nothing.

All Cass could do—all Dvorak could do—was wait.

For Emmett to return.

For Amir to call.

"Are you going to come in?" Dvorak asked, her gaze fixed on the fire. "Or are you going to stand there and stare at me?"

Cass took a seat in the armchair. He felt on edge, overly alert as he set one elbow on the armrest and took another drink of his coffee.

"Amir looked into you," she said, her tone detached. Devoid of emotion as she continued staring into the fire. "When your face first came on the news. After the Brysons were killed and you were connected to the bombing in Chicago. He discovered you weren't Cassian Ransom, but Cassian Gray. A fighter for the Underground with ties to Mordecai. Otherwise known as Nicholas Marks, a known member of Swarm."

"So you thought I was a member, too."

Dvorak nodded. "You were the guy. Pretty Eden Pruitt was nothing more than your sidekick." She looked at him, then. The expression in her eyes betraying the detachment in her voice. It was fearsome. And furious. "They do like young girls."

The coffee in his gut soured.

"But then you showed up, and *she* was the one with all the fire. *She* was the one who wanted the Monarch dead. Because he was after *her father*." Her fearsome fury morphed into suspicion. Like she'd been contemplating those final moments before the raid every bit as scrupulously as he had these past few weeks stuck in a prison cell. "Because he brought down Karik Volkova."

Cass gave her a steady, singular nod. But internally, his heart pounded.

Dvorak stared at him. "How did you enter the picture?"

He stared back, his gaze unwavering. What was the best way to lie? Weave in the truth. As much of it as possible. "You already made the connection."

"Mordecai?"

"He was looking for the Pruitts."

"Because Mr. Pruitt destroyed Oswin's test group."

She was close to it now. Eden. Her identity. The truth. "I thought someone should warn them."

"Why?"

"I don't like when bad things happen to innocent people." It was the same line he'd given Eden in Cleo's dorm room. He fed it to Dvorak now.

She didn't seem too keen on the flavor. She traced her thumb in figure-eights along the porcelain of her mug. "Where is the girl's father?" she finally asked. "Why is he letting his pretty little daughter traipse around the country to hunt down his hunter with someone like you?"

"He was shot. Twice. It made traveling difficult."

"How did you find us?"

"Francesca."

Dvorak narrowed her eyes.

"Several years ago, her path crossed with Cleo's. Francesca was being treated by Cleo's mother. Cleo asked Francesca how she got the glass eye. Francesca told Cleo the Monarch gave it to her. So we traced Francesca to the Brysons and the Brysons led us to Amir."

"And now here we are. All but destroyed." Her mouth tightened.

The fire popped.

Cass shifted in the armchair, eager to pivot the conversation, throw her attention in a different direction. "What's your story? How did you even know there needed to be a resistance?"

"I was a member of Swarm." A spark ignited in her eyes. A flame that seemed to burn from within. "Not that I was given a choice."

"How does that work?"

She took a long breath, as though settling in for a story. "When my father graduated high school, he was recruited into the United States army. There, he was recruited again. Swarm was targeting patriots. People with a profound love of country. My father believed the lies Swarm fed him—America was in danger. Politicians, protesters, rioters, the agenda-driven media. All of them were a cabal of extremists hellbent on tearing his beloved country apart, and only the Monarch knew how to stop it. My father joined the cause. They called themselves Invictus. They thought they were saviors. After his first tour ended, he began attending Thursday night meetings and there, he met my mother. A woman even more radicalized than he was. They got married. They had me. Twelve years later, my mother was killed in a random act of violence carried about by an illegal resident. You can imagine how much more extreme and devout my father became after such an event."

Cass imagined the man. Grief-stricken and bitter, having lost the woman he loved. He didn't agree with any of it. Conspiracy theories. Cabals. Extremism and radicalization. But he could see how all of it might shape a person into someone very strange.

"I was fifteen when The Attack happened. Over a million people were dead. And do you want to know what Invictus did?" She paused with her nostrils slightly flared. "They celebrated. They toasted to a new future. A new beginning. Predicted by their beloved Monarch, step one in the grand vision he had painted. A vision that included the destruction of the evil cabal. The next step came three years later. My father insisted I play a part."

Cass tilted his head, absorbed in the tale Dvorak was spinning.

"The Monarch was looking for women. Strong and healthy. With no genetic defects. Of child-bearing age. My father never asked if I wanted to participate. I never gave my consent. And yet, I was subjected to a series of medical procedures with no say at all. Many of the women died during these procedures. Many more failed to conceive. To my chagrin and my father's immense pride, my body succeeded. There I was, a pregnant virgin."

Cass stared, troubled by what he was hearing. Amazed, too.

Prudence Dvorak was a *Magnes Mater*. But her name wasn't on the back of the pamphlet.

"Amir called me Mary." Dvorak smiled a bitter smile, then shook her head. "I was placed in a cohort with five other women, each one as devout as my father. Lillian Kashif was the oldest. Her son, Amir, was only one year younger than me. We became close friends. Confidantes. Twice, my body attempted to reject the life that was forced upon me. Twice, I was forced to undergo more medical procedures that prevented it. Amir held my hand through it all. And then, the big day arrived."

"*Sanctus Diem*," Cass muttered.

Dvorak nodded, her expression grim. "We were taken to one of Oswin Brahm's underground facilities. All ninety-four of us. There, we were induced. My body was more than ready. I was the first to deliver. Lillian was the last. I watched as a doctor cut her open. I watched her bleed to death as they pulled the life from her womb. The babies were taken away and we were given medicine to drink. Medicine that would make us strong. Medicine that would make us *clean* so we could be reunited with our *special children*. I didn't want to be reunited with my child. I wanted nothing to do with it. I pretended to drink. Then I watched as one by one, these devout women—these *Great Mothers*—convulsed and died."

Cass's grip tightened on his mug. Ninety-three innocent women, dead because of a monster named Oswin Brahm.

"I escaped. I ran to Amir. I told him everything that had happened. He helped me hide. And that was the beginning. It took many more years of careful and meticulous planning before we became a respectable resistance. But now ..." She closed her eyes, like the effort of keeping them open had become too much.

Now the Resistance had dwindled egregiously.

Thanks to him and Cleo and Eden.

They led the government to their doorstep.

Because Mona had sold them out, just like she'd sold Cassian and his mother out all those years ago. He could feel the storm clouds brewing—gathering, darkening—as his grip tightened around his mug.

The door to the alley opened.

Cass and Dvorak turned toward the sound.

Footsteps clomped up the hallway.

Emmett appeared, looking even older than when he'd left.

Dvorak came to her feet. Her blanket spilled to the floor. "What's wrong?" Her attention dropped to Emmett's gnarled hand, which was curled into an upturned fist.

He opened it. A Monarch pin rested on his palm.

Dvorak stepped forward, a look of horror stretching long down her face. "Why do you have that? Where is Amir?"

Emmett looked up from the pin with soupy, haunted eyes. "He's dead."

36

The morning sun crested the horizon, painting the clouds in yellows and pinks as a team of Alexandrians extracted an unconscious Francesca from the steel shipping container. Her skin was burned. Her combat clothes were charred. Her boots half-melted. As quickly as possible, the team moved her onto a stretcher and wheeled her off to Kaiser. Lark went with, her injury much less dire.

Eden wasn't injured at all.

Not even a scratch.

Her hand moved to the tear in her tactical vest, covered in dried blood. *Her* blood. Where a scrap of metal had pierced through bone and organ. She felt Cleo's eyes upon her, but she didn't meet them. She couldn't meet them. Lest the wall she'd spent the last five hours building around her heart shatter. If she was going to continue this mission—if she was going to be a weapon and fight Oswin Brahm—she needed that wall to stand.

Birds chirped in the trees. Frost glittered on weeds. Somewhere further away, in the pink-yellow sky, a crow circled and cawed. They stood in a haphazard huddle that was pregnant with shock and defeat. Eden and Jericho, covered in grime and soot. Cleo, Asher, Dayne, and Nairobi were clean. But their faces were ashen. Their eyes, bloodshot.

Nobody spoke.

What was there to say?

They'd been working on this prison break relentlessly, and it had failed. Not just sort of, but flagrantly. Every one of those prisoners was dead, along with the four from Bunker Three. And that guard, who was very much not on their side. Eden pulled the ring from her pocket—the memory of the man's cries swirling with the cawing of that crow. She opened her hand. The ring caught the sunlight and glinted in her palm.

Asher took an aggressive step forward. "Where did you get that?"

"A guard was wearing it. He was by me after the explosion. I was with him when he … " She swallowed hard, her teeth clamped.

"It's like Amir's," Nairobi said.

"Do you think it's more than a ring?" Jericho asked.

Asher took the piece of jewelry from Eden's palm. The others drew nearer as he removed his chess piece and began comparing the two.

Eden remained in place, not a trace of curiosity within her.

"It has a button," he said, running the pad of his thumb across the backside of the butterfly. Running the pad of his other thumb across the button on his chess piece. The one that contained nanotech, and alerted them whenever a council member needed to meet in the war room.

"What happens if you push it?" Cleo asked.

"We shouldn't try without knowing," Asher said.

Nairobi's breath caught.

A small hitch only Eden could hear.

She looked and saw why.

Asher's chess piece was flashing.

He clicked the minuscule button on the bottom side of his

queen. It projected a red holographic code that floated in the air. "It's from Amir. He's waiting in the war room."

They wasted no time.

They rushed to the boardroom, where an array of technology blinked and hummed. They sat at the table and slipped on headsets.

When Eden opened her eyes, she was in the virtual space with six of its octagonal walls still covered. Someone was already there, waiting for them.

Only that someone wasn't Amir.

That someone was Prudence Dvorak.

———

Eden splashed water on her face. The grime left in swirls of smoky liquid that washed down the drain. She gripped the sides of the sink and met her reflection in the mirror. Drops of water slid down her cheeks. With trembling fingers, she combed through the snarled mess that was her hair. She tried commanding them to stop. Be still. But as she braided her locks into a plait, the tremble only grew worse. Until it wasn't a tremble, but a quake.

Heat billowed in her lungs.

Fire licked up her throat.

A sob tore free in a fast and furious exit.

She cupped her hand over her mouth to stop anymore from coming. But the tears couldn't be stopped. They pooled in her blue-gray-green eyes and tumbled down her wet cheeks.

Cassian was alive.

She removed her hand from her mouth and inhaled—a loud gasp that flooded her chest with oxygen and life and a paralyzing, tenuous hope that fissured the wall she'd erected around her heart.

Cassian was alive.

He was on his way to the airport with Prudence Dvorak.

Jericho was meeting them there now. Eden had insisted upon going. Jericho had insisted she stay. He knew how to get them here—to the IDA—unseen. She would only muddy the waters. So here she was, staring at herself in the mirror. Afraid to move. Afraid to blink. Afraid to hope.

Cassian was alive.

But not Amir.

Their mole had been killed in the same way the Brysons had been killed. In the same way the security guards at SafePad Elite had been killed. In the same way a bookie named Yukio had been killed. A cold-blooded bullet to the forehead. The prison transfer had been a set-up. Amir was fed faulty information. He passed that faulty information to the Resistance. The Resistance ambushed the convoy, which had been rigged with an explosive. As soon as that explosive detonated, suspicions about Amir Kashif were confirmed. He wasn't on Swarm's side. Amir was the leak.

Now, Amir was dead.

Eden should feel sad about this.

Prudence Dvorak certainly was.

But as she stared at herself in the mirror, Eden could feel nothing but this paralyzing hope. The news of Cassian's survival felt like a thing that was terrifyingly delicate. A wisp of flame that could be extinguished by the slightest breeze. What if Prudence Dvorak was playing a trick? Or what if this was another set-up? What if Dvorak's avatar wasn't Dvorak at all, just like King George hadn't been King George, but Asher hiding behind his avatar? Francesca wasn't there to ask her strange questions. Nobody else had bothered to confirm her identity. What if they were fools and Cassian really was dead at the bottom of the Potomac River and another ambush was on its way? She imagined curling her arms around the tenuous flame in an attempt to protect it from the barrage of debilitating what-ifs, determined to keep it alight.

She tore some paper towels from the dispenser and dried her

face. She set her shaking hand over her abdomen, took a deep breath that lifted her shoulders, and exited the ladies' room.

The boardroom hummed.

The television was on, playing Concordia National News.

Two carafes of coffee sat on the table. One empty. The other half gone.

A platter of food someone had fetched from the commissary remained untouched.

They'd been awake for going on thirty-six hours, but not a single one of them dreamt of sleeping. They were waiting on pins and needles for word from Jericho. They'd just received word from Kaiser that Francesca was stable and sedated. Two bones in her left arm were broken. Her burns were mostly second degree. Her hands and face had taken the brunt of the impact. Her combat clothes had offered protection to the rest of her body.

According to their sources, the Great Dismal Swamp was teeming with military personnel and search dogs. Everything within a hundred-mile radius was on lockdown. But no news of the explosion and six dead prisoners had touched Concordia's airwaves. For whatever reason, the 'powers that be' were keeping the botched prison break under wraps.

Asher and Cleo were sitting next to one another, studying the butterfly ring Eden had pulled off the guard. An exact match to the one Amir owned. The one he'd been given as a supposed member of Swarm. Apparently, it was Amir's ring that inspired Asher to alter his chess piece and Francesca's locket and Jericho's domino and Lark's bullet and Amir's pin. Each trinket embedded with nanotech, kept on their person at all times, enabling them to safely call for a meeting in the war room should the need arise.

They identified the guard to whom it belonged. He was already in their database of known Swarm members. He'd been part of the set-up. Now he was dead and they had his ring. But what could they do with it? They knew the guard used it to communicate. What they didn't know was whether the ring had an identifier. If it did, anyone they attempted to contact with it would know the ring's owner had died in the explosion. Pushing the button could very well jeopardize their location in Alexandria. So they didn't make any attempt. Instead, Asher was conducting a thorough examination, explaining each step to an attentive Cleo.

Nairobi and the last remaining survivor from Bunker Three excused themselves to check on the asset. It was time to administer another dose. Eden's jaw clenched. Her hands, too. She didn't know what to do about the asset. There was nothing she *could* do about the asset. So she tried her best not to think of the asset at all. It was a coward's solution.

On the table, Dayne's phone vibrated.

A rapid-fire succession of buzzing.

Buzz. Buzz. Buzz.

Just as he picked it up, the television blared with an Emergency Broadcast Alert.

Eden held her breath.

They'd been expecting this. News about the missing bodies of Cassian Ransom and Prudence Dvorak. By now, divers had to have commenced with the recovery mission. By now, they had to know there were no dead prisoners in the back of the submerged van.

Cleo turned up the volume.

A smartly dressed Chuck Perez sat behind the news desk. With late-breaking music playing in the background, he began his report. Only it wasn't about the recovery mission. It wasn't about the missing prisoners. This was about another toxin attack. Civilians were dropping like flies up and down State Street in Madison, Wisconsin. The National Guard was on the scene. As Chuck Perez spoke, Dayne's phone continued buzzing.

"I need to get to the media room," he said, his chair scraping against the floor. "The wire is going crazy with news from our contacts in Madison."

Cleo stood, too. "I'm coming with."

As they exited, she gave Eden's shoulder a squeeze.

Eden could do nothing but sit there, frozen in her seat, her stomach tying into knots. Madison was so unnervingly close to Milwaukee.

Drone footage showed first responders in hazmat suits, carting away the dead from Bascom Hill to Capitol Square. Eden remembered another scene in that same square. A protest turned violent.

This isn't right. Where is Dwight?

She'd been so shocked when she'd seen it. But not Cassian. Not Cleo, either. She'd been monitoring the situation, keeping tabs on any and all protests unfolding across the country. According to Cleo, there had been a considerable uptick over the past year. Cleo had a map in her dorm room flagging seven different cities where they had occurred. Fresno. St. Louis. Detroit. Seattle. Milwaukee. *Minneapolis. Madison.*

"He's targeting cities on the map," Eden said.

Asher looked at her.

She stood, the legs of her chair scrapping against the floor, too. She moved to the smart board and used her finger to scrawl the names of the seven cities. "Cleo's been monitoring uprisings. Protests and riots over the past year." Eden circled Minneapolis and Madison. "What are the chances that two of them have been hit with this toxin?"

There was a moment of silence as Asher absorbed what Eden had said.

The knots in her stomach tied into a brick again. It sat heavy in her gut. Milwaukee was on that list. Her parents were in Milwaukee.

Asher's walkie-talkie beeped.

Jericho's voice filled the room. "I've got Pru and Cassian."

The words were gasoline poured straight on the tenuous flame of hope in her chest. That hope ignited into a roaring fire. It wasn't a trick. It wasn't a set-up.

He had Cassian.

"We're on our way," Jericho said. "Over."

37

Cass and Dvorak met a man named Jericho at what was once the Reagan National Airport. Now, a relic of the past—a behemoth tomb that echoed when they walked. Jericho was dressed in black combat gear that looked like it had gone through war. He had a deep, soothing voice, a firm handshake, a no-nonsense manner, and even more information than Emmett, the bartender.

Dvorak sat in the passenger seat of Jericho's UTV, holding it together. But Cass wasn't fooled. He'd been there, in Emmett's back office, when Dvorak's knees had hit the ground. When a wail of lament had torn up her throat. When she'd taken the butterfly pin from Emmett's hand and thrown it—in a wild fit of rage—against the wall. After hearing Dvorak's story, Cass could hardly blame her.

She and Amir had been friends for decades. When pregnancy had been forced upon her, he was her confidante. When she ran from the abuse, he had been her safety. Together, they had built a Resistance to fight the cult they'd been born into. *Ad Astra Per Aspera.* Through hardship to the stars. Francesca's glass eye. The disturbing room in the Bryson's basement. Maybe not every Swarm member abused their children, but the philosophy sure lent itself to abuse. Amir and Dvorak had been bonded by proximity and trauma and purpose. And now, that bond had been severed. Her partner in crime was dead. Thanks to a prison break that never would have been necessary had he and Eden and Cleo not led the government into Washington, DC.

The truth set him on edge.

He listened carefully to everything Jericho had to say while riding in the back of the UTV on their way to the Potomac Yard. When news came across his two-way radio about a crisis unfolding in Madison, Jericho informed Dvorak about a similar crisis that had already occurred in Minneapolis. A crisis Cass and Dvorak hadn't been aware of while locked away in their cells. None of the prison guards felt compelled to share their copies of *Concordia Times*. But Cass recalled two of them muttering about Minneapolis on one of his trips to the showers. Now he knew why. A deadly toxin was being unleashed into cities and civilians were dropping like flies. The first attack had been in Minneapolis. Another was unfolding in Madison. The public believed Interitus was to blame. But Interitus didn't exist.

Jericho updated Dvorak on the state of the Resistance and the botched prison break that ended with their van plummeting into the Potomac River. Jericho had taken part in the prison break. So had Francesca, a woman named Lark, four more members of the Resistance. And Eden. She'd gone with Jericho. She was there when the convoy transporting six prisoners to South Mills, North Carolina, exploded.

Cass had questions. In what capacity had Eden joined the Resistance? What did they know about her? What had she told them? He bit his tongue, knowing those questions would only rouse suspicion. Dvorak was harboring plenty of that on her own.

His muscles were tense. His nerves, raw. These people wanted to take down the Monarch. In that, their goals were aligned. But their method of doing so included destroying the Monarch's soldiers. Cass couldn't care less about those soldiers.

The Resistance could destroy every single one and he wouldn't blink twice. Unless, of course, they included Eden among them. And they would, wouldn't they? She had the same design, the same potential. Most damning of all, the same proclivity to be controlled. If Cass were Dvorak, he'd want Eden destroyed like the rest. His hands curled into fists. If they wanted to get to her, they would have to crawl over his cold, dead body.

Jericho drove over a bump.

A pair of twin buildings came into view—their glass fronts reflecting the sun. Jericho wasted no time. He brought the UTV to a skidding stop in front of the building further east. Cass followed him and Dvorak inside. With his stride long and his heart beating like a drum, he trailed them through the building to a closed door on the ground floor. Jericho didn't knock. He barged into a boardroom with a long conference table. Only two people sat around it. The giant on the moped who'd led them to Washington, DC. And a tall Black woman dressed in the same combat gear as Jericho, only her fatigues were much less ravaged. The pair stopped in the middle of their conversation.

With a cry, the tall woman pushed to her feet and nearly tackled Dvorak in a hug. Dvorak stood there with her arms by her sides—for a beat, maybe two—before hugging the woman back. Cass looked past the embrace, searching for Eden, his beating heart beginning to pound. Where was she? He was about to demand an answer when his attention slid to the floor-to-ceiling windows lining the opposite wall.

He stopped breathing.

There she was, standing in a courtyard, dressed in the same battle-worn fatigues. Her hair braided over her shoulder. Her blue-gray-green eyes wide inside her perfectly clean, uninjured face. She was staring right at him, her lips slightly parted.

He didn't move. He didn't blink. He didn't breathe—positive if he did, the moment would vanish. He would wake up in his prison cell and despair.

Eden didn't move either. It was as though she feared the same thing.

Until the moment became too much. He had to touch her. Feel her. Hold her. His blood pounded with the need. Every nerve in his body begged for it until he could resist no longer.

He strode to the door and flung it open.

And there she was, her body colliding into his. He wrapped his arm around her waist. He lifted her off the ground as he slammed the door behind him and walked all the way outside. He pressed his face into the sweet, soft curve of her neck, their hearts beating in unison as she dug her fingers into his hair, and then his mouth was on hers. His body on fire as he kissed her and she kissed him back with a fervency that matched his own.

This girl he craved.

This girl he cherished.

This girl he loved.

So much, *he couldn't think straight.*

The monster's words slammed through him, shoving Cass painfully and mercilessly into sobriety.

He dragged himself away.

But Eden didn't let go. She kept her arms locked around his neck and looked up at him with swollen lips and flushed cheeks and a shy smile that made his fingers ache. He wanted to bury them in her hair. He wanted to keep kissing her, tasting her, feeling her until he was consumed with Eden Pruitt, this girl he had dreamt about, worried about. She was here, in his arms. So intoxicating he couldn't think at all, let alone think straight. Mustering every ounce of willpower within him, he unclasped her hands and stepped away.

"Does anyone know?" he asked.

"Dayne."

His body tensed. "How?"

"I told him."

"You told him?"

"I had to." She frowned at the ground between them, as

though annoyed by the distance he'd put there. "Barrett and Violet killed two highway patrol officers and a civilian on national news."

"*What?*"

"It was a fake. Dayne could spot it almost immediately. But the location wasn't. They were heading into Minneapolis. I needed to know why they were there. I needed to know if my parents were okay. Dayne knew how to reach Violet because she's a missing person in his newspaper."

Eden kept talking.

But Cass stopped listening. His ears were ringing. His mind spinning. Dayne Johnson knew the truth about Eden, and his literal job was to *share* news. "We have to leave," he said.

Eden's forehead puckered.

Cass glanced over his shoulder, toward the door several paces behind them, urgency burrowing beneath his skin. They needed to leave right now, before Dayne spilled the beans. But Eden didn't look at all inclined to go. "Brahm has an army."

"I know."

"Those guys in there want to destroy that army."

"I know that, too."

Her unflustered acknowledgement of this particular piece of news had the urgency burrowing deeper. "If they find out that you are part of that army—"

"I'm not, though." Her blue-gray-green eyes flashed. "I'm not part of that army."

"They won't see it that way."

"We don't know how they will see it."

Cass ran his hand down his face, unsettled by her choice of phrase. He would have much preferred, 'Don't worry. They won't find out.'

She stepped closer. "We can't leave, Cass."

"Yes, we can." Easily, in fact. There was a UTV parked in front of the building. They could hop on and go. They could leave right now while the reunion was unfolding in that board-room and the Resistance was distracted.

But she was shaking her head. "Where would we possibly go?"

He grappled for a suggestion. A legitimate possibility. But she gave him no time to grab one. "A team of divers is swimming to the bottom of the Potomac right now. Maybe they already have. At any moment, Concordia will announce your Houdini-like escape. If you were wanted before your imprisonment, think how much more rabid the country will be once they find out you got away."

Now he was the one shaking his head.

But she kept going. "This is the only safe place for us to be right now."

"It's not safe," he said, biting the words between his teeth.

"We can't run away from this. *I* can't run away from it. It's too big." She took his hand and looked at him beseechingly, painfully, like this was the last conversation she wanted to have. But how could they talk about anything else? "I can't go into hiding while other people risk their lives. We're in a literal war, and the vast majority of the country doesn't even know. I bring a considerable advantage." Her hand squeezed his. "But only if I stop hiding it."

Her words came like a kick to the groin.

He pulled away—emotionally, physically.

She seemed less hurt by the gesture than she was frustrated. Stubborn. Her resolve solidifying in the blaze of her eyes, in the hardening of her jaw. In the subtle lift of her chin. She looked fierce—like a warrior on a mission—and it scared the hell out of him.

"I want to tell them the truth," she said.

"No," he said back.

"I'm not asking permission." Her voice was firm but tender. Her eyes soft. Filled with a knowing compassion that made him want to shove his fist into a wall. "I've proven myself, Cass. By now, they know I'm on their side. They will see this as a good thing, and if they don't, we'll just have to convince them."

He wanted to shout. Curse. Take her face between his hands and tell her to stop being so reckless. But the door opened behind them. He turned quickly, positioning himself in front of her like a bodyguard. Like they had superhuman hearing and had eavesdropped on their conversation. If they so much as attempted to harm a single hair on her head, he would fight every one of them.

But they weren't moving toward Eden. They were striding past her.

"Dayne just received news from our contact in Milwaukee," Asher said, marching toward the west tower. "There are boots on the ground."

38

The news room bustled with people and movement and commotion and the thick scent of coffee. Eden made a beeline for Dayne, who stood at one of the round tables, conferring with two of his journalists. If boots were on the ground in Milwaukee, then the toxin had to be there, too.

"What's going on?" she asked as soon as she reached him, trying hard not to choke on her escalating panic.

"We think the toxin is in Milwaukee." His answer came like a wallop to the chest. Even though she'd braced for it, it knocked the wind out of her.

"It hasn't been reported on the news yet," a journalist said.

Eden's attention darted to the flat screens. Some featured somber-faced reporters. Others, drone footage of emergency vehicles with their red and blue lights flashing up and down State Street. So far, the attack on Madison had resulted in more deaths than the sum total in Minneapolis. Eden set her hand over her stomach, unwilling to fathom it.

Dayne dragged his palm down his stubbled face. "We keep trying to reach our people in Madison, but they've gone silent."

The community in Minneapolis went silent because the community in Minneapolis had been wiped clean. They were gone, all of them. Eden imagined a mass grave. When she lay in bed at night, between yearning for Cassian and worrying about her parents, she pictured bodies tossed inside a giant ditch and covered up like they didn't matter. Like they were of no consequence at all. Now Madison had gone silent. Would Milwaukee be next?

The door leading into Dayne's office opened with a swoosh.

Cleo swept into the room with a stack of printouts, her long braids wrapped in a thick bun on top of her head. The scratches and scrapes on her face from the air raid in Washington, DC, had long since healed. The only sign that she'd endured any trauma at all was her limp and the fresh scar above her right eyebrow. Still, Eden could feel Cassian studying her, cataloging her injuries.

When Cleo finally looked up from the papers and saw him, she yelped. The printouts scattered as she catapulted herself into his arms. Cassian received the hug the same way he had when they'd arrived at Cleo's dorm room all those months ago—like a stoic big brother. This time, though, he had a bruise on his temple. A cut on his opposite cheek. The structure of his face was sharper, more pronounced, as though his time in prison had shaved all excess away. Dvorak's face had the same gaunt look to it. While the effect gave her a sickly appearance, it only made Cassian more devastating. A perfect sculpture chiseled from stone. At the moment, that sculpture was furious, and that fury was directed at Eden.

Asher watched the embrace with a frown as a familiar tune filled the newsroom. Every flatscreen cut from the crisis unfolding in Madison to Chuck Perez sitting behind his news desk. Breaking news on top of breaking news. Concordia's chief anchor was coming on air with an update on the recovery mission in Montgomery County, Maryland. A team of divers had successfully retrieved the body of thirty-two-year-old Milo Guthrie, a prison guard from Annapolis. They had found no trace of the two prisoners who should have been secured in the back of the van. At this, pictures of Cassian and Dvorak came on the screen.

Eden could practically feel the panic rising across the country. The regime they believed to be responsible for the catastrophic attacks upon Minneapolis and Madison had freed two of their most valuable players. Right from beneath the government's nose.

Chuck Perez welcomed Chairwoman Kendra Cruz to join the live feed. She sat behind her own stately desk—dressed like a high-powered businesswoman—and addressed the nation. She urged the public to stay calm. She encouraged citizens to stay at home until the government could get a better grasp on the developing situation. As Eden suspected, she tripled the bounty on Cassian and Dvorak's heads.

"Why aren't they saying anything about the prisoners who died?" Nairobi asked, bending over to pick up the fallen printouts.

Surely, this would have been viewed by the public as an Interitus fail. The regime had attempted to free all eight of their players. They'd only managed to free two. Six had perished. Along with several more who'd been part of the prison break. If the government truly wanted the public to stay calm, this would certainly help. But not even a whiff of the botched ambush was making the airwaves.

"Brahm is too smart for that," Dvorak said, her eyes like black stone. "He's not interested in calming the public. His plans work better if they're terrified."

Nairobi handed the papers to Dayne.

The newswire beeped.

So did Eden's back pocket.

It was the gadget. The one she'd used to contact Barrett and Violet. It hadn't so much as vibrated since the last time they'd communicated. With so many noises happening around them, nobody seemed to notice. Except for Cassian. His golden eyes met hers. He followed her as she exited the news room.

Cleo caught on and followed, too.

They found a private corner off to the left of the elevator. Eden pulled the gadget from her pocket and answered the call.

Barrett appeared—his round, friendly face going bright with excitement. "Hey! I've got her! She's right here."

He moved out of the frame.

His projection disappeared.

Another replaced it.

Someone so unexpected, so wholly longed for, Eden had to cup her hand over her mouth to muffle her own exclamation.

It was her dad.

She was looking at her father—his face lined with tension and anxiety that was melting away before her eyes.

Beside him—but not in view—someone cried.

"Mom?" Eden whispered. "Is that Mom?"

"Yes," Dad said, beaming. "She's right here." He looked off to his left with a reassuring smile. Eden imagined Dad taking Mom's hand and giving it a jubilant, reassuring squeeze. "The Foresters are here, too. So is Ben. And Violet."

"Where *are* you?" Eden asked.

"We got out of Milwaukee just as the National Guard was rolling in. We reached the Damen Silos not more than ten minutes ago."

She choked on her relief.

The Damen Silos.

"Is Mona there?" Cassian asked, the question filled with such sharp urgency, Eden was taken aback.

Dad must have heard him.

His brow furrowed. "Was that—are you with Cassian?"

"Yes," Eden said. "He's here. He's alive."

And he was holding out his hand—a nonverbal request to take the gadget.

Eden passed it to him.

"Mr. Pruitt," he said, "is Mona at the Silos with you?"

"Not yet. But there's a kid here who tells us she'll be back soon."

"You need to leave now. Before she returns."

"Why?"

"Mona can't be trusted."

Eden and Cleo gaped at one another.

Ever since bombs had dropped on their dummy location, Eden had suspected Mona of betrayal. Cleo had defended her, insisting Mona would never betray them. Now, here Cass was, his tone and expression simmering with something dark. Something threatening. Cass and Mona weren't close. Their relationship was devoid of warmth. But there wasn't animosity either. He had no way of knowing about the attack on their dummy location, unless Jericho had mentioned it en route. But even then, why would he pin such an attack on Mona?

The furrow in her father's brow deepened. "Where are we supposed to go?"

Eden touched Cassian's arm. "They should come here. It's the only safe place."

"Where are you?" Dad asked.

She opened her mouth to give him their location, but Cass cut her off with the lift of his hand. "We can't say. Not while you're using Mona's network."

"You're both overreacting." Cleo set her hand on her hip, clearly annoyed. "We don't have any proof Mona is the one who sold us out."

"She sold *me* out, Cleo," Cassian said. "My mother, too."

"What are you talking about?" Cleo asked.

"My father came for a visit while I was in prison."

Eden covered her mouth.

Cleo's eyes went round as saucers.

"Mona's the reason he knew we were alive. She told him where he could find us in exchange for cash."

Eden shook her head, trying to process this information. This awful, sickening information.

But Cass gave her no time. "Where's the closest safe house?"

She drew a mental map in her mind, a replica of the one she'd seen in Mona's office. There were five safe houses spread throughout the Chicago area. The closest was in Beecher. Eden gave Cassian the name and the address. She could hear the scribble of a pen as Dad wrote the information on one of Mona's sticky notes.

"Get there as quickly as possible," Cass said. "Contact us as soon as you arrive and we can tell you where to go next. If Mona intercepts this, she will know where you went, which means you need to get in and get out fast. We have to stay ahead of her."

Her father nodded.

"Dad," Eden said, coming right beside Cassian so her father could see her. So she could see him. Her mother did the same, smiling tremulously as tears spilled down her cheeks. Eden could only look at her for the briefest of moments lest she break down, too. "Did you bring the device with you—the one Violet fixed?"

"Of course."

"Keep it close. We're going to need all the information we can get from it." She gave them her bravest smile. "I love you."

"We love you, too, kiddo. Talk soon."

With a resolute nod, Eden ended the call.

39

Shock and fear rippled through the room.

Violet shut off the device she'd been examining—specifically, the movement and pattern of blinking dots—and slipped it inside the pocket of her new, clean coat. Ellery slid off the headset she'd been using to study the map of off-the-grid communities and safe houses across the country. Everyone stared at one another inside Mona's underground office, none of them sure what to do.

Cassian was alive.

The Damen Silos weren't safe.

Mona couldn't be trusted.

They needed to get to the address Alexander had written on the sticky note. They needed to get there as quickly as possible. Meanwhile, a radio played somewhere beyond the sheet hanging in the doorway.

"While biowarfare threatens the Midwest, authorities across the country are celebrating a much-needed victory. RRA officials raided a community of illegal residents late last night in Madison, Wisconsin. According to officers on scene, it was a hotbed of gambling and fighting and what is believed to be a major recruiting ground for Interitus."

Madison.

They'd been there on their trek to Dr. Norton's cabin. Now the toxin was there. It had followed them from Minneapolis. Then it followed them to Milwaukee, too.

"In light of this discovery, Wisconsin officials have mandated fingerprints and retinal imaging for all citizens under the age of eighteen."

The radio coverage switched to a young mother inside a neonatal unit.

"For those of us with nothing to hide—law-abiding citizens," she said. "I don't see why we wouldn't fully cooperate. I will do whatever is necessary to keep my child safe."

Alexander drew his gun and loaded a magazine. He stepped next to the wall and peeked around the sheet. "We need to get to the truck quickly and quietly."

Nobody objected.

They fell in line without saying a word. Alexander led the way. Barrett and Violet took up the rear. They didn't meet anyone in the damp, torch-lit hallway. Not even the tall, skinny kid who had led them to Mona's office. There weren't many people here in the Silos, and the ones that were had made their way to the cafeteria for breakfast.

They reached the stairwell.

Up above, the sky was dreary and overcast.

Alexander peeked above ground to make sure the coast was clear. Then he waved them up. They hurried up the stairs in single-file. On the fifth step, Violet stopped. She grabbed Barrett by his elbow, yanking him to a halt as a dart whizzed through the air and hit Ellery in the neck.

She crumpled to the ground.

Annette screamed.

Jack roared.

Violet dropped down the stairs. She scuttled backward with Barrett, ducking into the pitch-black shadow of the stairwell as a gun fired and crows cawed and Ruth's scream joined Annette's.

There was a flood of headlights through the dreary sky. The roar of two vehicles.

Violet couldn't see, but she could hear. So well, she could track every movement as she hid in the dark, holding on to Barrett's hand. There were ten officers. Ten guns. All of them yelling, "Hands in the air! Drop the weapon!"

Alexander's handgun thudded in the grass.

The officers closed in.

Arms were wrenched behind backs.

Annette cried and begged as a guard tore her away from her daughter.

Jack objected.

There was a quick scuffle followed by the sharp crack of metal against bone. The crunch of cartilage. The spurting of blood as knees hit the ground. A face being smashed into the dirt. An officer's boot pressed against someone's spine and Annette sobbing incoherently.

Violet could smell the salt of her tears, the iron in Jack's blood.

"Identify the girl. Make sure she's not a fake."

An officer removed an object from his belt. Pants creased as he crouched low. An eyelid was pulled apart, followed by the hum of an infrared scan. "We've got one of them. There should be two more."

Boots shuffled, as though the officers were looking around. And then, an angry demand. "Where are the other two?"

"I don't know who you're talking about," Alexander replied, squeezing the words between clenched teeth.

Ruth whimpered.

"Don't play dumb with me." There was a soft, subtle click. The cock of a gun. "Barrett Barr and Violet Winter. Where are they?"

Violet swallowed a squeak.

They knew her name.

The barrel of the officer's gun shoved against flesh. "Tell me now or I will pull this trigger."

Violet squeezed her eyes shut.

Alexander Pruitt was about to be shot and killed.

Because of them.

They needed to walk up the stairs with their hands raised. They needed to surrender. Right now, before that officer squeezed his trigger finger. She tried to get Barrett's attention, but his body was rigid and unmoving beside her.

And suddenly, the gun turned in a fast whirl. Based on the sudden silence of Ruth's whimpers, she was the new target.

Violet's heart pounded.

She shook her head.

Not her. Not the nice mother.

She tried to pull Barrett up, but he wouldn't budge. Heat and tension and panic seeped from his pores as he bore down like gravity might betray him. Like it had the power to yank him up by his feet and hurl him into the sky.

If the guard expected Ruth Pruitt to crack under such pressure, he was in for a rude awakening, for when she spoke, her voice came in a low, menacing tremble. "My husband already told you. We. Don't. Know."

There was a silent face-off.

Hearts pounded.

And then the officer lowered his weapon.

"Load them into the truck," he shouted. "Search the grounds. They're here somewhere."

Violet yanked Barrett to his feet and they ran. They raced through the torch-lit corridors, dodging open-mouthed residents who had just finished breakfast, until they reached tunnels that weren't torch-lit. Water splashed beneath their boots as they turned wildly, losing themselves in the labyrinth, until they found another exit.

They ascended the stairs on silent feet.

Across a fifty-yard span of waist-length prairie grass, two

RRA vehicles idled with an officer standing guard in front of each. Violet communicated her plan to Barrett using made-up sign language. He began shoving the journals he hadn't yet memorized under his coat and into the waistband of his jeans. He left the rest in the rucksack behind, and together, they slithered like snakes around the edge of the fence until they reached the back of the vehicles. The two officers remained unaware, despite their vigilant postures with guns at the ready.

Violet could hear Annette sobbing and Jack moaning in the vehicle to the left. Along with the rattle and tug of metal as Alexander and Ruth and Dr. Norton tried and failed to break their restraints. Violet and Barrett crawled beneath this vehicle and pulled themselves up and out of sight, clinging to its undercarriage, breathing just barely.

Thirty minutes later, the other officers returned.

"The tunnel system is expansive. They could be anywhere down there."

"We'll have to send in a crew of dogs. Jake and I will take these guys to Fred. Baz and Ike will take *her* to command. The six of you can start evacuating. Remember, these people aren't going to any of the facilities. Handle them with care."

"But they're illegal—"

"They won't be for much longer. Paperwork's already in process. Keep a close eye on the exits. Barr and Winter are down there somewhere. Don't give them a way out." The officer climbed behind the wheel.

A second officer—Jake—got in beside him.

The doors shut.

The engine shifted into drive.

The officer drove through the gate, completely unaware that the two they were looking for had helped themselves to a ride.

40

Eden, Cleo, and Cassian stood in silence.

He'd seen his father—the monster-of-a-man who had killed his mother, then beat him within an inch of his life. That monster had visited him in prison. And during that encounter, he'd told Cassian Mona sold them out. *Mona.* The woman Eden had first seen in a picture, wearing a jaunty hat while an adorable six-year-old boy smiled at the camera, sandwiched safely between his effervescent mother and the woman who had taken them in. That woman had sacrificed an innocent mother and her innocent child. For what? To feed more mouths?

Eden's stomach churned. Perhaps she might believe that Mona was regretful for such a cold-hearted move if not for the air raid that had occurred two miles south of the Potomac Yard. If *America Underground* hadn't had the foresight to create a dummy location, they would have been completely decimated. There would have been nobody left to resist Oswin Brahm. He would have had free rein to carry out his psychotic plans.

"Dayne needs to know she can't be trusted," Cleo said. She didn't wait for Eden or Cassian to agree. She turned on her heel and marched inside the newsroom with only a ghost of a limp.

Eden touched Cass's arm. She wanted him to look at her. She

wanted to ask him about his dad, about Mona, but he refused to meet her eye as he turned and followed Cleo.

Together, they congregated in Dayne's office. There was no need to alarm everyone in the newsroom. At least, not more than they were already alarmed.

"The leader in Chicago is not on our side." Cleo shut the door behind her, then turned around to explain.

When she was finished, Asher cursed.

Dvorak looked ready to snap. Her mouth was tight and quivering, her eyes two laser beams of fury.

Jericho looked deeply troubled.

"She has the location of our safe houses," Nairobi said.

"And every off-the-grid community across the country," Cleo added.

An unsettled silence fell upon them.

If Mona was a sell-out—and it seemed she most certainly was—she had enough information to make a fortune. Thus far, they'd kept the Resistance private. They'd only shared with the people of Alexandria, a decision with which Francesca took issue. Never mind spreading the word across the entire off-the-grid network, the girl with the glass eye didn't even want to clue in their newest bedfellows. Francesca needn't have worried. The people in Alexandria stepped aboard with no hiccups. Eden wasn't surprised. The people in Alexandria were illegal residents. Illegals were natural allies. Except, of course, for Mona. Oswin Brahm was exterminating their natural allies and that woman was all-too-eager to point her finger at known infestations.

"Except us," Eden reminded them. "Mona doesn't know *this* location."

"It's the only safe place to be right now," Dayne agreed.

"How is that useful?" Asher asked. "Are we going to find some busses, tell everyone to pile inside, and start driving east?"

Nairobi rubbed her chin. "That won't work. Not with patrol officers manning state borders."

"I wasn't serious," Asher said.

"We can start small," Cleo interjected. "Like … with our safe houses. What if we used them to create some sort of Underground Railroad that could bring people east?"

"Small, huh?" Asher replied, a bite in each syllable.

Cleo wheeled on him. "Do you have a better suggestion, or are you just resigned to being a jerk wad?"

"A *jerk wad*?"

"Mona knows the location of our safe houses," Jericho said, ignoring the antagonistic exchange while he slowly scratched his goatee. "But Brahm hasn't gone after any of them."

"Yes, he has." Dayne frowned. "Elmer and Eloise Miller."

"That's only because he thought *we* were there," Cleo said.

Thanks to Mona.

That sweet couple was dead because of that woman. The mere thought of her brought a bitter taste to Eden's mouth. She could only imagine how much more so for Cassian. She tried again to make eye contact. But he was resolutely avoiding her.

Jericho took a seat on the edge of Dayne's desk. "He seems to be targeting larger communities."

"He's targeting specific cities," Eden said.

Boots on the ground in Milwaukee proved her theory. A third city on Cleo's map was under attack. It couldn't be a coincidence. When she finished sharing, Cleo's eyes shone with excited agreement. "He's punishing dissent. Any city that's had a protest or a riot is coming under attack."

"Have we checked on safe houses in Minneapolis or Madison?" Jericho asked. "Have we tried contacting them?"

Everyone looked at Dayne.

"I've sent correspondents to the community in Minneapolis, but I didn't think to have them check on our safe houses."

"Can we?"

"Of course." He opened his office door, letting in a whoosh of noise, and asked one of his journalists to send out messages to every safe house in Minneapolis, Madison, and Milwaukee.

"What were the other cities on the map?" Nairobi asked.

"Fresno, St. Louis, Detroit, and Seattle," Cleo replied.

"Then those are the ones we have to evacuate," Dvorak said. "I'll get in touch with Harlan. He'll be able to help. If safe houses are still safe, we can use them to move people in this direction."

"It's going to get crowded," Asher said.

"We have plenty of room," Cleo shot back.

Her aggravation was understandable. Amenities in Washington, DC, and Alexandria were luxurious compared to Chicago. Asher had never seen Chicago. He was accustomed to luxury. But he'd just have to get over it. They were in the middle of a war. Sacrifices had to be made. Starting with the one Eden needed to make now. No more hiding who she was. *What* she was. It was time for the cat to come out of the bag, no matter how badly Cassian wanted to keep it a secret. She needed to reveal who she was. It was the only way she could be the weapon Brahm had created her to be. It was the only way she could use her superhuman abilities against him.

She took a breath. "I have a group of people who are willing to be the first travelers."

Dvorak narrowed her eyes. "Who?"

"My parents," Eden said. "Along with a family of three and a gentleman named Dr. Benjamin Norton."

"All three men have military experience," Cass added.

"Right," Dvorak said dryly. "One of them was in the CIA."

Her tone was so redolent with mistrust, Eden's face flushed. Dvorak's suspicion only confirmed Eden's decision. They were going to find out sooner rather than later. If not from her, then on their own. Better from her. She took another breath. "They will have two more with them. A young woman named Violet Winter. And a young man named Barrett Barr."

"The kid who shot the patrol officers?" Asher quipped.

"*Kid*?" Cleo rolled her eyes. "They're like, three seconds younger than you."

Asher rolled his eyes back. "My bad. The *young adult* who shot the patrol officers?"

"What are you two going on about?" Dvorak asked.

Jericho stepped in to explain. "Barrett Barr is the missing eighteen-year-old who was all over the news this summer. He and his female companion shot and killed two patrol officers outside Minneapolis."

Dayne shook his head. "It was a deep fake. He didn't shoot anyone."

Asher didn't seem very comforted by the news. He turned on Eden. "How are you connected with these two?"

Beside him, Dvorak stood with her arms crossed, waiting for an answer. She looked fierce and frail all at the same time.

Beside Eden, Cassian stood with *his* arms crossed, exhibiting no frailty at all. Tension rolled off him in waves. She could physically feel his anger. And yet, she knew that anger was a front. Beneath his fury, he was scared. Possibly terrified. She would be, too, if their roles were reversed. But their roles weren't reversed, and she couldn't let her concern for his feelings keep her from doing the right thing. Emotions could not cloud her judgment any longer. Not hers. Not Cassian's, either. Brahm was on the attack. He was making bold moves. If they had any hope of defeating him, they needed to use every advantage at their disposal. She was a distinct advantage. So were Barrett and Violet.

It was time to come out with the truth. "Barrett and Violet are Subjects 003 and 004."

Cleo made a strangled sound.

Dayne shifted.

Cassian's heart rate accelerated.

Eden pulled back her shoulders. "And I'm Subject 006."

It took a moment for Dvorak to register the implication of Eden's words. When she finally did, her face paled. "The test group?"

Eden nodded.

Asher's eyes went wide. "Holy—"

"The test group was destroyed," Dvorak interjected.

"Two of them were destroyed," Eden said. "The rest of us survived."

Nairobi gaped. "You're one of Brahm's soldiers?"

"No. Never," Eden said. "I'm just … designed in the same way."

Jericho wound his hand around the back of his neck. "Does Brahm know?"

"Of course he knows," Dvorak spat. "If he didn't know, her mug wouldn't be on the news. There wouldn't be a deep fake of this Barrett Barr and Violet Winter." She pressed her lips together, her jaw clenched like she was chewing on a mouthful of rocks. "I can't believe we didn't put the pieces together. We were so busy looking at him, we didn't think to look into her." She flung her hand accusingly at Cass, like it was his fault they'd wandered off course.

"Digging into me wouldn't have gotten you anywhere," Eden said. "I'm not a threat. We're on the same side."

"You're part of the Electus."

A growl rumbled in Cassian's chest.

Eden was confident only she could hear it. But hear it, she did. She held up her hand in a gesture of peace and kept her voice calm. "I wasn't raised like them."

Nobody seemed to take any solace in the words. She looked at Asher, hoping he might offer some support. But he looked more mutinous than Dvorak, as though her revelation personally offended him.

Eden's frustration mounted. "If you want me to defend myself further, I will. But I promise you, it's a waste of time. I'm not one of his soldiers. I'm not part of the Electus. Until three months ago, I thought I was a regular girl with two regular parents. But then a gambler named Mordecai found me and forced me to attack them."

As soon as the words were out, she realized her mistake. She had shared too much.

Cassian realized it, too.

"He needs her location in order to control her," he said, his voice low and filled with authority. "He doesn't have her location."

"Locations are easy enough to find," Asher said.

"Apparently not for you guys," Cleo muttered.

He glowered.

She lifted her chin. "How many failed recon missions have you gone on now?"

Eden pursed her lips, then lifted her hand higher. "We're getting off track. Everyone in this room wants the same thing."

"It doesn't matter what you want," Asher said. "Not if he controls you."

The growl in Cassian's chest deepened. "He can't control her."

Asher jabbed his upturned palm at Eden. "You just admitted he can if he has her location."

"And we just established he won't find it," Cass replied, the two of them squaring off.

Eden imagined them going toe-to-toe. Asher was half a head taller, with considerably more weight on his large frame. Even so, she knew Cassian would come out the victor.

"At ease," Cleo said, stepping between them. "We're on the cusp of a discovery that could make this whole conversation moot."

Dvorak raised her eyebrows. "What discovery?"

"A man named Jack Forrester has been studying her network."

"*What?*" Asher barked.

Cleo gave her head a smug toss. "He got in. In a matter of days, in fact."

"Who is this guy?"

Eden's internal temperature was skyrocketing. Now wasn't

the time for their snarky back and forth. "You'll meet him soon enough. The point is, he's been scrutinizing our networks—all three of them—and he discovered that Violet's network is different from mine and Barrett's. We have a master node. That master node is the mechanism used to control us. Violet doesn't have one."

"Why not?" Nairobi asked.

"That's the question," Eden said. "Let's get them here and together, we can figure it out."

41

Eden dressed quickly and towel dried her hair, feeling jumpy and nervous, like she'd had one too many cups of coffee. Cassian was in her apartment. They were alone together, away from the uneasy looks that had dogged her since making her announcement in Dayne's office. She had become a source of tension—a thing to be watched. The more they watched, the more tightly-wound Cassian had become, until finally, she decided to remove herself from the equation.

Tomorrow, the outlook would be different. This was what she was trying to tell herself, anyway. A night of sleep would help everyone see the situation with more clarity. She wasn't a threat. On the contrary, she gave them an advantage. Once the shock wore off, once Dvorak and Asher and the others settled down, she felt confident Cassian would, too.

With a shaky exhale, she slipped out of the steamy bathroom and stopped at the end of the hallway, where it opened into the living room. He wasn't sitting on the couch, or the armchair Cleo liked to claim. He was in the kitchen, leaning against the counter. Standing in the dark.

Nerves fluttered in her abdomen.

She tried her best to ignore them.

"You can sit down if you want," she said, her voice a tiptoe as she set her hands on the back of the sofa. Then she looked over her shoulder, toward her bedroom. He was clearly exhausted. He probably wanted to sleep, but she'd left him out here. "Or if you'd rather lay down, my room is—"

"I'll sleep on the couch."

Heat rushed up her neck. She wasn't sure what embarrassed her more—her own suggestion or his outright rejection. She'd spent the last three weeks longing for him. With such potency, it had been a physical ache in her bones. She wanted Cassian to be here with her. Now, here he was. Alive! And furious. She understood why. He was upset—fear disguised as anger, which, for Cassian, almost always presented itself as animosity.

It didn't intimidate her.

At least, it never had before.

She took a steadying breath and made her way around the couch. "So, you spoke with your father."

His jaw went tight, a familiar muscle tick-tick-ticking into the silence.

She joined him in the kitchen and turned on the light.

His hair had grown longer. The sides curled over his ears.

She wanted to go to him. Trace the bruise on his jaw. Take his hand and whisper his mother's words. *Voila. Tout au mieux.* She wanted to pour them into his ear over and over until the animosity was gone. The dark circles beneath his eyes, too. They were disturbingly dark—a testament to the toll his time in prison had taken. Instead, she remained where she was. "Do you want to talk about it?"

"There's nothing to say."

His words were a slap. A shove. So cold and detached, her eyes burned. Of course, there was plenty to say. His father paid him a visit. But he was locking it up behind tightly drawn shutters.

A large part of her considered letting it go. Leaving it be. Give him space to process. To breathe. To deescalate. But another part of her was worried about her parents and defensive about her decision to tell the truth, especially considering the second-guessing she'd done in the shower, and frankly, annoyed that he was punishing her for doing what she felt was the right thing to do.

This was the part that won.

"Cass," she said without a smidge of quaver in her voice. "Your father came to visit you while you were imprisoned. You haven't seen him since you were twelve when he—"

He looked at her then, his eyebrow lifted in a dare. "When he what?"

She swallowed and stretched her fingers by her sides, refusing to let them fidget. "That had to dredge up some feelings. Especially when he told you Mona—"

"I don't want to talk about Mona."

Her heart sank. Her shoulders, too. Gone was the warmth, the intimacy, the ease they had established at the Millers. This boy she cared so deeply for was here and alive and a million miles away. She wanted to go to him. Tear down the wall he had built. Bridge the gulf he was creating. Wipe the animosity from his face. But she could see it was a losing battle. He wasn't budging. Not tonight.

The door opened.

Cleo limped inside with a box of Mike and Ikes, muttering under her breath about Asher and how much she wanted to punch him in his smug face. She paused when she saw them, smiled a little devilishly—like perhaps she had interrupted a make-out session, which she so clearly hadn't—then cut between them to grab a Diet Coke from the refrigerator.

"He's so arrogant," she said, cracking open the can. "It's a wonder nobody's done it yet."

"How do you know they haven't?" Eden asked, thankful for the distraction.

"His nose is too straight." Cleo took a slurp, then eyed the communication gadget on the countertop. "Any word?"

Eden released a heavy sigh. "Not yet."

Cleo twisted her lips to the side and tapped her soda can. "None of the safe houses in Minneapolis or Madison have responded either." She set her soda next to the device and opened the box of Mike and Ikes. "The toxin attack in Milwaukee was just hitting the airwaves when I left the newsroom."

Eden looked at the black flatscreen in their living room. She didn't have the stomach to turn it on. Chuck Perez's voice had become grating.

Cleo rattled a few candies into her palm when something beeped.

For a millisecond, Eden's hope leapt. So did her heart—right into her throat. Her attention darted to the gadget. But the gadget was silent. The beeping was coming from the intercom in their apartment.

Her hope crashed in a heap of fiery disappointment. To keep herself from growling, or screaming, or pulling out her hair, she marched to the intercom and jabbed the button.

Asher's voice crackled through the speaker. "We're having a meeting in the boardroom."

"I thought we were done for the day," Eden said.

"There's been a new development."

She glanced over her shoulder—toward Cass and Cleo—then turned back to the intercom. "I'll be there in a minute."

She prepared to go alone, or with Cleo. Cass could stay here. Get some sleep. *On the couch.* Whatever the development, she could catch him up later. But he was already grabbing his jacket and shoving one arm into a sleeve.

Cleo scooped up the gadget and handed it to Eden at the door.

She slid it into her back pocket, willing her parents to call. *Please call.*

As they made their way to the IDA, Eden tried to convince herself that her parents were fine. It would take time to move carefully. Maybe they'd intentionally delayed making contact. They were traveling to the next closest safe house and there they would call. Wouldn't Eden rather they take precautions and keep her in suspense than take risks just to ease her mind? She breathed in the evening air and took solace in the fact that Cassian was with her. Hostile and closed off, but with her all the same. And if that was possible, then anything was possible.

When they reached the boardroom, the door was already open.

Eden could see Dvorak and Jericho sitting at the table. Jericho looked uncomfortable, like whatever he'd eaten for dinner wasn't sitting well. Lark was still missing in action, most likely in Kaiser getting her leg treated. Asher was out of view.

As Cass stepped through the door ahead of her, a strange feeling somersaulted through her gut. Something like a premonition rose up her throat, but before she could capture it on her tongue, Asher stepped out from behind the opened door and stuck Cassian with a needle.

Eden saw red.

She charged at Asher like an angry bull, so consumed with outrage she didn't hear the dart. It hit her square in the neck. The pain that followed was so excruciating, she turned feral.

Eden dropped to her knees and clawed at her skin. She rolled and writhed on the floor, desperate to put the fire out. But the flames were inside. Coursing through her veins. Stabbing her bones. Scorching her lungs. Searing her from the inside out. With her tendons bulging, she screamed and she screamed and she screamed until her world turned to ash and everything went black.

THE RETRIBUTION
OF EDEN PRUITT

K. E. GANSHERT

ABOUT THE AUTHOR

K.E. Ganshert is an award-winning author of clean fiction filled with mystery, adventure, romance, and the fantastical. Her stories are perfect for readers who crave unexpected twists, strange happenings, high stakes, and romance that runs deep but never explicit. She lives in eastern Iowa with her husband and their two children.

WICKED IS THE HOLLOW
A SUPERNATURAL MYSTERY

Ever since her mother vanished, Selah Whitlock has been drawn to the unexplained. So it feels almost fated to live in Foggy Hollow, a place where mystery abounds. Even more so when her father accepts a job at the Vandenberg estate, the epicenter of the town's most infamous cold case.

Moving into the estate's carriage house pulls Selah into the orbit of the Vandenberg cousins: Jude, the brooding heir with a tragic past, and Rafe, effortlessly charming and undeniably dangerous.

Then a centuries-old portrait surfaces bearing Selah's exact likeness. Suddenly, she isn't just chasing a mystery. She's caught in the heart of one. As the town prepares to celebrate its bicentennial, Selah and Jude are pulled into a secret that spans generations. Something sinister is stirring beneath the golden leaves and carved pumpkins. And the deeper they fall, the deadlier the consequences.

9 798993 987644